Old Enough to Die

Also by Ridley Wills II

A Walking Tour of Mt. Olivet Cemetery (1993)

The History of Belle Meade: Mansion, Plantation, and Stud (1991)

Belle Meade Bloodlines, 1816–1904 (1990)

Old Enough to Die

Ridley Wills II

HILLSBORO PRESS

Franklin, Tennessee

TENNESSEE HERITAGE LIBRARY
Bicentennial Collection

Printed in the United States of America

00   99   98   97   96   6   5   4   3   2   1

Library of Congress Catalog Card Number: 95-81701

ISBN: 1-881576-81-7

Cover by Bozeman Design

Illustrations used by permission: page 13—*Cities Under the Gun,* James A. Hoobler and page 154—*Architecture of the Old South: Mississippi-Alabama.*

Published by
HILLSBORO PRESS
an imprint of
PROVIDENCE HOUSE PUBLISHERS
238 Seaboard Lane • Franklin, Tennessee 37067
800-321-5692

To my dear wife

Irene

who has supported me in all
my endeavors. She is a credit
to her Bostick ancestors.

CONTENTS

Foreword   *ix*
Preface and Acknowledgments   *xi*
Prologue: An Ill-fated Generation   *3*
    1. Who Are Their People?   *12*
    2. On to Virginia!   *18*
    3. Western Virginia—Lee's First Campaign   *25*
    4. Winter Campaign   *37*
    5. The Peninsula Defense   *53*
    6. Joe and Litton Join the Fight   *67*
    7. Life in Occupied Nashville   *76*
    8. Kentucky and Tennessee   *86*
    9. Chickamauga and Missionary Ridge   *96*
    10. The Atlanta Campaign   *107*
    11. Home to Tennessee   *134*
Epilogue: Life Goes On   *145*
Endnotes   *156*
Bibliography   *172*
Index   *173*

FOREWORD

FEW WARS HAVE BEEN MORE WRITTEN ABOUT THAN THE
American Civil War. It is a mark of its special attraction that we can greet
another account with pleasurable anticipation. In this account, Ridley Wills
II does for a family at war what he has already done for a family at peace in
his gripping history of Belle Meade Plantation and the people who lived
there. His narrative focuses on the experiences of a single albeit extended,
family which he manages to integrate into the larger picture of a nation
divided against itself.

His cast is headed by the Bostick brothers: Litton, Joe, Tom, and Abe,
ranging in age at the onset of war from thirty-five to twenty-one; they are
supported by cousins Jim Cooper, Jim Thomas, Jake Thomas, and Bill
Robinson, and by their brother-in-law, John Early. The womenfolk include
their mother, old Mrs. Bostick, widowed in that secession winter, and sisters
Catharine, Mary Anne, Eliza, and Mag, together with a wife, Bettie.

The first year of war is seen principally through the eyes of the youngest
Bostick brother, Abe, whose literate and often lengthy letters are interesting
not because they are unique, but precisely because they are so familiar. We
find him chafing at the tedious inaction which is the common experience of
infantrymen in all wars; complaining of incessant rain, cold or shortage of
supplies; and noting with some regularity that he writes more letters than he
receives. We also note a tendency he shared with Confederate soldiers every-
where to underestimate his enemy. He longed for battle and the "fine times"
it would bring; he dismissed as "cowards" Union troops who retreated to
fight another day; and he was confident that the "Yankees can't stand steel."
Of the righteousness of his cause he entertained no doubt. East Tennesseans
who did not share his views he dismissed as laboring under delusions brought
about by incorrect information. He could not contemplate living in a
defeated South, taking for granted that the whole family would move in that
eventuality "to some other country where we can at least be free." Given his
eagerness for battle, fate dealt Abe a card from the bottom of the pack: after
twelve months of fruitless marching and camping he was killed at the very
start of his first major engagement in June 1862.

The themes Abe articulated so clearly were to surface in the letters of his
brothers. Litton also, on occasion, expressed his frustration at inactivity and

the weather. He, too, utterly failed to comprehend that Northerners were every bit as committed to the cause of the Union as he was to that of the Confederacy. The fall of Vicksburg, he wrote, will not break the rebellion, and when that fact becomes evident "a reaction will take place in public opinion in the North and they will learn at last that the subjugation of the South is an impossibility." Litton's letters, indeed, are characterized by an incurable optimism, even during the dark days of Sherman's Atlanta campaign.

Nor is he just whistling in the wind: the optimism shines through the long, detailed accounts he writes of the engagements in which he was involved—some of the best participant accounts to be found anywhere. It is sadly ironic that Litton, with his optimism, should join Abe, with his zeal for the fight, as the only two of the Bosticks' extended family to be killed. Jim Cooper was wounded four times, but he and the other brothers and cousins survived to face the uncertain future of the post-war South.

While the men marched and fought, their womenfolk suffered that war-induced nightmare so common in our own century, being driven from their homes, turned into refugees and forced upon their own resources. Old Mrs. Bostick and her oldest daughter, Catharine, decided to stick it out in occupied Nashville where they suffered insult and harassment. Eliza already lived in Mississippi; the other women fled there in early 1862. We see through Eliza's eyes the dawning recognition that this was a total war in which "the women will be as brave soldiers as the men before this war is over. I am willing to do anything now rather than yield and although I gave up a great deal when I gave up my husband, I should not have him back now."

The Bostick correspondents do not speculate about the overarching themes of the Civil War which preoccupy historians today, and which preoccupied political leaders then, themes of slavery and aristocracy, of secession and constitutional freedoms, of political rivalries. What we see is a deep loyalty to community, a sense of shared values. If their apparently unquestioning acceptance of the Confederate cause and its implications is chastening, their loyalty, courage and fundamental decency is also heartening.

Ridley Wills II provides us with the background of the Bosticks and with a brief account of their post-war history. In between he embeds their correspondence in a clear narrative of the war-time operations in which they were involved. This is a humane, touching and illuminating book which can be read and enjoyed not only by the Civil War buffs but by anyone who feels for the human condition in times of war.

—Duncan MacLeod
St. Catherine's College, Oxford

PREFACE AND ACKNOWLEDGMENTS

FOR MOST OF MY ADULT LIFE, I HAVE MADE AN AVOCATION of studying family genealogies. For the past two decades or so, I have enjoyed writing and teaching local history. Soon after my marriage to Irene Jackson in 1962, I learned about a large packet of Bostick letters which had been passed down through her father's family. In 1966, I transcribed and footnoted those letters which were written by various members of the Bostick family. Now, nearly thirty years later, I have written and edited this book. Its completion fulfills a long-standing desire I have had to do this. Having read a number of books consisting primarily of Civil War letters, I have been struck by how articulate the Bostick brothers were and by their devotion to their family and to the Confederate cause which they supported so valiantly.

What I should have realized when I transcribed the Bostick letters was how close a feeling I would come to have for the four brothers and their families. Learning details of their everyday lives helped foster a feeling of kinship. Finding out that John Bostick bought land in 1830 where Monteagle, Tennessee, is today, and that his granddaughter, Catharine Halbert, spent her summers there after 1895 strengthened the bond. Irene and I own a cottage in the Monteagle Sunday School Assembly. Our grandchildren, Meade and Ridley Wills IV, represent the seventh generation of Irene's family to spend part of their summers there. I also had no idea in 1962 that Irene's great-grandmother's brother, Dr. Joe Bostick, lived in Marion County, Tennessee, only eighteen miles from where we own property.

Other discoveries brought the ties even closer. In recent years, I realized that my long-time friend John Ransom, of Sewanee, Tennessee, is a distant kinsman of Irene's. His middle name is Bostick and he is descended from James Alfred Bostick through a daughter, Martha Elizabeth, who married George Washington Ransom.[1] Irene and I are fortunate to live at Meeting of the Waters, an historic Williamson County home built between 1800 and 1809 by Thomas Hardin Perkins, a brother of Bethenia Perkins Bostick. She was the wife of Absalom Bostick and the mother of John Bostick, who came to Williamson County about the time his uncle completed Meeting of the Waters. In our dining room, we have a sugar chest thought to have been owned by the Bostick family of Hardeman Cross Roads, Tennessee. In 1994, Irene was given by her mother, Henriette Weaver Jackson, a Washington Cooper portrait of John Bostick, the grandfather of Abe, Joe, Litton, and Tom. Its coming to Meeting of the Waters coincided nicely with the completion of this book and seemed, in my mind, to symbolically complete a cycle.

Since moving to Williamson County, it has been a pleasure for Irene and me to get to know Miss John Bostick, who is the sole member of the Bostick family still living in the county who carries that name. I appreciate the stories she has told me about growing up in Triune, Tennessee, where she attended grammar school in the red-brick building on the hill that earlier housed the Bostick Female Academy.[2] I am also indebted to B. D. "Bill" Kidwell of Fort Worth, Texas, whose research on the Bostick family greatly facilitated the completion of this book.

Old Enough to Die

BOSTICK FAMILY TREE

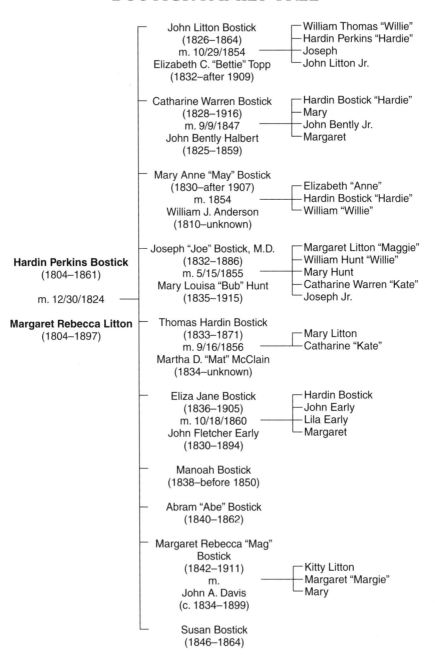

Hardin Perkins Bostick
(1804–1861)

m. 12/30/1824

Margaret Rebecca Litton
(1804–1897)

John Litton Bostick
(1826–1864)
m. 10/29/1854
Elizabeth C. "Bettie" Topp
(1832–after 1909)

- William Thomas "Willie"
- Hardin Perkins "Hardie"
- Joseph
- John Litton Jr.

Catharine Warren Bostick
(1828–1916)
m. 9/9/1847
John Bently Halbert
(1825–1859)

- Hardin Bostick "Hardie"
- Mary
- John Bently Jr.
- Margaret

Mary Anne "May" Bostick
(1830–after 1907)
m. 1854
William J. Anderson
(1810–unknown)

- Elizabeth "Anne"
- Hardin Bostick "Hardie"
- William "Willie"

Joseph "Joe" Bostick, M.D.
(1832–1886)
m. 5/15/1855
Mary Louisa "Bub" Hunt
(1835–1915)

- Margaret Litton "Maggie"
- William Hunt "Willie"
- Mary Hunt
- Catharine Warren "Kate"
- Joseph Jr.

Thomas Hardin Bostick
(1833–1871)
m. 9/16/1856
Martha D. "Mat" McClain
(1834–unknown)

- Mary Litton
- Catharine "Kate"

Eliza Jane Bostick
(1836–1905)
m. 10/18/1860
John Fletcher Early
(1830–1894)

- Hardin Bostick
- John Early
- Lila Early
- Margaret

Manoah Bostick
(1838–before 1850)

Abram "Abe" Bostick
(1840–1862)

Margaret Rebecca "Mag"
Bostick
(1842–1911)
m.
John A. Davis
(c. 1834–1899)

- Kitty Litton
- Margaret "Margie"
- Mary

Susan Bostick
(1846–1864)

AN ILL-FATED GENERATION

he year 1860 found Hardin Perkins and Margaret Litton Bostick with every reason to be proud of their four sons. In an era when Tennessee's economy was predominantly agrarian, their boys—Litton, Joe, Tom, and Abe—had all chosen and successfully entered prestigious professions. John Litton Bostick, the oldest son, whom everyone called Litton, was married to the former Bettie C. Topp, of Columbus, Mississippi. Their children, William, Hardin, and Joe, were all small. He was practicing law in Nashville with his father.

Litton was born on May 6, 1826, in Williamson County, Tennessee, where his parents were living on a farm near Hardeman Cross Roads. Litton received his early education in private schools, one of which was Mrs. Ripley's School in Franklin. A good student, he went on to graduate from the University of Nashville in 1843 and from Harvard Law School four years later. A year or so after his graduation from Harvard, fabulous stories were circulating about gold discovered on the south fork of California's American River. Accounts were published in all the major American newspapers of the richness of the gold-bearing veins along that and other streams on the western slope of the Sierra Nevada Mountains. A California congressman named George W. Wright[1] wrote Tennessee's governor Neill S. Brown, that one gold vein there was so rich that it "lasted for twelve miles." Wright said that finding it was no more difficult than "finding any post office or country village in Tennessee." Litton was one of thousands of American men who, succumbing to the lure of finding a mother lode, soon became known as "forty-niners." He went to New York and from there to San Francisco by sailing ships, interrupted by a 22-mile-long land passage across the isthmus of what is now Panama but was then the Republic of New Grenada.

Litton described the road across the isthmus in terms his family would understand. He wrote, "Take any of our Tennessee turnpikes, imagine it 10 feet wide in its original state, let it be traveled 100 years by mules without repairing till it had worn down in many of its 'cuts' to a foot in width, while at other places it remained perfect, and you will get some idea of this road. . . . Any one who has ridden over the Sam's Creek hills or the knobs between Williamson and Rutherford Counties can snap his fingers at the road from Cruces to Panama."[2]

Litton arrived at San Francisco on the steamer *Tennessee* in June 1850. After gathering supplies, he and his partner, a fellow Nashvillian Dr. J. H. Harris, set out for what he called "my exploring expedition." Soon adventurous dreams met dreary reality. Litton found the whole country full of miners and not a stream that was "not muddied by the ruckus of miners, nor a mountain or valley that had not resounded to the noise of the pick and the shovel." During July, he ran into a party of Forty-Niners from Clarksville, Tennessee, and John F. Pate, a trader from Williamson County. Litton and Dr. Harris employed Pate to examine a vein on Rattlesnake Creek. They instructed him to enter claims for them if he found any value. He didn't. Meanwhile, Litton's own efforts were equally fruitless. After ten days of the hardest work he had ever done—digging quartz, pulverizing it with a hand mortar, and washing the particles in a pan—Litton concluded that Mr. Wright's accounts, which "astonished and excited the whole Union," were the "grossest misrepresentations."[3] Although Litton wrote his father not to say anything "of our disappointment," he undoubtedly wondered if he had come thousands of miles for nothing.

After spending a largely unproductive period of weeks or months looking for gold, Litton did what some other frustrated miners did—he opened a store to supply goods for the miners who continued to pour into the territory. Three years later, Litton was running the store in Arum City, California, in partnership with a man named Miller. When business was slow in the summers, he spent his time working on a ranch he had bought. He called it Tule Ranch. Litton also was admitted to the California Bar and represented several clients. One day in court at Stockton, the District

Attorney walked up to Litton and asked him if he was Litton Bostick from Tennessee. The man introduced himself as William Porter. He and Litton had been schoolmates at Mrs. Ripley's School in Franklin.[4]

Litton wrote his mother in June 1853, that, when working on Tule Ranch, he spent his days "mowing, raking, pitching, hauling and stacking hay by day and fighting mosquitoes by night."[5] That month he also wrote a long letter to his nineteen-year-old brother Tom telling him either to come to California immediately or not at all. It turned out that Tom was already on his way; he arrived in

Young Tom Bostick.

California within weeks. In the letter to his mother, Litton also reflected on his naiveté when he left home in 1850. "What a great mistake I made and how little of life did I know when I thought more than three years ago that I could come to California, engage in a difficult & uncertain business & at the end of 18 months cut myself off at one stroke from all my new associates & tastes & return to be just what I was when I left." Despite ambivalent feelings about leaving California, Litton told his mother that he intended to return home in the fall and asked her about several of his female friends, including "sweet little Bettie Topp."

Litton's departure for Nashville was delayed for some time because of Tom's arrival. When Litton first saw him he appeared "tall, slim, delicate & 'wishy-washy' resembling the ghost of a dandy."[6] Actually, Tom was sick. Because of that and because business was dull, the brothers soon decided to close the store.[7] With Tom's approval, Litton then set his little brother up on his 320-acre ranch where Tom could regain his health by strenuous work outdoors. It worked. Within weeks, Tom's weight was up to 150 pounds and he was "strong and healthy." Litton didn't mind that Tom was then wearing his clothes as Tom's no longer fit. Litton was also amused that Tom usually shaved only every other week or so, which caused the fuzz on his cheeks to resemble that of a ripe peach. Tom liked to think he had a goatee.[8]

Although setting Tom up first in the store and then on his ranch took more money than expected, Litton was determined not to leave his brother until he was "in a fair way of making money if it takes all that I have as it now seems to do."[9] It seems likely that Litton left California that fall or winter for home.

Before leaving, Litton wrote his brother-in-law, Bently Halbert, the following description of himself.

> I look pretty much as I did when I left home except that I am more robust, somewhat sunburnt & perhaps a little older. I am dressed in checked cashmere pants (good article)—black silk vest (well made)—light calf skin boots—white shirt— fine cravat (the one mother sent)—a good stand-up collar (a little turned down today, however, it is Sunday)—a straw hat such as I wore at home and a brown frock coat (off at this time for convenience sake). Lastly, my beard is of civilized length about the same as the 'goatee' I once wore at home and my hair is always cut by a good barber being a shade or two thinner than you last saw me.

Upon his return to Nashville, Litton began courting Bettie C. Topp, the girl he mentioned in his letter to his mother a year or so earlier. Bettie, the second oldest of five children of Dr. and Mrs. William W. Topp, wealthy residents of Columbus, Mississippi,[10] may have been living in Nashville at the time. She and Litton married in Columbus on October 29, 1854.[11] Following their marriage, they lived in Nashville where Litton and Bently formed a law partnership with offices at 45 North Cherry Street. The relationship lasted until a fatal illness forced Halbert to give up law practice two or three years later. After Bently's death in 1858, Litton practiced law with his father.

One of Litton's closest friends was Randal W. McGavock, his Harvard Law School classmate. In early 1856, Bostick and McGavock spent two hours writing the by-laws for the Robertson Association, a charitable organization which McGavock founded to help the poor in Nashville. On New Years Eve, 1857, Bostick accepted McGavock's invitation to lecture before the Robertson Association. Litton's speech, "An Ethnological View of the Negro," was delivered to a disappointingly small crowd but was "very fine" according to Randal. After the lecture, Bostick, McGavock,[12] and Francis Fogg went to Thompson's room to play euchre and watch the New Year arrive.[13]

Litton and Bettie lived at 73 North Summer Street in a house he bought in 1855 or 1856.[14] Their first child, William Thomas, was born about the same time. Three years later, they had a second son, Hardin Perkins. While her small boys occupied most of Bettie's time, Litton focused his efforts on practicing law, attending meetings of and lectures given to benefit the Robertson Association, and, for a short time in 1858, campaigning for Randal McGavock in his successful mayoral campaign. On election day that September, Bostick and other friends stationed themselves at the polling places with tickets promoting McGavock's candidacy. For relaxation, Litton enjoyed playing euchre, poker, or whist with friends in the evenings.

By 1860, Litton's standing in the professional community was well recognized. When Tennessee seceded from the Union the following spring, the thirty-five-year-old lawyer hoped to continue his law practice. By then, he and Bettie had three sons with the addition of Joseph, born in 1860.

Not long after Litton returned home from California, Tom concluded that California was not the place for him. His admiration for Litton undoubtedly influenced his own aspirations to become a lawyer. Accordingly, he sold the Tule Ranch and returned home in 1854 and entered the Department of Law at Cumberland University in Lebanon, Tennessee, that fall. Three months following his graduation in 1856, Tom married Martha "Mat" McClain, daughter of Josiah and Martha McClain of Lebanon.[15] Mr. McClain had been secretary of the Board of Trustees of Cumberland University since its founding, and a member of one of Wilson County's most prominent families.[16] As their new son-in-law was just embarking on a legal career, the McClains invited Tom and Mat to make their home with them. The young couple did so and soon had two daughters—Mary Litton, born about 1858; and Catharine ("Kate") a year younger—much to the delight of both sets of grandparents.

Joseph "Joe" Bostick, M.D., the second oldest son of Hardin and Margaret Bostick, was born April 1, 1832, at Hardeman Cross Roads. After moving with his parents and siblings to Nashville in 1842, he continued his education in private schools there. The Davidson County census of 1850 confirmed his status as a student. For the 1851-1852 school year, he studied medicine at the Medical Department of St. Louis University, where his uncle, Abraham Litton, was on the faculty. Following graduation, the Hospital of the City of St. Louis admitted him "to the practice of this institution for one year." Toward the end of that academic year, Joe was uncertain whether to continue in medicine or go to the iron works on the Ohio River that his father had recently purchased. Litton, having heard in California of Joe's indecision, wrote his mother that Joe should stick to his profession and leave "iron mines, gold mines, politics and speculations of every description to take care of themselves."[17] Joe took that advice and returned to Nashville.

After coming home, Joe began attending dances at the Athenaeum, a girls' school in Columbia, Tennessee, forty-one miles to the south. There, he met his future wife, Mary Louisa "Bub" Hunt, daughter of Henry W. and Mary Darwin (Trotter) Hunt of Columbus, Mississippi. Joe fell in love with Bub and quickly dropped his plans for post-graduate medical study in Europe. On May 15, 1855, the young couple married in her hometown.[18] For a year or so, they lived in Nashville, where their first child, Margaret Litton, was born April 10, 1856. Joe and Mary wanted to rear their children on a farm, free of the evil influences of the city. Consequently, they focused their attention on Marion County, Tennessee, where Joe's grandfather, John Bostick, had owned a large tract and where Joe may have visited as a boy.

Joe and Mary found the land they wanted near Brock's Cove on the stage road from Jasper, the Marion County seat, to Huntsville, Alabama. There, in 1856, Joe bought three tracts of land encompassing 2,500 acres from the East Tennessee Mining and Manufacturing Company for $6000.

One parcel, called the River tract, was fertile river-bottom land along

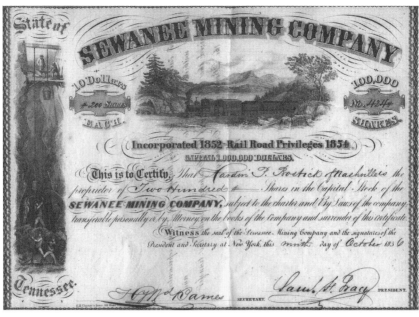

Stock certificate owned by Hardin P. Bostick.

the Tennessee River. It was here that Joe and Mary lived in a house on the west side of the Jasper-Huntsville Road. A second tract was on the side of a spur of the Cumberland Mountains. The third and largest tract encompassed 2000 acres of uncleared land on top of the mountain. In a separate purchase, Joe bought another 122 acres adjacent to his river-bottom land below the mouth of Battle Creek.

In 1859, Joe sold a fifty percent interest in his land and twelve slaves to his brother-in-law, William Barry "Will" Hunt, who had come up from Mississippi to live with his sister and brother-in-law.[19] Will, who had just graduated from the College of New Jersey, assumed much of the responsibility for managing the farm, which enabled Dr. Bostick to devote most of his time to practicing medicine. Mary assumed primary responsibility for rearing their three children—Margaret, born in 1856, William Hunt, born in 1858, and Mary, born in 1860. Joe Bostick's farm partnership with Will continued until the Civil War disrupted their lives and both men joined Confederate companies.

The youngest Bostick brother, Abram, nicknamed "Abe," was born at Hardeman Cross Roads November 18, 1840. Before his second birthday, his family moved to Nashville where he received his education in private schools and at the Western Military Institute of the University of Nashville. Abe was one of eight young men who graduated from the military college in 1859. He did so with an A.B. degree and only five demerits, the second lowest number given anyone in his class.[20] Interested in writing prose and in public speaking while in college, he was a member of the Agatheridan Debate Society. In his senior year, he participated on the winning side in a debate on the resolution that "the Indian has greater cause for complaint than the Negro." Abe's society took the affirmative position in the debate, which was held at the university's Agatheridan Hall.[21] In another debate with James Trimble on the question, "Affirmed that if the next President is a Black Republican, there will be a dissolution of the Union," Abe took the negative position.

Abe was a member of McKendree Methodist Church, where he worshiped regularly with his family and where, as a child, his Litton grandfather was a prominent layman. At the time of his graduation from the Military College of the University of Nashville in June, 1859, Abe stood 5'11" tall, had gray eyes, light hair and a fair complexion. That fall, when he began teaching school in Nashville, he was viewed as an attractive and outgoing young man with a bright future—a future to be dramatically changed less than two years later.[22]

*Eliza Jane Bostick Early
(1836–1905).*

The Bosticks also had five daughters whom they loved dearly. Their eldest daughter, Catharine Halbert, was a widow and Nashville school teacher. She and her children, Hardin, Mary, and Bently Jr., were living with the Bosticks in their large home on the Charlotte Turnpike. Soon after Catharine's husband, Nashville attorney John Bently Halbert, died in 1858,[23] Litton had a portrait of his former brother-in-law and law partner painted by his and Catharine's uncle, Washington Cooper, a noted Nashville artist. Litton's close friend, Randal W. McGavock, whose red hair was the same shade as Bently's, sat for the portrait.[24]

Mary Anne Anderson, the second oldest daughter was living in Mobile with her husband, William J. Anderson, a fifty-year-old cotton broker, their two children, Anne and Hardin, and her two stepchildren. Before moving to Mobile, Mary Anne and William, a native Virginian, had lived in Mississippi, where Hardin was born.

The three youngest daughters, Eliza, Mag and Susan, were all single, although Eliza was engaged to be married that fall to John Fletcher Early, a young man from Lynchburg, Virginia, who was associated with the Southern Methodist Publishing House in New Orleans.[25] As the oldest daughter still

John Fletcher Early
(1830–1894).

living at home, she had assumed a primary role for the past couple of years in running the household.

Eliza's two younger sisters, Margaret "Mag" and Susan, both teenagers, were also living at home.[26] Mag was in school, most likely at the Nashville Female Academy, where Catharine and Eliza had gone, while Susan, who had severe health problems, probably was never able to attend school.

Despite some financial reverses in the late 1850s, the Bosticks were a tight-knit, happy family surrounded by brothers, sisters, aunts, uncles, and first cousins.

CHAPTER ONE

WHO ARE THEIR PEOPLE?

Hardin and Margaret Litton Bosticks' home, where they were living in 1860 with five of their children—Abe, Catharine, Eliza, Mag, and Susan—along with three Halbert grandchildren—was on the north side of the Charlotte Pike between Bostick and Robertson Streets and about a mile west of Nashville's public square. It was a handsome, two-story brick house with an attic and a wooden shingle roof. The first floor plan featured two double parlors on either side of a wide central hall at the end of which was a circular staircase to the second floor. There was a spring house in the front yard and several cabins and a stable behind the house. A little farther north, about 400 feet behind the house, lay the tracks of the Nashville & Northwestern Railroad.

Nashvillians considered the Bostick home as part of a Litton family enclave. Hardin and Margaret's immediate neighbors to the east on the north side of the Charlotte Pike were Mrs. Bostick's sisters, Ann (Litton) Cooper and Elizabeth (Litton) Thomas, and their families. The three Litton daughters' homes stood on large lots facing a commons area across the turnpike.[1]

Ann and Washington B. Cooper, her husband of twenty-one years, lived in a large home on property immediately north of the Bosticks. They had two sons and a daughter. One son, James Litton "Jim" Cooper, would become one of five first cousins connected with the Twentieth Tennessee

Infantry during the Civil War. Mr. Cooper, a tall, big-framed man, whose weight fluctuated between 240 and 260 pounds, was Nashville's most famous artist. Only a year earlier, his portraits of Tennessee governors were exhibited by the Tennessee Historical Society in the State Capitol.[2]

On the other side of the Coopers, another sister, Elizabeth Thomas, lived with her family.[3] Elizabeth was married to Jesse Thomas. He was U.S. Collector of Internal Revenue in Nashville. Jesse and Elizabeth had eight children. Their oldest son, James "Jim" Thomas, would be another of five first cousins in the Twentieth Tennessee Regiment. Elizabeth's only other son to participate in the Civil War was Jacob Thomas, whose nickname was "Jake."

Margaret Litton Bostick's parents, Catharine and Joseph L. Litton, were natives of Ireland. In 1817, they left a comfortable life in Dublin to emigrate to the United States, arriving at the Port of Philadelphia.[4] The following spring, they moved to Nashville, where they joined McKendree Methodist Church and became steadfast and valuable members.[5]

Margaret Litton Bostick had six siblings who did not live in the compound on the Charlotte Pike. A third sister, Susan, was married to James C. Robinson. Twenty years earlier Mr. Robinson sold his cabinetmaking and undertaking businesses in Nashville and moved to a 550-acre farm in Williamson County. The plantation, known as Blue Springs Farm, was in a bend of the Harpeth River off the Natchez Road.[6] Their log house, which

H. P. Bostick Home on the Charlotte Pike in Nashville.

Margaret Rebecca (Litton) Bostick (1804–1897).

had been covered with planks, had two lower rooms connected by a dog-trot and two rooms above. Jim and Susan Robinson had seven children, including a daughter, Kitty, and two sons, James Jr. "Jim," and William "Bill" Joseph. Both boys would fight for the Confederacy, Bill in the Twentieth Tennessee Infantry with his four cousins.

Margaret's brother Isaac "Ike" Litton, was well-known to his contemporaries as treasurer of the Missionary Society of the Southern Methodist Episcopal Church. His name is familiar today as the person for whom Nashville's Isaac Litton High School was named.[7] Ike and his family lived three miles north of town on the Gallatin Pike. His son, George Litton, would served in Tyler's Brigade of Hood's Army of Tennessee.

Margaret Litton's oldest brother, Benjamin, was a wealthy Davidson County farmer whose personal estate was valued at $45,000 in 1860. His home, Litton Place, was where Vanderbilt University is today. His daughter, Jane Litton Taylor, sold the farm to Vanderbilt in 1873 following her father's death.[8]

A third brother, Abram, was a college professor, first at the University of Nashville and later at St. Louis University's Medical Department where

John Bostick (1765–1850).

his nephew Joe Bostick studied. Margaret's two other brothers, Joseph Jr. and Jacob, died relatively early.

Margaret Litton Bostick's husband, Hardin Perkins Bostick, was born in Stokes County, North Carolina, on December 30, 1804.[9] His parents, John and Mary Jarvis Bostick had moved there from Pittsylvania County, Virginia, in 1778 or 1779 when Stokes County was still part of Surry County.[10] After moving from Stokes County to near Hardeman Cross Roads, Tennessee, with his parents and siblings in 1809, Hardin attended the Harpeth Union Male Academy and King's Chapel Methodist Church.

At the time of his marriage to Margaret Litton, in 1824, Hardin was living in Franklin where he had just opened a general store. During their early years of marriage, he was an active mason and, for two years, Franklin's town recorder. In the early 1830s, Hardin and several other Franklin men successfully petitioned the State Legislature to open a bank branch there. The Union Bank of the State of Tennessee opened the doors to its Franklin branch in 1833.

Later in the decade, the Bosticks moved to Hardeman Cross Roads, where Hardin had grown up. There he operated a general store and a

175-acre farm with the help of seven slaves. He, Margaret and their children lived in a house on a separate seven-acre tract. Hardin took advantage of the 1837 agricultural depression to buy more land at a depressed price. To do so, he borrowed $950 from his father[11] with a one-year note. Soon, Hardin was feeling the economic pinch and was unable to pay off the note. Tennessee banks were quickly losing the public's confidence. Customers at his store could not afford to buy what they normally did. After pondering his alternatives, Hardin tried to obtain a federal political appointment. If successful, he would get out of both farming and the mercantile business.

So, in the winter of 1840-1841, Hardin left for Washington, armed with letters of reference and testimonials which he hoped his congressman, Meredith Gentry, would present to influential members of the Whig administration. After stopping in Baltimore and Philadelphia to pick up additional recommendations from prominent business acquaintances from earlier buying-trip days, Bostick went on to Washington in order to be there for the inauguration of President William Henry Harrison.[12]

Hardin Bostick did not get the appointment he sought. As the agricultural depression gradually deepened, he quit farming, closed his store, and moved to Nashville. He and Margaret were attracted to the state's largest city by the far greater business and educational opportunities available there. They were living in Nashville in September 1842; that month Hardin identified himself as a resident of Davidson County.[13] The following spring, he bought 45 acres on the Charlotte Turnpike, where he and Margaret built the home he would live in for the rest of his life.[14] There his younger children grew up playing with their Cooper and Thomas first cousins, sometimes in Lick Branch, a creek that crossed the Charlotte Pike at the foot of the hill toward town, or along the railroad tracks behind the house.

Hardin apparently was successful in establishing a business in Nashville as he had sufficient leisure time during his first few years there to become a Royal Arch Mason in Cumberland Lodge No.1 and a Knight Templar.[15] A decade later, he was an iron manufacturer, owned an iron mine on the Ohio River, and had interests in iron furnaces and real estate. He also speculated in the Sewanee Mining Company on the Cumberland Plateau and out-of-state silver mines. In the process, he prospered.

Late in the 1850s, Hardin Bostick suffered serious financial reverses. To raise needed cash, he subdivided his unimproved property along the Charlotte Turnpike and offered 40 building sites for auction. He even put up his own home, complete with its four acres of land, garden, orchards, and spring house for sale.[16] When the auction took place in November 1858, a large crowd of spectators, speculators, and Nashvillians interested in suburban living showed up. Mayor Randal W. McGavock, who attended the sale, noted in his diary that Mr. Bostick sold his house for $13,050 and got $16 per foot for some of the best lots. For some reason, the house sale fell through, and the Bosticks remained in their home. Hardin held another sale six months later. This time, lots in what was advertised as Hardin's addition "went off slowly and low."[17]

In 1860, Hardin was practicing law with his oldest son, J. Litton Bostick, on North Cherry Street. His unusual career change probably was related to disappointments in either the iron business or real estate or both.

Hardin Perkins Bostick died on February 22, 1861, at age fifty-six, leaving a widow and nine surviving children. His funeral was held two days later at his home on the Charlotte Pike.[18] The *Daily Nashville Patriot* reported that he died of typhoid fever after an illness of four weeks.[19] An unsubstantiated account said that he was murdered and that his alleged assassin, William Nolen Jr., was charged with the act but never convicted. Hardin's death, although a devastating blow to his widow, was but a prelude to other tragic family events that would be brought about by the War Between the States that broke out that spring.

CHAPTER TWO

ON TO VIRGINIA!

When Tennessee left the Union in May 1861, Abe Bostick was convinced of the righteousness of the South's cause. He also looked upon the army as an adventure, one he didn't want to miss. Certainly, he would have found it difficult to choose to stay home when all his friends were fighting for the South. Accordingly, he enlisted on May 20, 1861, for a one-year tour of duty. Two first cousins, William Joseph "Bill" Robinson, and James W. "Jim" Thomas, enlisted about the same time, Bill in Company A and Jim in Company C with Abe. All three boys were sent to Camp Trousdale on the Louisville & Nashville Railroad in Sumner County, Tennessee, only a few miles south of the Kentucky border. There ten companies, including theirs, were organized into the Twentieth Tennessee Infantry Regiment.[1] Abe was delighted to be a part of this.

Abe's brother Tom married and, with two small daughters, was not as free to volunteer. Nevertheless, he too felt a sense of duty to the South. Tom immediately put aside his law practice in Lebanon and, along with his brother-in-law, Rufus P. McClain,[2] joined the "Blues," the first company organized in Wilson County. Its captain was a prominent Lebanon attorney, Robert Hatton.[3] Tom was elected lieutenant and Rufus quartermaster sergeant. Along with five other Wilson County companies, Lt. Tom Bostick and the "Blues" left Lebanon on May 20 for Nashville where they spent the night at the fairgrounds and by chance met Abe, Bill, and Jim. The following evening, they all went to Camp Trousdale for instruction. There, one thousand men pitched their tents on high ground near plenty of water. On the twenty-eighth, the six Wilson County companies, two from Sumner, and one each from Smith and DeKalb Counties, were organized into the Seventh Tennessee Infantry Regiment. When Captain Hatton was elected colonel and regimental commander, Tom Bostick succeeded him as captain of Company K, "The Blues."[4] Abe, a private, desiring to serve with Tom, asked for and received permission to transfer to the Seventh Tennessee's Company K from the Twentieth Tennessee.

The Seventh Tennessee Regiment[5] remained at Camp Trousdale until July 14, drilling and training for six hours daily. Because there were widespread cases of measles and mumps in the camp, the commander, Gen. Felix F. Zollicoffer, warned his officers not to allow children, who had not had those diseases, to visit. Nevertheless, crowds of wives, children and other family members from Wilson County visited almost daily.

The men slept in tents and, by early June, were armed with Mississippi rifles, which Col. Hatton felt were the best guns in the service.[6] By July, most soldiers in other regiments were "armed with flint-lock muskets that would actually shoot if it wasn't raining."[7] The Mississippi rifles would prove to be a problem, however, because of difficulty in obtaining ammunition. Nevertheless, it would be two years before they were replaced with Springfield and Enfield rifles.

When a demand was made for all available Tennessee troops to rush to Virginia to reinforce Gens. P. G. T. Beauregard and Joseph E. Johnston at Manassas and the lightly defended western front beyond Staunton, the First Tennessee Brigade was formed, consisting of the First, Seventh, and Fourteenth Tennessee Infantry Regiments. Samuel R. Anderson, of Davidson County, recently commissioned as brigadier general in the Provisional Army of the Confederate States, was its commander. Anderson's Brigade first traveled to Nashville on July 14, where they paraded down the streets of the city with the band playing and flags flying. One of the spectators lining the streets to wave the soldiers good-bye was Bishop E. W. Sehon of the Methodist Episcopal Church. He recognized Abe and stepped into the street to shake his hand.[8] The next morning, Abe and Tom were bid tearful farewells by their family at the Nashville & Chattanooga Depot. From there they traveled by rail through Chattanooga to Knoxville, arriving on the evening of the seventeenth. The brigade remained at Knoxville four days, hopeful of going to Virginia but cognizant of the possibility of being diverted to the remote and uninvolved Cumberland Gap.

On Sunday evening, the twenty-first, their cars left for Virginia on the East Tennessee & Virginia Railroad. At Bristol, they heard the glorious news that a great battle had been fought and won at Bull Run. Quickly, they were put on an express train and rushed to Lynchburg, Virginia, covering the distance of 250 miles in twelve hours. The brigade spent all day Tuesday in Lynchburg, leaving that night on a freight train that climbed and descended the Blue Ridge so slowly that most of the soldiers were able to sleep while lying on the floors of the cars. The next morning they arrived in Charlottesville where for the first time they saw the sick, the wounded, and the dead from Bull Run. Abe and Tom enjoyed talking to veterans of the successful battle and being fed and entertained in a private home by a hospitable Charlottesville family. That night, with mixed feelings of homesickness and excitement, they made the short trip by rail to Staunton.

The three letters, which follow, chronicle the eight-day trip from Chattanooga to Staunton through the observant eyes of Pvt. Abe Bostick, Company K, Seventh Tennessee Infantry.

━━━━►▷·◊·◁◄━━━━

Knoxville, Tennessee
July 18, 1861

Dear Mother,

We arrived at Chattanooga on Tuesday morning and that night about 1 o'clock started to Knoxville. We had a heavy road and an up grade and the rails being wet we made very slow progress, traveling but 21 miles the first 6.5 hours. We reached Knoxville in the evening and came out to this place about 3/4 of a mile from town, to camp. Our reception in Knoxville was not very warm; about half a dozen boys came down to the depot to sell pies and cakes and 4 or 5 men, who looked as if they felt no interest in any of us. I must confess that I was very agreeably disappointed, however, in the people between here and the Cumberland Mountain; at almost every house we passed the inmates came out and cheered us. At little log huts, where one accustomed to better would imagine not more than one could live comfortably, a dozen little whiteheaded, fat faced, shirt-tailed fellows would run out and, arranging themselves along the fence, would clap their hands and hurrah for Jeff Davis, while the old lady would wave her handkerchief and bid us God-speed. There was one little fellow in particular that arrested my attention; he was standing on top of a shed with a flag in his hands and as we passed he waved his flag and gave "three cheers" for Jeff Davis; he was just learning to talk and it was really amusing to see him; we approved of all he said. Such little things as these seem to have a wonderful effect upon the soldiers; it cheered them up and makes them prouder of the cause in which they are engaged to know that the hearts of the women and even the youngest children are enlisted with theirs. There was one sight that enraged the men as much as anything I ever saw. A little fellow (whose Southern heart had not been tainted by the foul precepts of his father) was waving his handkerchief to us as we passed and the old Tory came out and kicked him and drove him in the house. The men who saw it would have treated him very roughly if they could have laid hands upon him. Judging from what we saw, the people near the road are "all right," but judging from what we heard, the people in the interior are not. One man told me that there was a regiment in Bradley County who were Union men and there were [Union] companies all through this portion of the state.

If it is only the people who cannot see and hear for themselves that are against us, I have no fear of the final result of East Tennessee. They will come right as they are gradually informed.

I do not know when we will leave here or where we will go. If I could decide it to suit myself, we would leave for Va. today. You need not write until you hear from us again.

I am very well and agreeably situated. Tom wrote to sister Mat[9] this morning. He is well.

Your affectionate son
A. Bostick

Knoxville
July 21, 1861

Dear Mother,

Tom is going into Knoxville in a few minutes to church and I concluded to write a few lines to you as I have this opportunity to send [the letter] to the Post Office.

We will leave here tomorrow for Virginia: we will stop a day or two at Haynesville, Tenn.[10] to wait for the artillery company from Nashville: We will join Col. Maney's Reg. and one or two others; these with 2 or 3 Cavalry; Companies will form Anderson's Brigade.[11] It is thought that we will go from Haynesville to Lynchburg [Va.] and will remain there a short time. In that event I hope to see Miss Fannie Early.[12]

I was afraid that we would be sent to Cumberland Gap to spend the summer, which would have been the equivalent to burying our Regiment for we would never have seen a battle; but we will have a fine chance now. The whole Regiment are delighted at the idea of going to Virginia. We expect to have fine times up there.

We marched through Knoxville yesterday and when I got back, I was as wet as if I had jumped into the river; my coat pants and everything I had on was wet. I tried to dry by a fire before bedtime but did not succeed and had to put on dry clothes to sleep in.

Tom is waiting for my letter. We are well. Direct to Haynesville, Washington County, Tennessee, care of Captain Bostick, Col. Hatton's Regiment[13] and if we leave before I get it, it will be forwarded to me.

Your affect. son
A. Bostick

Staunton, Va.
July 26, 1861

Dear Sister,[14]

We have been at this place since Wednesday night. We spent Wednesday in Charlottesville; it is the most hospitable place I have ever seen. The citizens met us at the depot and took the soldiers to their houses and treated them like princes. All the day long the soldiers were feasting upon the best the country affords. The city is now a large hospital in which every house is a chamber for the sick and wounded; business is almost entirely suspended and the men, women and children are engaged in waiting upon those who have been brought from the battlefield.[15] While we were there 150 wounded men were taken into their charge. The wounded men gave some very amusing accounts of the fight. Almost everyone had some trophy he had taken; one man had a guitar, which he said the Yankees had brought to play on at the springs this summer; he said that they made a charge on them [the Yankees] and took almost a wagon load of champagne and the finest brandies he ever saw; he said that they had hair dye and pomatum [pomade] and everything else that a dandy would take on a trip of pleasure—Poor, deluded creatures; their doom was very unlike their dreams!

As we passed along the road from Charlottesville to this place the men and women came out to see us and threw baskets full of the nicest bread and butter into the cars I ever saw. The man who would not fight for such people is not a man.

The country through which we have passed, though not altogether so rich is the more beautiful than our own state. It is a very hilly country and abounds in the most sublime scenery. Staunton like all the towns I have seen in this state is built upon steep hills. Some of its streets are very steep. We are encamped upon a hillside opposite the city; it is very rough and steep. We all had to scotch ourselves upon a rock to keep from rolling out of our tents. I slept with Tom and Lieut. Toliver[16] last night and we had to lie up and down the hill or we would have rolled entirely away; this, however, did not alleviate the difficulty. We slided [sic] down feet foremost. Tom and Lt. T. propped themselves against their trunks which enabled them to sleep pretty comfortably. I did not happen to strike a rock larger than my head and consequently slipped from under the cover and like to have frozen

(Last night was the coldest night I ever knew in the summertime).

We will probably have to leave here tomorrow for Western Virginia. We will have to march about 150 miles on foot, into an unfriendly country where the people, worse than savages, because they have more sense—are said to worm themselves along in the grass and weeds so closely that it would take a fine comb to get them out and shoot our men, almost without danger to themselves. I did hope to help in the taking of Washington City, but I fear that I will be disappointed; if we do not get there, however, we will meet McClellan who is said to be their best general.[17]

Your affec. brother
A. Bostick

CHAPTER THREE

WESTERN VIRGINIA— LEE'S FIRST CAMPAIGN

onfederate concern was great in June 1861 for the western part of Virginia in and beyond the Allegheny Mountains. That vast area, whose streams flowed into the Ohio or its tributaries, was strategically important. It was also wide open to the Federals. By controlling the line of the Baltimore & Ohio Railroad, Union forces under Maj. Gen. George B. McClellan could advance southward from Grafton and threaten Staunton and the upper Shenandoah Valley. Were this to happen, railroad communications with Kentucky and Tennessee would also be endangered. Sentiment was divided in this mountainous area with most of the people, many of whom came from Pennsylvania, open in their support of the North. Only the relatively few slave-owning planters who lived in the river valleys shared the states' rights and secessionist views of Midland and Tidewater, Virginia. Because the majority of the inhabitants were Unionist, the Confederacy had poor intelligence as to the movement of Union troops.

On June 1, three weeks after having been given command of all forces in Virginia, Robert E. Lee heard the rumor that Grafton had fallen to the Federals. A few days later, he learned that Phillipi, fifteen miles south, had been captured by Union forces. Lee realized that, unless the Federal army was checked, their forces could advance to Staunton only 120 miles away by road, and isolate Southwestern Virginia. To counter this move, Lee ordered Brig. Gen. Robert S. Garnett, C.S.A., to Staunton to assume

command of Northwest Virginia. With only twenty-three companies of
infantry, miserably armed and poorly disciplined, and a single battery,
Garnett advanced through the mountains and occupied passes on Rich
Mountain and Laurel Hill. Soon he was forced to abandon these positions
by the numerically superior Federal forces under Gens. McClellan and
William S. Rosecrans. Flanked by their forces and closely pursued, Gen.
Garnett and some of his troops were cut off and killed at Carrick's Ford on
Shivers Fork of Cheat River. Garnett thus gained the dubious honor of
becoming the first general officer on either side to be killed in the war.
Conversely, the Union victory helped establish McClellan's reputation as a
"winning general" and secure his appointment as commander of the Army
of the Potomac. The victory also gave the Union control over Virginia's
northwest counties.

The portion of Garnett's command who escaped death or capture
retreated through uncharted wilderness to Monterey, only forty miles from
Staunton. Among them were members of Atlanta's Gate City Guards, a
unit so decimated by the ordeal that its surviving members were mustered
out of service never to serve again as a unit.[1]

Virginia was now threatened by Union attacks on three fronts—in
Western Virginia by McClellan's army; in Northern Virginia, where Brig.
Gen. Irvin McDowell was mustering a large army on the south bank of the
Potomac; and in the Tidewater area by forces under Gen. Benjamin F. Butler
and later under Gen. John E. Wool. In response, President Jefferson Davis
and the War Department took responsibility for the defense of Northern
Virginia, concentrating their forces around Harper's Ferry and Manassas
Junction. Robert E. Lee took responsibility for the defense of Richmond and
Eastern Virginia, while Lee and Davis shared responsibility for the western
front. Lee realized that, because of the dangerous situation arising in front of
Manassas Junction, he had few Virginia troops to spare for the west. Those
he dared release were quickly rushed to Staunton and put under the temporary command of Gen. William W. Loring, whose charge was to cling to the
mountain passes, to protect the railroad, and to organize a counter offensive
as soon as he could. To further support Loring, Jefferson Davis called for
troops from Tennessee and the other southern states to hurry to that front.
When the Seventh Tennessee Regiment, including Tom and Abe Bostick,
arrived in Staunton on July 24, 1861, following their nine-day trip from
Nashville over the Nashville & Chattanooga, the East Tennessee &
Virginia, and the Virginia Central Railroads, they found a disorganized command of dirty, exhausted, and discouraged men.

Four days later, Gen. Lee arrived to coordinate the Confederate war effort on the front. During the following weeks, he and his soldiers would encounter incessant rain, sodden roads, hard marches, beautiful but lonely country, and a Confederate commander, Loring, who showed no disposition to move quickly against the enemy. This period included a failed attempt to engage Union forces at Cheat Mountain. Lee's consent to allow an inexperienced officer, Col. Albert Rust of the Third Arkansas Regiment, to lead an attack against a position that no experienced soldier had reconnoitered, was a major factor in his first campaign being a failure. Following the non-battle at Cheat Mountain, Lee focused on bringing together all the troops then commanded by two feuding generals—Henry A. Wise and John B. Floyd—and taking the offensive against Rosecrans' troops in the Kanawha Valley. Part of the challenge was accomplished on September 20, 1861, when Gen. Wise was ordered to turn his command over to Gen. Floyd and report to Richmond. The other challenge was tougher. Plagued by continuing rains, knee-deep mud, supply difficulties, and hungry, shivering, and sick soldiers, Lee concluded by early October that an offensive against Rosecrans, who had succeeded McClellan in command, would gain nothing and that the time had come for him to leave. He would keep Loring's brigade and enough other troops in the fog-enshrouded mountains to protect the passes. Soon, Floyd would be transferred to Albert Sidney Johnston's army in Kentucky. Lee returned to Richmond, never to see Floyd again. Lee's failure to drive Rosecrans out of the area cowed the secessionists and encouraged the pro-unionists in Western Virginia. On October 24, a majority there voted to establish the state of West Virginia, thus losing the area to Virginia and the Confederacy.

The following letters, written by Abe Bostick to his mother and sisters, chronicle daily activities on the western front during the late summer and fall of 1861.

Huntersville, Virginia
August 4, 1861

Dear Mag[2]

I received a letter from mother yesterday the first I have received. We reached this place yesterday after a hard march. We have marched three days; forded a number of streams, which were full on account of recent rains, crossed three high mountains (spurs of the Alleghany's [sic]) and halted yesterday, pretty nearly broken down.

Night before last after marching 15 miles I had to stand guard. The next day I had to start at sunup; when I had marched about 10 miles, my knapsack and gun began to feel pretty heavy I assure you; added to all this our reception to this place was anything but pleasant; it was a very cool one; it threw a damper over all our feelings, for when in about a mile from town it began to rain, and for about half an hour it rained in torrents; we halted till it ceased and just before we got here we had to wade a large creek. After marching through the town,[3] which is about the size of Triune,[4] we went out to our campground and just as we reached it, it commenced raining again, out tents were in the wagons behind us, and we were in a field, where there wasn't a tree; I took my seat upon a stump and sat there till the rain was over. We got our tents up by night and although our blankets were wet we slept soundly and this morning are all right again. We will not move today; they gave us today to wash our clothes. I expect to spend my time by cleaning my gun and mending my clothes.

Maney's Reg.[5] and a Clarksville Reg.[6] are here; we will all move together. The enemy are about 35 miles from here. We expect to clean out all this part of the country and then go to Washington and catch old Abe.

I have not seen or heard of Bush. I hope that he will be in our brigade.

General Loring[7] is here; he will take command of the forces here. We have great confidence in him, and are confident of success. Everyone here vows that he will not come home without a Yankee to carry his knapsack and gun.

Tom has gone to church. He is very well and has been ever since we came to Virginia.

Give all the girls my love. Judie in particular.

Direct to Huntersville, Pocahontas County, Virginia, care of Captain Bostick, Col. Hatton's Reg.; I have written to mother four times, Sister C,[8] Eliza[9] and Litton.

When I get into a battle, I will send you a portion of my booty, such as rings, breast pins, etc. Write soon.

Your affec. brother,
A. Bostick

Polecat Hollow [Va.]
August 13, 1861

Dear Sister,[10]

I wrote to mother a few days ago and told her that we expected a fight in a few days; but we are still here and no better prospect for a fight than when I wrote. The rains have been so incessant and the roads are so bad that it is just as much as we can do to get provisions enough from one day to another and it would be madness to attack the enemy without several days provisions ahead, and, besides, we are at the foot of a mountain, which we will have to ascend, and it is almost impossible to get heavy artillery up. In all my letters lately I have written about the rains; I have never seen anything in the wintertime to equal the rain here now. It rains nearly all the time. I was on guard yesterday and last night, and it rained on me all the time. The people who live here say that it rains this way all the year; they say that it rained 362 days last year, and if it was to fail to rain for three or four days they would expect a famine. It is turning cold now and I hope that it will stop; it feels more like a winter day than I have ever felt at this time of the year before. In my letter to mother, I told her that some of the boys had named this place Starvation Hollow, but they have no fear of starving now, for there are enough polecats here to feed us for a season yet. One man said that he saw 40 while standing guard the other night; he said that he would have seen more but it wasn't a good night for them. He killed one with a rock. The woods are full of "varmits." We see them prowling around us all the time we are on guard; one says he saw a bear; another a panther; others wild-cats, etc. I do not vouch for the truth of these assertions, but there certainly are many of them about here.

The enemy have made no movements yet. We sent out 180 men under Col. Maney today. I tried to go with them, but could not get off. We all hope for some movement after their return. It is said that the Yankees are very strongly fortified and because they have whipped the Virginians and Georgians, they are very impudent. I hope we will be allowed to cool them soon. It is thought by some that we will not attack them at all, but will be ordered back to Warm Springs. I hope this is not true. I do not believe that there is any foundation for it. Were such an order issued there is no telling how discouraging it would be to our troops.

Mrs. Cockrill was here a few days ago. Joe Stones came up a day or two ago to bring a letter to Gen. Anderson;[11] he will go back tomorrow, and I will send this letter by him.

When you write tell me all about the school. Did Jake[12] get a place? Why don't he write? Where is Bush? How are you getting along at home? What has become of old Pearl? How is Bayless? Write long letters and give me all the news. What is Kentucky doing? Are there any prospects for peace? How did our state vote? We don't know anything. Direct to Huntersville as before. Give my love to all the girls (Miss Dunham). Write soon. Write to Joe[13] for me. I seldom get a chance to send a letter.

A. Bostick

I enclose a letter to Joe. Please forward it.

━━━➤◦⬤◦⬅━━━

Big Spring, Virginia
August 20, 1861

Dear Mother,

I wrote you a long letter Sunday, but as one of our men, who has been discharged on account of sickness, is going home tomorrow, I concluded to write again.

I have just returned from a blackberry hunt.[14] I did not succeed very well in finding blackberries but found a good many gooseberries, they are larger and better than those we have at home. It is now nearly night and we have orders to cook provisions for 48 hours and be ready to move at a moment's warning: no one knows where we will go: it is thought that the Yankees have retreated some distance and so we are all at a loss to know what we are going to do. It is reported that Maney's went to take two hundred Yankees who were encamped near here last night. I have not heard the success of the expedition. A Yankee prisoner was brought into camp today; he was taken about 60 miles from here: the men flocked around him like it was some wild animal; he is the first "live Yankee" we have seen.

Lieut. Toliver returned from Richmond a few days ago: he says that Richmond looks like a vast army camp; he says that it would be impossible to form any idea of the number of arms taken at Manassas without seeing them, but thousands of them were ruined, some broken in pieces, some bent double some with bullets sticking in them. The more we hear of that victory the greater it appears: it will stand forth in history as one of the most brilliant ever achieved. It is said that when the New Orleans Tigers charged Elsworth's [sic] Zouaves[15] they could have been heard screaming for a mile. They hid behind a fence until they were very near them, fired off their guns and then charged them with their bowie knives. The Yankees can't stand steel.

I have written to every one in the family and to you—I don't know how often. I have written to Jake and Bully; but I have received only three letters. I have nothing to write—wrote to let you know that we were well. Our P. Office will be Huntersville, in fact the letters will come to us from almost anywhere. I will write when we halt if I can find a chance to send my letter. Write soon to your afft. son.

A. Bostick

August 21st—we will not leave here for some time yet.

Near Mingo Flats, Virginia
September 7, 1861

Dear Sister,[16]

I received a letter from you and also one from mother a week ago, but have had no opportunity to answer until now. We received orders to cook provisions for two days last Monday evening and the next morning were marching toward the enemy to relieve a regiment which had been stationed as a picket guard.

We crossed Talley Mountain and the country once more began to look like the hand of civilization had been there. For the last several weeks we have seen nothing but mountains and the wildest country I ever saw. There we saw a beautiful valley, teaming with crops of corn, hay and oats—a large frame house, and a woman (a good sign of civilization).

We made a rapid march of 12 miles. We came to a halt in a thick woods. We were not allowed to make any noise as it was a great object to remain concealed because we knew nothing of the situation or number of the enemy and we did not wish to put them on the alert. We were not allowed to have any fire, and, at night, to talk. We had to sleep on our arms as it was not known what moment we might be attacked. We were all tired and although bugs were crawling all over and occasionally a snake (one man waked [sic] up and found one on his head) we were soon asleep. We had not slept long when we were awakened by rain, not a slight shower, but a real old Virginia rain, which almost washed a fellow out of bed; it rained the rest of the night. The next morning I was told that there was a house about a mile off and taking coffee pot and my gun I put out and found the house. I made my coffee and dried my clothes.

During the day a party of 30 or 40 were seen to leave the hill on which the Yankees were encamped, and move toward our left: fifteen were selected from Williamson's company[17] and 15 from ours and we started to meet them: we expected to have a nice fight; but when we came upon them we found, to our chagrin, that they were our men, who were out scouting. Late in the evening a picket fired off his gun and we thought the Yankees were on us. I never saw the regiment formed so quickly in my life: this proved to be a false alarm. Three of the Yankees had crept along a bluff and when within close shooting distance of our pickets, they raised and were about to fire when our man gave the alarm: he was excited and had to shoot so quick he did not kill either one of them. When this man was detailed to guard that place, I went to him and begged him to let me take his place, but he refused as everyone wanted it; I think that I would have plugged one of those gentlemen. That night it rained and we could not sleep and the next day it still rained down.[18]

The second day we were out we went inside of the enemy's pickets and from what they could see concluded that there were not more than a regiment of them on a hill in front of us and another regiment to their right. General Anderson then went to General Loring and asked permission to attack them and promised that if he did not "bag them" he would take them back to Tennessee. General Loring consented and Maney's and Forbes's[19] regiments were ordered out day before yesterday. That evening as our provisions were consumed, one man from each mess was sent back 1.5 miles to cook, we sent a negro for our mess, but as I had been wet two or three days, I went to dry: we had only five skillets to cook for 80 men and it was 2 o'clock when we were through. It was so dark that we all broke ranks and each man put out for himself; and of all the walks I ever took in my life it was the most unpleasant. I had to go 1/2 a mile through a dense woods on a little path and every ten steps I ran against a log or in a mud-hole: if it had not been that we were to start at day-break I would have laid by for the rest of the night. When I got to camp, it was nearly day and I sat down in the mud and leaning against a tree slept until day. We expected to leave at sunup to attack the enemy. Our regiment was to go up the mountain on which they were encamped in front—the 1st regiment in the rear and the 14th on the side. Nobody was to be in the fight except Tennesseans and we intended to give it to them—and it was all the men talked of, each one had selected something that he intended to take; some a pistol, some a Manards rifle, some one thing and some another, I was going to have a pair of pants as I burn[ed] all the bottom out of mine while drying them the day before and I had nothing to "half sole" them but bark. I intended to pull them off the first Yankee I caught. It would have amused you if you could have heard them talk. The men all rose early and such rubbing up of guns I never saw before; but lo and behold: an order came from old General Loring postponing the show indefinitely, and we were ordered to fall back seven miles. The men have been mad ever since. We lost one apparently of the finest chances. I fear we will never see such again. We were in sight of the Yankees three days and some of our men were fired upon, (but missed) and when our arrangements were all made to take them we were ordered back. General Loring doubtless had some good reason for it but none of our officers know what it is.

We have had pretty hard times for want of something to eat. One morning I made my breakfast off a piece of meat, no bread, which I refused several days earlier because I did not think it good. I had nothing to eat today except blackberries and corn until 2 o'clock when we accidentally found some flour in a chest. This scarcity of provisions is owing to the bad road; we have started men for provisions and we will get plenty this evening. We have had a hard time of it, but no grumbling till we were ordered back. We are now encamped in a good place and are all well and straight again. The only thing of which we will have to complain is inactivity; while the right and left is doing so much the center wishes to do something and would do it if permitted.[20]

General Loring complemented our regiment very highly; he said that we were the best regiment he had and had found out more about the enemy than all the rest.

In a letter to Eliza I wrote for what I needed. You can send them by

Rex Vick,[21] our Quartermaster, who is in Nashville and Lebanon providing for our regiment. Send me a pair of strong, cheap pants well lined, and a pocket knife.

I expect that you are having fine times eating fruit: we never see anything of the kind. A man has just brought Lieutenant Powell[22] a bundle of newspapers; they are a great rarity and very acceptable.

There is a tree here that I wish you could see; it is a wild cucumber: it is a large tree loaded with cucumbers which are a beautiful red.

Sunday morning

I had to stop writing yesterday and intended to write a longer letter to you today, but there is a man going to leave today and I have no time.

I suppose you are now teaching school. What room are you in? And what is the Home School of which you write? Did Jake get a place? Why don't he and Bully answer my letters? Who is Bully going to school to? It is reported that Battle's[23] regiment is at Camp Trousdale.[24] If that is true, I reckon Bush is snorting.

Why don't Litton answer my letter? How is Sister Bettie?[25]

My man is about to start and I must stop. Love to all. Tom and I are well—write soon.

Your afft. Bro
A. Bostick

Direct as before until I give you further instructions.

———◦———

Big Sewell, Virginia
Oct. 5, 1861

My Dear Sister,[26]

If you will look at a map of the corner of Fayette County where a chain of mountains terminate, you will see where we are. We are on Big Sewell Mountain in full view of Gen. Rosecrans' army: we can see them drilling, can hear them cutting wood, can see the "Stars and Stripes" floating amongst their sea of tents, and they serenade us every night with "Yankee Doodle" etc. We do not know their number, it was thought they had 15,000 several days ago and they have received reinforcements since. We have about 12,000 men here. Day before yesterday a woman by name Mrs. Tyne (a relative of Aunt Lucinda) saw about 5,000 Yankees going to reinforce Rosecrans, and got upon her horse and rode along with some of the officers and found out that they intended to attack us yesterday or today: she got away from them and came around to our camp and told Gen. Lee about it. She did the same thing twice before and saved Gen. Wise.[27] Fortunately for the Yankees they didn't attack. We will slay them if they attempt such a thing. I do not think we will attack them. They have more cannon, more men, and are strongly fortified, and although I believe we would whip them, it would cost too many lives to suit General Lee. He values the lives of his men even to a fault. On our way here we passed through a beautiful country and had an abundance of fruit (the first of this season). A good road, a level country, farms and farm houses infused some spirit among the men and made them feel that they had something to fight for, besides mountains and mud and made them lively and cheerful again. We have not got our clothes yet. What I have are worn out, but if one of our regiments had good clothing the rest would not know him. The Yankees call us "the ragged Tennesseans."

We have been hard run for something to eat lately but our men won't starve. I went hog hunting yesterday but had no luck! One of them just came in with a big pumpkin and a bag of corn. We haven't got any salt but we have got some brine out of a barrel of pickled pork and we use that to salt our beef and biscuit. I don't know where we will winter; we will have to leave here soon or freeze. Bayless just got here, he brought me a letter from you and one from Jake. I didn't get the pants or Mag's[28] letter: he knew nothing about them. Alex Read has not been with us for some time; he has not been well. Tell Jake I will write the first opportunity: I have written to him three times and have received two letters. Why don't you sell my horse? If you can get anything for him sell him. When I left home, Litton owed me $80. Tell him to pay to mother what is left. I told him to pay her a portion of it monthly. He may have forgotten it. We don't get any pay out here and if I did it is only 11 dollars per month. I never see anything like money out here. I often reproach myself for leaving you all as I did but it is too late now. You are justly entitled to pay more than your assistant. Lay your case before Litton and he can have it increased.

Tell Bully I want him to join our company and that he must not join any other before I write him, which I will do as soon as I find out where we are to spend the winter.

It is reported this morning that the Yankees have all left. We can hear nothing nor see any smoke or tents over there. It may be a Yankee trick.

When will Eliza start back? Write soon. I get very few letters from home now. You do better than all the rest. Write me a long letter and tell me all about home affairs. This is all the paper I have. I have been carrying this in my cartridge box. Direct to Lewisburg, Va. Tom and I are well.

Yours,
A. Bostick

CHAPTER FOUR

WINTER CAMPAIGN

For several months following the great Confederate victory at Manassas in July, the Northern and Confederate armies seemed content to marshal their forces. Fresh from his success in Western Virginia, Maj. Gen. George B. McClellan, hailed as a young Napoleon, took command of Federal troops in the Washington area. By early fall, his Army of the Potomac had grown to an astonishing 168,000. In November, General-in-Chief Winfield Scott finally resigned and McClellan was named commander-in-chief of all Federal armies. Meanwhile, the West Virginia region was made a department by the Federal authorities. There, Commanding General Rosecrans reorganized his forces as a result of three-month enlistment volunteers going home and new soldiers being received.

After eleven days of cold rains in late October, Confederate Brig. Gen. John B. Floyd took advantage of Rosecrans' failure to occupy Fayette Court House and Cotton Hill, in a mountainous area between the New and Kanawha Rivers. Floyd crossed the New River with 5000 men, moved down its left bank and made a demonstration against a Union force at Gauley Bridge. On November 10, Rosecrans' troops, hoping to trap Floyd, flanked the Confederate force and moved against him from the front. Floyd, realizing his vulnerability, withdrew his artillery and, on the twelfth, began a retreat to the railroad in the

Shenandoah Valley. Following this, both armies then went into winter quarters and, although some fights occurred, a status quo ensued in West Virginia. The only significant action was a fight at Buffalo Mountain, on December 13, where twenty Union and twenty Confederate soldiers were killed.[1] Abe missed that fight. At this time, the Seventh Tennessee, as a part of Gen. Loring's Division, was stationed at or near Staunton.

Stonewall Jackson, whose orders were to rid Northern Virginia of the Union presence, moved his troops, including the Seventh Tennessee, to Bath, Virginia, which the Federals occupied. Upon the Confederates' approach, the Union forces evacuated the town and retreated across the Potomac to Hancock, Maryland. Unable to bridge the swollen river, Jackson shelled the Union position at Hancock, burning the town. The Confederate general then moved his forces up to Romney, also held by the Federals. They too retreated into Maryland. Having rid this area of Union forces and plagued by cold weather, deep snow, and an over-extended supply line, Jackson pulled his forces back to Winchester.

For Abe Bostick, November and early December was a period of waiting, of uncertainty as to where he would spend the winter, and of boredom, tempered by the balming influences of a sojourn at Warm Springs. The latter half of December and January were filled with hard marches, bitter cold, and, on too many occasions, a lack of food. Light casualties and youthful exuberance mitigated Abe's suffering, however, and kept aflame his hopes of capturing Washington and ending the war. Nevertheless, for however long it lasted, he was committed to seeing the war through as a soldier.

Tom missed the sojourn at Warm Springs because he was home on furlough. By mid-December, he was back with his company, then near Staunton. Despite the fact that Abe wrote his mother on the sixteenth that he and Tom were both well, that seems not to have been the case with Tom. Eleven days later, Col. Hatton wrote his wife: "I heard, however, through Capt. Bostick's letter, that on the 17th he was regarded as out of all danger. I hardly knew how much I thought of him, until I heard of his extreme illness. There never was a kinder father, and I don't think there ever was a boy who thought more of a father than I do of him."[2] During January, Tom was still on the sick list in Winchester. By the first of February, he was reported by Col. Hatton as "looking quite improved." Several days earlier, Abe wrote his mother that Tom was sent to Winchester largely as a precautionary measure to keep him from getting really sick. Tom completely recovered and was with Gen. Anderson and Col. Hatton in Richmond on March 5.[3] Although there are no known letters from Tom Bostick written during the winter campaign of 1861-1862, there are eight letters from Abe, which are transcribed below.

⟶➤⬦⬥⟵

Greenbrier River
Nov. 6th, 1861

Mrs. J. B. Halbert[4]
Dear Sister,

 When I last wrote, we were expecting to leave this place any day, but no order came and many are beginning to fear we will have to remain all winter; I do not believe we will have to stay, because there are several Virginia regiments here and I don't believe that we will have to stay, and, they be permitted to go elsewhere. We are 46 miles from the railroad and during the winter months we might as well be 500, for all communication will be entirely cut off. I walked up to Huntersville last Sunday for my clothes: when I first opened my bundle I could not imagine why you sent me the brown jeans coat, but it is well you sent it, for the blue would not begin to meet: I was very sorry for it was a beautiful suit of clothes. I gave it to Tom, but it was too small for him & I gave it to Bob Bugg (for Aline's sake). When I came to my hat I threw my cap in a mud-hole; I then hung my old coat up on the road side and left it. My clothes came in good time, for it is winter here now. Day before yesterday when we awoke the mountain tops were covered with snow: it is said to be 18 inches deep on Cheat Mountain, where we had a little battle some time ago. It has been hailing and snowing & raining all day and we expect a snow tonight; but we all say let it come; we are well clothed now and don't care how cold it gets: we slept pretty cold before we got our supplies, but Tom got a large counterpin[5] from home and Lieut Powell with whom he slept got several blankets and comforts and so they turned over a blanket to me, then Baird[6] our Lt got a couple of blankets and these with what we had (we sleep together) make us a bed that would compare with what you have at home. The bundle you sent, or rather thought you sent by Bayless reached me last night: it came with the supplies of the 1st regiment. You sent the books that I would have selected for myself had I been chooser. They are quite a treat I assure you. I have all the clothes I need or will need during the winter; all our regiment are well supplied by their friends at home. We have a noble set of women to fight for, and if this war does no other good, it will develop the character of our people and teach us that we are of a noble race. Tell Hardie, Mary and Bently,[7] that their box of candy was the best thing I have had since I have been here: it with a box Tom got and some preserves and pickles sent to our Lieuts were the only good things we have had for a long time. Since we received our goods we have been living in style—something to wear, something to eat and good beds and something to read.

The night we got our goods all in, we dressed up and had a big dance—a stag dance—we had an old cracked fiddle and a rough place, but we had a fine time.

Today is election day and our company just sent up their vote for Davis.[8] An old fellow, who is running for Congress in this district came along yesterday and we made him think we could vote for him and got him up on a good box and made him speak: he is a great old fool (just the man to represent this district) and we had our fun out of him.

I wish you would look up my skates and get Jake[9] to have the straps fixed for if we stay here I will want them. The citizens tell me that the river is frozen up all the winter; they say it sometimes freezes over this month. I hope we will not stay here, however. I would rather go South, than anywhere else, because we will see more active service there than we can see in a colder climate. I wrote Eliza Saturday. Tom wrote to mother Monday enclosing five dollars. Mr. Blythe who brought out clothing to the regiment starts back tomorrow and I send this by him. Enclosed I send ten dollars to mother. We drew a portion of our wages a few days ago, will draw again soon and I will then send more. Tom and I are both very well. Love to all. Write soon and direct to Staunton.

> Yours,
> A. Bostick

Sweetbrier Cottage
Warm Springs, Virginia
Nov. 30th 1861

My Dear Mother,

We are now pleasantly located in a neat little brick house: it contains four rooms, one of which is occupied by a mess of privates and the other by the officers' mess. We have a new cooking stove, which we found here and our cook is a negro man who never did anything else; he was formerly a cook for the City Hotel at Nashville. I never saw anyone so proud as our cook since he got into a room with a stove. I have seen him upon several occasions invite the other negroes belonging to the regiment into the room to look at his stove. We are just opposite the bathrooms connected with the Warm Springs; it is the most delightful place to bathe I ever saw: the water is just as hot as one can stand but not hot enough to be unpleasant; the water contains a considerable quantity of sulphur. The name of our house is Sweetbrier Cottage. Lieutenant Powell[10] is in command of our company now; he is the only officer with us, the other Lieutenants being sick. He fills the place well; he is a clever gentleman, an energetic man and a fine officer. He has been down town and just returned with good news; our brigade is ordered to Staunton and from thence we will go either to Manassas or the coast of South Carolina; it is thought that the place is Manassas. I never believed that we would be kept here, now we are pretty certain to leave western Virginia. We are ordered to leave today but I do not think we will get off before tomorrow because our wagons are not here. Tell Tom that if he has any message to send to old Abe to write immediately. I expect to call on "Bob" when I get to Washington and Christmas night I expect to dance with one of his gals. Owing to a scarcity of officers, Lieutenant Powell has appointed me Lieutenant till Toliver and Tarver[11] get well and as the regiment will march to Staunton (about 50 miles) I expect to take charge of the sick and go by way of Millboro; I will have to walk only 15 miles. Some time ago I wrote for my skates: if we go to South Carolina I will not need them, but if to Manassas you will please send them by Tom. Col. Hatton had a slight attack of typhoid fever, he is getting better and I hope he will be well enough to be with us soon. He is the finest officer I know of and I never saw a man so universally beloved as is Col. Hatton. His men would follow him anywhere or do anything for him. If it were left to the men to choose a colonel I believe that two thirds of Maney's and Forbes'[12] men would join our regiment. Our company is in good condition once more: nearly all the men are well.

You said in a letter to Tom that Aline had knit me a pair of socks and wanted to know how to send them. Tell Tom to be certain to bring them with him. I will wear them when I dance with old Abe's gal in Washington and dance in my stocking feet. Tell Mag to give her my love.

I hope you have succeeded by this time in getting a house; it will be much better to move before Christmas, if you can get one.[13] Tell Tom I wrote to him day before yesterday and would have written again today but Lieutenant Powell will write to him.

We will start today. I haven't time to write more. Love to all. Direct to Staunton.

Your affect. son
A. Bostick

——➤-◦-◄——

Camp two miles west of
Staunton, Va.
December 10, 1861

Dear Sister,[14]

In the past few letters that I have written I have mentioned very cold weather, but for the past few days the weather has been warm for wintertime. I wish that we could be traveling this pleasant weather for it is extremely unpleasant in open cars without fire in cold weather, but I am not complaining for we are pleasantly situated and as for waiting—it seems that the "waiting policy" has been adopted by all our rulers; this however is a matter of very little importance, for it only cost about 1,000,000 per day to wait.

I received a letter from sister C and also one from Mag a few days ago. Sister C although she generally says she has nothing to write, writes longer letters and more of them than anyone of the family. From their accounts Nashville must be a horrible place.[15] They must have converted it into one large hospital, and I think a hospital is a horrible place. It is a good thing for me that I have had good health, for I believe it would kill me to have to stay with so many sick soldiers. As much as I detest hospitals I would be very much tempted to get sick if I had some of the nurses Mag mentioned in her letters. It would not take much of an effort to get as sick as many you find in the hospitals. A severe march is contemplated. The probability of a battle, the expectation of any kind of extra work or danger have caused more than half of the invalids who have frequented the hospitals in West Virginia and I expect elsewhere. There are many, many poor fellows who are sent to the hospitals because they are sick and they all have my sympathy, but on the other hand there are enough lazy vagabonds in the hospitals in the C. States, who go there because of laziness and cowardice, who are an expense and burden to the government, to make a large army if they could be collected. I would like to see this army collected and, when our army crosses the Potomac, for a bridge to be made of their bodies. If it were only these men that were killed, and, the war did no other good, I would think that we had been paid for our loss of time, trouble and expense.

The rest of our Brigade has not come yet, though it will in a few days. We have no idea where we will be ordered from here or when.

I just heard that one of Mr. Early's brothers[16] was the stationed preacher in the Methodist Church at Staunton. I will call on him tomorrow if I can get off to town.

Does Hardin talk of joining the army soon?[17] Give love to all the family, to Mr. Early and the rest of your family. I would like to see the figure you make acting mother. I have no doubt you look very old and dignified. I send this by our chaplain[18] who is going home on furlough.

Write soon.

Your affect. Brother
A. Bostick

Direct to Staunton.

Near Staunton, Va.
December 16th, 1861

Dear Litton,

We have been encamped here about ten days waiting for orders. We expected to be ordered to the Southern coast. General Donaldson's brigade[19] has been sent to Charleston, South Carolina, and we were ordered to join him (so says report) but General Loring sent a Virginia regiment to Donaldson and kept us with him, very much to the dissatisfaction of our regiment as we were very anxious to go to that place.

Yesterday evening orders came for us to start today to Strasburg, about 75 miles from this place, and there await further orders. I expect that we will be held there as a reserve force to be thrown to Manassas or Winchester, as circumstances may demand. We will probably spend the winter in our tents as the lateness of the season will not justify us in building huts. The order has come for us to strike tents and I have not time to write more.

Love to all. Direct letters to Strasburg, Virginia, Colonel Hatton's regiment and not to Anderson's brigade.[20]

Tom and I are both well.

Yours,
A. Bostick

As our regiment has not taken enough exercise during this campaign, we will march through, instead of taking the cars.[21] 2,000 of our men were attacked a few days ago by 3,000 Yankees: the latter were repulsed with the loss of several hundred, our loss inconsiderable.

Colonel Maney's, Forbes' and three Virginia regiments go to Strasburg with us. Our regiment is to be the outside regiment of the left wing of the Army of the Potomac.

Strasburg, Va.
December 22nd 1861

My dear Mother,

On last Monday at 10 o'clock we left our camp 2 miles beyond Staunton and yesterday at ten we reached this place, having travelled 77 miles in five days. We had a good turnpike all the way, which was decidedly better for the wagons than for us: heretofore all our marches have been on dirt roads and the hard turnpike was not very good walking, for on the evening of the second day nine tenths of the men were limping like they had been shot through the leg or foot. Our feet got better on the third day and afterwards we made it finely.

The country through which we passed is the oldest settled portion of Virginia; it is a beautiful country, thickly settled and well cultivated: the settlers are mostly Dutch (Lutherans and Dunkards): they are a very hospitable people; in all the villages, which are scattered along the road 8 or 10 miles apart; we were greeted by waving handkerchiefs and the smiles of all the girls. At Woodstock,[22] a place about the size of Lebanon, the people all "turned out" and fed us bountifully upon the best the country affords: we halted in the town and the Dutch girls, many of them very pretty ones, handed around the provisions in waiters: we were treated so well that many of us came off minus a heart, and all agreed that Woodstock should be called Goodstock. I noticed a great many women and some old men crying as we passed by: I do not know whether they were crying on account of sympathy for us or for the loss of some relative soldier; a great many of the first volunteers from this part of the country were killed in the Battle of Manassas: in a village about the size of Nolensville a company of 54 was raised and in that battle 20 of them were killed. I don't know why they should cry for us, for we are decidedly better off than those we left at home. We are well fed and clothed and the duties we have to perform now have become a habit with us and we regard them as something very insignificant.

The weather has been fine for the past three weeks. The citizens say it is usually very cold at this time of year, but we have had no rain or snow for three weeks and it has just been cold enough to make it pleasant marching. I think that Providence has favored us in this as in all things else and if we could have such weather all the winter, Loring would see the termination of the war. Unless it turns very cold I hope they will prosecute the war for although we may suffer from the cold, it will not be as bad as the heat of summer and the diseases and sickness which will be certain to visit the camp in the summer season. Our regiment is in better condition now than it has ever been.

General Jackson[23] is now in Maryland: he has destroyed two of the locks in [the] canal which leads into Washington. Many think we will be ordered to join him. I hope we will for I would like to assist in setting Maryland free.

Ten thousand Yankees surrounded two thousand of our men yesterday. Our men cut their way through them, but with a loss of 300 men.[24] I have not heard the particulars of the fight. We are several miles north of Washington City. I do not know anything about our future movement. We are waiting here for orders.

We will have dress parade this evening and as I have promised to write a letter for one of our men I must close. Love to all. Write soon and direct to Strasburg, Virginia.

Your afft. son

A. Bostick

Tuesday [Dec. 24, 1861]

I left my letter open thinking that I might hear some news. Sunday night it sleeted all night and the mountains now present one of the most beautiful sights ever beheld: they are covered with ice and the trees are all hanging with icicles. Monday was very cold and windy: the wind blew so hard that all the tents in the encampment were blown down once or more times. One mess had to put up their tent six times. Saturday night Captain Douglas[25] came round to our tent after we had gone to bed with a bucket of oysters and although it was snowing we got up and built a fire (we had to put out all the fire for fear of burning up our tents; the wind blew the fire about so much several were burned up); we built a fire and cooked and ate to our satisfaction. We then pegged our tent, as we thought securely, but about 3 o'clock the wind blew it down, and as it would have been folly to have erected it then we slept the rest of the night with our house on top of us: this did very well except when the wind got under the tent cloth and whipped us with the poles (They felt like the North Poles). When we got up we found that we were not the only ones who were houseless for nearly all the regiment were in the same fix. These little things do not hurt us, however, for, as I said before, getting cold will soon become a habit and we won't mind it.

Tell Mag that Clack Harrison,[26] the man they used to laugh at Panth McClain[27] so much about was killed last night by the accidental discharge of a drunken man's gun. The ball passed through his heart and he never spoke. I was with him a week ago at Millboro in charge of goods belonging to the regiment and I never saw a young man I liked better. He was buried today.

All the regiment are making preparations for a big eggnog tomorrow. As I can't indulge I expect to go to the country and eat my Christmas dinner with some pretty Dutch girl. I wish I could be with you tonight.

Yrs.
Abe Bostick

Camp near Romney, Virginia
January 18th, 1862

My Dear Sister,[28]

I know you would laugh if you could see how I am fixed for writing. I am using a piece of half tanned leather as a writing desk, a stick for a pen handle and a wet plank for a seat. We got the leather from a tannery which the Yankees destroyed when they left, having burned the house and cut up the leather. I borrowed the pen and ink and begged the paper.

Today is the first pretty day we have had in a long time and it has been raining and sleeting this morning, but it is considerably warmer and the snow is melting fast: the ground has been covered with snow for more than two weeks. We reached this place day before yesterday after one of the worst marches we have ever made: the road was a sheet of ice and each company had to push its wagon nearly all the way. The drum would beat for us to rise two or three hours before daylight and we would begin to march at light and march till darkness making, generally, about 8 miles: one day we made only one mile.

We found this country a perfect desolation. The Yankees have burned all the houses of the Secessionists and have made of Romney, once a beautiful place, almost a total ruin. Where once were fine houses and beautiful yards are now defaced walls and stumps of shrubbery. They heard of our coming and beat a precipitate retreat, leaving about 500 tents and a great quantity of flour, etc. The name of Jackson is a terror to the Yankees.[29]

The country is mountainous but well cultivated, not very rich here, but we are on the eastern end of one of the most fertile valleys in Virginia. I suppose it is the intention of General Jackson to drive the Yankees out of this portion of Virginia this winter. We never know what we are going to do till it is done. When we start on a march we don't know where we are going till we get to the end of our journey and we don't know when we are at the end. There were about 7,000 "Yanks" in Romney, and it was strongly fortified, but the cowards couldn't stand. We had about 11,000 men but a large number of them are sick at Winchester. We are in camp about 3 miles from Romney. We have plenty of wood and good water and are better satisfied than if we were in winter quarters.

The Yankees are said to be about 10 miles from here, about 10,000 in number. No fight is anticipated.

Tom [Bostick] is in Winchester: he is not very well and went there to "get out of the weather." I got a note from him last night; he had greatly improved and intended rejoining his company soon.

General Anderson[30] will start home tomorrow; he intends stopping in Richmond a few days.

I received your letter last night (the first from home in nearly a month) in which you seem to be at a loss to know how to rear your children in order to give them good constitutions. In my opinion children like all other animals and like plants depend upon the manner in which they are reared: if they are delicately reared they will be delicate in mature years. Had I been reared like Tommy Summers (trained to take cold when my feet got wet) I would either be dead or in the hospital at Winchester now. Don't expose them unnecessarily but let them "take it rough and tumble." I have slept on the frozen ground, before a fire, without a blanket, while it was snowing in my face. I have marched day and night in the sleet and rain with icicles hanging to my hair and this so far from injuring me, has been the means of making me the more hardy. You may say I have a good constitution and this enabled me to do this. I admit that, but I owe more to the good sense of my parents than to nature for my good constitution. Nature may give a child sense, but if that child is kept away from books and the world his sense will never be developed. And so it is with the delicate constitution of a child: if outward influences are not allowed to act upon it, it will be just as delicate in the full grown man as it was in the infant. If you want your children stout and hearty, don't make hothouse plants out of them. And while I am on the subject, let me advise you to take as much exercise as possible. You are entirely too near your schoolroom if you come from your schoolroom and stay in the house all the evening. You will die in less than a year. The way to keep alive is to keep moving. With this I end my lecture on the subject of health.

I received a letter from Ann Thomas[31] last night. Tell her I will answer it as soon as I can get time and paper. When you write again tell me all about your new house and how you are pleased.

Tell Hardie[32] I answered his letter soon after I got it. It is getting cloudy and I think we will have more snow. I hope I will never see any more snow.

Lieutenant Toliver wants me to go to Winchester tomorrow after some goods for the company. I do not know whether I will go or not. It depends upon the movements of the army. If we move, I will not go. I will send this letter by Bob Bugg. He starts home tomorrow with General Anderson. I am very well and so fat you would not know me.

Write soon and direct to Winchester as before. Write me a long letter. Although I am in the army and haven't near the facilities for writing that you all have I write four letters for every one that I receive. Give my love to all at home, to Carrie Eastman and Miss Dunham.

Yours
A. Bostick

Tell Hardin[33] not to let my dogs out of the yard. In your next letter tell me how you disposed of the horses and buggies and all the things you had to sell. I wish I was able to buy Uncle Ed,[34] his hire would pay for him in two or three years. Tell mother she owes it to her children to go about more and take more exercise.

                                                  Near Romney, Virginia
                                                  January 31st, 1862

My dear Mother,

    I have had no paper, no time to write, and no way to send off letters for a long time: and left it to Tom [Bostick], who had been in Winchester, to do all the writing. I have managed, however, to write an occasional letter. I wrote a long one to Sister C soon after we arrived in Romney, in which I gave all the details of our journey to this place. We are now 5 miles north of Romney (further North than any other troops in the C. S. Army) one mile from a wire bridge across the South branch of the Potomac. Our tent is on a hillside and we have dug it down and put the mouth of our tent up the hill: at the mouth of the tent we dug a square hole and put up logs on three sides and piled up dirt against them: we then built a log chimney across the end opposite our tent; a wagon cover serves as our roof; our tent is set in the open side of our house thus making a pretty snug house with two rooms; the room answers the purpose of kitchen, sitting room and dining room; the back room is our bed chamber: to one accustomed to better our house would not deserve the name of house but to us it is more comfortable than a palace is to a King. Our fireplace extends across the end of our house and our chimney is larger than the rest of the house, which occasioned some dispute at first. As some said it was a house with a chimney to it and others said it was a chimney with a house to it. We have an abundance of straw and plenty of blankets and quilts which makes as good a bed as a man wants and although they sometimes issue us poor beef and "Revolutionary" crackers we have been fortunate enough to purchase some meal, fresh pork, hominy, rice, sugar and coffee (coffee sold in Romney at 14 cents per pound).

    We have had only one bad job since we got here and that was night before last. Just as we were preparing to go to bed, an order came around to hold ourselves in readiness to march with our guns and cartridge boxes at the tap of the drum. We got our guns and cartridge boxes and at one tap on the base drum we formed in line. The night was very dark and it was sleeting; the mud in the road was ankle deep everywhere and in many places knee deep. News had been received that a large band of Yankees were moving on us to cross at the wire bridge: about 11 o'clock we started to the bridge; not a man was allowed to speak as it was intended to surprise the enemy and their scouts had been seen prowling around in every direction across the river in the evening. It was an imposing sight to see a large dark mass of armed men moving slowly and silently at the hour of midnight through the snow. When we reached the bridge [we] put in [place an] ambush just this side expecting the enemy to attempt a passage any moment, but no enemy came. Our feet were wet and it was impossible to keep warm by walking because the mud and snow was over our shoes: we couldn't have fire because we didn't want the enemy to know our whereabouts. We couldn't sleep for fear of freezing as it was very cold and, to make the whole thing worse, it was sleeting. I got on a log and managed to keep from freezing by "marking time" till day-light when Forbes' regiment came up and relieved us: we got back to camp about 9 o'clock and got our breakfast when an order came for four scouts from our company to go across the river and find out the number, as near as possible, and the whereabouts of the enemy. I made one of the four from our company but when we got to the bridge we were sent back and the cavalry was sent in our place. I have not heard the result of their trip, but it is rumored this morning that the Yankees have retreated from where they were encamped on the R. R. 17 miles from here and that the force which we expected to attack us the night before came up here to prevent us from pursuing them: large bodies of Yankee scouts came to Springfield, which is a mile beyond the bridge very often; they drove in our pickets a few nights ago.

We have no fears of being driven from this place unless they surprise us, which will be hard to do: we are so situated that our regiment can hold any force that can be brought against us, till Maney and Forbes come up (they are about a mile back toward Romney). There are three Virginia regiments in Romney and four more 3 miles beyond.

Romney was surrounded with fortifications which were built by the Yankees and all along the road between here and Romney, and fortifications built for them to fall behind in case they had to retreat, but the poor fellows didn't get any good out of their work: when they heard we were coming they forgot all about their fortifications and went off in double quick, the band playing their "National An[them]." "He that fights and runs away," leaving provisions, tents, and great quantities of cannon balls, shell and grape shot.

The boxes which Lieut. Toliver brought as far as Winchester came up day before yesterday. Among them was one for Zack Thompson, a nephew of Lieut. Toliver and a member of our mess. It contained a bushel of apples, a jelly cake about the size of a can of preserves and a bushel of sweet potatoes: the potatoes had rotted but the other things were good, and I assure you it was a treat.

When Eliza gave him my skates, the boxes were nailed up, and he couldn't bring them; he knows nothing of a cap which you mentioned in your letter to me: he gave the bundle, which Eliza gave him, to the clerk in the Commercial Hotel,[35] who promised to send them to you.

Tom is still in Winchester, will be up in a few days. One of our men has just got here from Winchester and says Tom told him he was entirely well; says he looks better than he has in a long time. Had Tom been very sick, I would have written you all about it. I consider it wrong and foolish to conceal anything of that sort and, if Tom or I ever get sick or wounded, you may rely upon what I write as being correct. He went to Winchester not because he was too sick to stay in camp, but to keep from getting so: he will come to us as soon as the weather moderates: the ground is covered with snow and has been so nearly all this year. I tried to get Tom to go back sooner than he did but he disliked to leave his company because there was a probability of a fight.

That trip to Bath was a terrible one. It has already killed two of our company and another one will die shortly.

I have applied for a position in the regular army,[36] as Litton has doubtless told you; it is very doubtful whether I succeed. I only want it while the war lasts. I will be much obliged to remain in the army till the war closes anyhow and it will all be much better for both you and me if I succeed.

Love to all and accept much for yourself.

Your Afft. son
A. Bostick

CHAPTER FIVE

THE PENINSULA DEFENSE

hile at Winchester, Virginia, the three Tennessee Regiments learned of the fall of Fort Donelson. In response to that defeat and the earlier one at Mill Springs, Kentucky, Col. George Maney's First Tennessee Regiment was ordered from Virginia to Middle Tennessee to report to Gen. Albert Sidney Johnston, Commander of the Army in the West, near Nashville. Gen. S. R. Anderson's Seventh and the Fourteenth Tennessee Infantry Regiments then joined the Army of Northern Virginia near Manassas. There, a replacement regiment, Col. Peter Turney's First Tennessee, joined the other two Tennessee regiments to form what became known as the Tennessee Brigade. The brigade was assigned to the extreme right flank of Gen. Joseph E. "Joe" Johnston's army near Dumfries, a landing on the Virginia side of the Potomac near Washington. There, the Tennesseans supported by heavy batteries planted along the river, were charged with interrupting Union supplies.

After a few days of duty along the Potomac, the Tennesseans were ordered first to Fredericksburg and then to Yorktown, where Confederate forces were being massed to contest McClellan's anticipated thrust up the James River to capture Richmond.

The Tennessee Brigade was assigned a position midway between the York and James Rivers in front of Yorktown. A month-long siege of the town by McClellan's Army of the Potomac ended with the much smaller Confederate force retreating.[1] Less than a week later, the Army of Northern Virginia abandoned Norfolk. About this time, Gen. Anderson resigned as a result of ill health. He was replaced by the beloved Col. Robert Hatton of the Seventh Tennessee. Numerous other field officers also received promotions.

Under Gen. Hatton the Seventh Tennessee got its first real baptism under fire. This was at the fierce but inconclusive Battle of Seven Pines, fought on May 31. Here, Hatton was killed[2] and Stonewall Jackson severely wounded. The latter casualty resulted in Robert E. Lee assuming command of the Army of Northern Virginia, a position he held until its surrender in 1865. Meanwhile, the Seventh Tennessee remained at Seven Pines until the first of June when it took a new position closer to Richmond. Now under the command of an unpopular Texan, Col. James Archer of the Fifth Texas, who was promoted to brigadier general on June 3 to replace Hatton, the Tennessee Brigade figured large in Lee's plans to relieve the siege of the Confederacy's capital.

A daring and skillful reconnaissance by Jeb Stuart's cavalry, which passed entirely around the Federal army, gave Lee the intelligence he needed to plan to assault the Federals at Mechanicsville. Here, in a successful assault, the Seventh Tennessee suffered considerable losses. The next day, the brigade was given an even tougher assignment—to charge, with other brigades under A. P. Hill and James Longstreet, a nearly impregnable Federal position near Gaines Mills. After two unsuccessful attempts, the Confederates carried the enemy's position on their third try. At a terrible price, Lee won a great victory for the South and the relief of Richmond. Among those Southerners who died in the first assault was Abe Bostick, the twenty-one-year-old schoolteacher from Nashville. Only a month earlier, he had been promoted to sergeant major.

Here are Abe's last letters to his family, written during the Peninsula defense, as well as a number of letters and telegrams advising family members of his death.

Fredericksburg, Va.
March 17th 1862

My very dear Mother,

It is with but little hope of your receiving this letter that I write, but I have a shadow of a chance to get it through, and when I have I will never fail to write. I will lose nothing if they are intercepted and the Yankees will gain no information.

I have heard nothing from home since Nashville was surrendered except that Mag was living in Columbus [Miss.] and Litton was in the army.

We are living in one of the great historical epochs of the world and the crisis of the time is now upon us: the next sixty days will in a great measure decide our destiny: I don't mean that we, in the event of continued disasters,[3] will be subjugated: that can never be done: but it will decide in a great measure upon what terms our independence will be obtained. These disasters, which have lately attended our arms, although they may add to the length of the war, will make the men more desperate. While the war lasts, I expect to be in the army: and should we be subjugated (I never entertain such an idea), I expect to [go] to some other country: for if my country is subject to the North, and I am spared to witness such degradation, we can go to some other country where we can at least be free. I say we, I consider your and my destinies as one. If you find it unpleasant to live in town,[4] I would advise you to go to some of our relatives in the country: but not knowing how you are situated I don't pretend to advise you. Never fail to incur any expense if by doing so you can make yourself and Sister C more comfortable and happy, making me responsible for the debt. If you need money, borrow from Uncle Jimmie[5] or anyone else you can and, although I can't repay it right away, if I am spared, I will pay it with interest some day or other.

We are so situated at present that you can't hear from me often but don't allow your fears to get the better part of reason: there is a God who ruleth the destinies of each and all, who doeth all things for the best, who I trust will soon permit us to be reunited.

After this the rest of my service will be in Tenn. until it is free, which time I hope is not too far distant.

Try to keep my writing desk and guns. Write to me every opportunity and if you can get a letter through tell me all about my friends in Nashville. Direct to Fredericksburg, Anderson's Brigade. Tom and I are both very well. Love to all and a great deal to your dear self. It is late and I am writing by a tallow candle so I must close.

Your afft. son
Abe Bostick

---

near Richmond, Virginia
May 23rd 1862

My dear Mother,

 Ann Thomas[6] wrote to me that she could send you a short letter from me, and I gladly avail myself the opportunity as you doubtless are anxious to hear from us. I would that I could write you a long letter; but I am limited. Tom is Aid [sic] to Gen. Hatton (who has lately been promoted)[7] with the rank of Major. The position is decidedly easier and better for him than that of Captain of a company. Our captain is a clever fellow. His name is Norris.[8] J. F. Goodner is our Colonel. I mess with our 1st Lieut. Baird: a big fight is daily looked for.[9] We are confident of success. Tom and I are very well. Write whenever you can: we are very anxious to hear from you. Never read the Northern news, and never allow yourself to become uneasy about us from any reports. I heard from Joe[10]a short time ago; he was very well. I don't know where Litton is.[11] Love to all and accept much, from

Your afft. son,
A. Bostick

Camp near Richmond, Va.
June 20th, 1862

Capt. T. H. Bostick
Dear Tom,

John Peyton[12] reached us a few days ago bringing me a letter from you. I was sorry to hear you could not get home with the body of Gen. Hatton[13] His command has never been able to fully appreciate his services until now. Our newly appointed general (General Archer formerly Col. of the 5th Texas Regt.)[14] is so much his inferior in every respect that the men really hate him. Col. Goodner[15] says he knows nothing but severity. His headquarters are 1/2 mile from his command and he indulges in all the formalities of an old army officer. He is cool and reserved to every one who approaches him. He is not the right kind of man for Tenn. Vols. The whole command looks like it was lost; there is not the joviallity [sic] and alacrity in performing duty as formerly existed. Twenty-four men have been reported as deserters in the 1st Regt., some from ours and some from the 14th. These men didn't leave to get out of the service, but they wished to go into Tenn.— a laudable desire, but a bad way to gratify it. Our Brigade reports about 700 for duty. It is thought by many that the three Regts. will be made into one after the non conscripts leave. I think this very probable: the War Dept. will not pay the number of officers necessary to a Brigade when there are scarcely enough men for a Regt. I hope, however, this may not be done. I came into this Regt. a perfect stranger and all the acquaintances I now have are newly formed, and were I to be forced into a Regt. composed of three (which will be the case with all except Con. off.) I would have to begin anew. I now see the folly of the step I took when I came to this Regt. What do you expect to do? Where is Litton and what does he intend doing? Were I you, I would go into Tenn. and raise a guerrilla company: I think it could be done in East Tennessee or even in Middle Tenn. If a man wants to benefit his state and country that is the way to do it: if a man wants to make himself a name that is the way to do it. If we are whipped here we will be compelled to resort to this manner of fighting altogether. If McClellan can't silence the battery on Drury's Bluff, I don't think he will attack us here. I would not be much surprised if the whole fight were shifted to the valley. I wish you could get into Tenn: something must be done or mother and the family will suffer. $40 per month is not enough for their support, and this will stop by the end of this month, and I doubt whether the school will be continued next session. Had I any way to send it, I could send my bounty and clothing money to them.

I would like you to send me the two pictures in your trunk the first opportunity; until then take good care of them. I got Steed's carpetbag.

Write to me all about the family and my friends: where is Uncle Jimmie and Ike.[16] Was Joe reelected Capt?

The position of Sgt. Maj. is not by any means an enviable one, but decidedly preferable to me to staying in our old company. I have had both my own and George Howard's[17] duties to perform since the fight.[18]

We are still on the line of battle near the enemy, skirmishing every day, but no prospect of a decisive fight. I direct this to Marietta, will write by Andrew Martin when he starts. Love to Uncle Jesse's family.[19] Write soon and often.

Yours & etc.
A. Bostick

June 22nd

The field officers of the three Tenn. Regts[20] have petitioned the War Dept. to send us to Kirby Smith[21] I understand they are considering it favorably. It is reported that Andrew Ewing[22] and Gov. [Isham G.] Harris are in Richmond trying to get us to Tenn. I hope this may be true. I received a note from Willie Hunt[23] his morning; he was wounded in the Battle of Seven Pines in the muscle of the left breast and in the left arm, and now has ensypelas [sic] in his arm. He is at the 3rd Ala. Hospital in Richmond. A great many of our wounded are getting furloughs. Capt. John Allen[24] is in a dangerous condition. It was thought for a while that Capt. Dowell[25]would lose his arm but it is better: he acted very bravely in the battle field. Mort Baines' wound was very slight: it only kept him from the Regt. two days. The day after the fight was a terrible one to us—the few who were with the Regt. We were not close enough to take an active part in the fight but had to lay in a swamp, where the water was in many places knee deep, and dodge bombs all day. If there's no thing that I hate to do more than all others, it is to have to be shot at and not be able to return the fire. A. P. McClain[26] was killed that day in a few feet of me by a bomb.

Col. Howard[27] has been too unwell for the past week to be with us. Capt. Williamson[28] is also absent sick.

All is quiet along the lines today. No news. Write soon.

Yrs.

Abe

—◦—

Near Drury's Bluff, Va.
June 30, 1862

Miss May Bostick[29]

This note is to inform you of the death of your brother Abe who fell on the evening of [the] 27th while gallantly charging the enemy's fortifications with [the] 7th Tennessee Regt.[30] The shot which proved fatal took effect just above his left knee passing through and cutting the artery. He might have been saved if he could have received attention at once but we were repulsed on the first charge and before we could rally and drive the enemy from his works he had expired from loss of blood. He also had a slight wound on his left arm and in the left forefinger.

We dressed his remains and interred them at a church about ten miles NE from Richmond and have marked the place so that it may be easily found. Although we could by no means procure a coffin yet we interred him as neatly as it was feasible to do under the circumstances.

It is painful to us to make the communication to you because we who have been intimately associated with him for twelve months past know something of the sorrow you must feel at the loss of a brother, whom it must have been so great a pleasure to have loved but we can heartily recommend two sources of consolation.

First, he was a Christian and maintained his profession amid the temptations of the army. He has therefore exchanged the turmoils of this inhuman warfare for a world of peace and happiness.

The second is he was a brave and chivalrous soldier and fell while gaining a noble victory for the South. The Regt. testifies to this by the universal sorrow produced at his loss. We felt like we had lost one like unto a brother and will long cherish him in our memories.

Your brother requested us before going into battle to write to you if he were killed. This I have done imperfectly while resting on our way to the battlefield again.

I am very respectively
E. L. F. McKenzie[31]

P. S. Some money was taken out of your brother's pocket before we got him. We saved his watch and badge, and will dispose of as directed by any one of the family.

E. L. F. McKenzie

Chattanooga
June 30th, 1862

My Dear Mother,

I have just received a dispatch conveying to me the painful intelligence that Abe was killed in the battle on Friday the 27th. I would go to Richmond if I did not know that it would be impossible to get his body home now. You have my dear mother the consolation of knowing that he died bravely and was prepared for that dreadful hour. I never saw such a boy in my life. Most boys of his age in the army have either become dissipated or very wicked. I never saw Abe do anything inconsistent with his religion. He was a model boy and to be candid I loved him better than I did any brother or sister I had. How could it have been otherwise when I was so intimately associated in camps for thirteen months and have no other relation in the army with me.

I have telegraphed my friends there to have him buried if possible so that I can get his body hereafter. He will be buried long before I can get there and if I were there I could not bring him home now. If it is possible he will be buried so we can get his body.

In the first fight I lost my best friend Genl. Hatton. In the second I lose my dear brother. Mother you can't expect to have all your boys in

Received at June 29, 186[2] at _____ o'clock, _____minutes,
By telegraph from Richmond 28 to Capt. T. H. Bostick
Abe killed yesterday. Our fight thus far successful.—
J. D. Fry [sic][32]

Received at June 29, 1862 at _____ o'clock, _____minutes,
By telegraph from Richmond to Capt. T. H. Bostick
Abe was killed in the battle of twenty seventh Col Howard seriously wounded
Capts Williamson Walsh[33] and Curd[34] wounded. Lt. Col. & Maj. of 1st Tenn.
regts killed —R. P. McClain[35]

the army and not lose some of them. I pray God you may never be afflicted with the death of another. I do not know how Abe was wounded. I will write you all the particulars as soon as I get them.

So far as we have heard we have gained a great victory. Such a one as will cause our recognition by England and France. McClellan's whole army will either be captured or destroyed. McClellan's army is surrounded and he has to surrender or his whole army will be destroyed. Col. John K. Howard of Lebanon was seriously wounded. I don't know how. Please write to Mat,[36] tell her I am well and waiting here expecting her every day. She can come all the way in a buggy or carriage and she must come. Tell her to get Baily [sic] Peyton[37] to bring her. I mean little Baily. I have not heard from Mag and Eliza & Mat since I wrote. Kate, Anne and Uncle Jesse[38] were well last Sunday. Write to me dear Mother. Direct to Marietta [Ga.] care Uncle Jesse. Give my love to all.

Your affectionate son
T. H. Bostick

━━━◆◦◆━━━

Chattanooga, Tennessee
June 30, '62

Mrs. T. H. Bostick
Lebanon, Tennessee
My Dear Mat

I have just received a dispatch from Rufe McClain telling me Abe was killed in the fight on Friday 27th. I wish I had been there. I have the consolation to know he died bravely and was prepared for it. Write to Mother. Col. John K. Howard was seriously wounded. Capts. Williamson, Walsh, and Curd wounded. Lt. Col. and Major of 1st Tennessee Regt. killed. This is all I have learned. I have telegraphed for the particulars but will not get an answer before evening. We have gained a complete victory. McClellan[39] is surrounded and will have to capitulate or [have] his whole army destroyed. Our prospects are brighter than ever.

I have been waiting here expecting you every day, but alas I am disappointed every day. Why don't you come? You can come all the way in a buggy or hack. They come through every day. Be certain to come. I will be here or at Marietta. You can telegraph me. You can get there in a few hours on the cars. Kiss the children for me. God bless you.

Your fond husband
T. H. Bostick

Received at July 1st, 1862 at _____ o'clock, _____minutes,
By telegraph from Richmond 30 to T. H. Bostick
Abe buried to himself & grave marked Howard[40] shot in breast doing well—
J. D. Fry [sic][41]

[July 1, 1862]
Chattanooga, Tenn.

Mr. Tom Bostick,
My dear Cousin
    I received your letter an hour or two ago but the sad intelligence it contained reached us this morning. Mr. Claiborne told Pa[42] that you had received a dispatch. There is no need to tell you how much we feel this sad affliction for Abe was, you know, like a brother more than a cousin to us, we have had him near us always until the last year and so we loved him dearly. Then too our sorrow is made still greater when we remember what he was to you, to all his family and to Aunt

Margaret[43] and cousin Katharine[44] especially. And this sad bereavement comes to you when your family circle is divided and you will feel so deeply the separation from loved ones. Truly the ways of Providence are mysterious. I heard of the news of the victory at Richmond[45]with joy, without dread, for I thought the only relative I had there was safe from harm. I could not believe that yet another sorrow was to be added to Aunt Margaret's load of grief. Yet God so willed it. She is so good and Abe was too that we must believe, if we believe in a Providence at all, that much as it grieves us, hard as it seems to us to be, that yet it was done in wisdom and in love. I know how very trying his loss is to you, he has been so intimately associated with you for some time past, and I wish I could say or do something that would help to comfort you, but the greatest consolation any one can have, you have, for you tell me he was ready to go, and left behind the memory of a life so devoted to the right and noble that you who knew best can say he was the best boy you ever saw. I will write to Brother Jimmy[46] this evening. Next to you all, there is no one who loved him better and will feel his loss so much. They were always dear to each other and Jimmy never ceased to regret that he [Abe] left his company[47] on his own account, though he knew Abe would be happier and more comfortable with you. I have not heard from home since you left. The war news you hear sooner than we as probably. I am glad we are victorious so that an end may soon be to these scenes of bloodshed that are making so many hearts sad, so many homes lonely. I hope Matt [sic][48] will come out to see you. If she does, bring her to see us. She will be more comfortable here and we would like very much to see her and the children. We will expect you if she does not come. Brother Jimmy is said to be at Vicksburg.[49] We have not heard from him. I dread the effects of the climate for Jimmy is more apt to be made sick by bad water and unwholesome food than by any other hardship. Ann[50] sends you her love. She feels her own bereavement is yours, for she has lost one of her best loved friends. Pa joins us in wishing you to know how much we feel with and for you. Write to us if you hear anything further. May God be with you and all yours to comfort and bless prays. Your loving cousin.

Kate Thomas
Marietta, Ga.
July 1, 1862

Chattanooga
July 4th 1862

My dear Mother,

    I have written home several times since I reached this place. The last time I wrote to you I told you of the death of Abe. I do not know that you have received my letters. Abe was killed in the fight on the 27th. He died bravely fighting for his country and was prepared for the dreadful hour. He was a noble boy and a good Christian. For the past thirteen months we have been very intimately associated and I loved him better than any brother or sister I had. How could it be otherwise when my troubles were his and his pleasures were mine. He is buried in a grave to himself and his grave marked so that his body can be gotten and taken to Nashville and placed beside that of his father. He had a great many friends in the army and they attended to this before I could telegraph to them. Mother we must expect this. Some have to be killed in a war like this and all of your boys could not expect to escape. Abe was better prepared to die than any of us and and it may be that a just God took him from you for this reason. God grant that the rest may be spared to comfort and make your life a happy and pleasant one. In the other battle I lost my best friend.[51] In this I lost a dear brother. May this battle end this terrible war. I received a letter the other day from Abe written a few days before the battle. I will keep it and send it to you by Mat when she returns. It is the last he ever wrote. My dear mother I know this is a hard blow to you but your children will love you the more if such a thing is possible.

    Mat got here yesterday. She left the children and will return in two or three weeks. I will write to you again by her. It is a hard trip for a woman to take but she stood it finely. Mrs Miller of Lebanon came with her. She is trying to see her son who is in the army. I heard from Joe a day or two ago. He is at Morristown E. Tenn. and [is] very well. Litton, Mag and May are at Columbus [Miss.] and [were] all well at last accounts. Eliza is at Raymond, Miss. with Early's uncle. She is very pleasantly situated and she and child [were] very well when I last heard. I telegraphed Mag of Abe's death.

    We have gained a great victory.[52] The enemy routed and it is supposed McClellan's entire army will be captured or killed. They are still fighting but the enemy are trying harder to get away than to whip us. Up to Tuesday night the loss of the killed, wounded and missing of the enemy was estimated at fifty thousand.[53] Our loss very heavy but nothing like as great as that of the Federals. I hope I will see you soon. Give my love to all. God bless and protect you my dear Mother is the prayer of your afft. son.

T. H. Bostick

Write to me at Marietta care [of] Uncle Jesse[54] and he will forward the letter to me if I am not there. He Kate & Anna[55] all well. I will take Mat there this evening.

CHAPTER SIX

JOE AND LITTON
JOIN THE FIGHT

hree months after his brothers, Abe and Tom, and his brother-in-law, Will Hunt,[1] joined the army, Dr. Joseph "Joe" Bostick set aside his medical practice in Marion County, Tennessee, and organized a company of men from the Bridgeport area of adjoining Jackson County, Alabama, for service in the Confederate army. Just as Tom had been elected captain of his company, Joe was elected captain of Company A, "The Davis Guards."[2] His was one of ten companies mustered into Confederate service by Col. William M. Churchwell at Camp Sneed in Knoxville, Tennessee, on August 19, 1861.[3] First known as the Fourth Confederate (Tennessee) Regiment, the unit's name was changed in November to the Thirty-fourth Tennessee Regiment because another Fourth Tennessee had already been organized in West Tennessee. The new designation never attained general recognition, however, and in most field reports the regiment would continue to be called the Fourth Tennessee Infantry Provisional Army.[4]

A month after his enlistment, Joe got a furlough to visit his family in Nashville. When he left Nashville at the end of September to rejoin his regiment at Knoxville, he was accompanied on the train by his seventeen-year-old first cousin, James Litton Cooper, who had decided to cast his fortunes with Company C of the Twentieth Tennessee Regiment, then stationed at Cumberland Ford, Kentucky.[5] The presence of another cousin, Jim Thomas, in that company naturally was an inducement for Jim to join.

When Capt. Joe Bostick and Jim Cooper reached Knoxville, they found that Joe's regiment had already started for Cumberland Gap and was camped about sixteen miles from town. In the company of several other officers from the regiment, Joe and Jim set out by foot to catch up. They reached camp about ten o'clock that night. From there, the regiment went on to Cumberland Gap the next day, after which Jim reached Cumberland Ford and his company a day later. Jim Thomas was there to greet him. Joe Bostick's regiment remained at Cumberland Gap that fall and winter. It did not participate in the Battle of Fishing Creek in January, but Jim Cooper was wounded and captured[6] and Jim Thomas and Bill Robinson fought and survived unscathed. Later at Camp Chase, Ohio, where Jim was imprisoned, he met a man from Marion County who had two sons in Joe's company.[7]

Joe's regiment remained in the mountainous area along the Tennessee-Kentucky border until the middle of June. At that point, it moved to Bean Station in Grainger County, Tennessee, skirmished at Jones' Station and Walden's Ridge, and spent July and August at Woodson's Station, about forty miles from Morristown.[8] A transcribed copy of Joe's letter to his mother, written on July 17, is included in this chapter.

J. Litton Bostick was the last of the Bostick brothers to enlist under the Confederate banner. This was natural as he was the oldest of the brothers, having reached his thirty-fifth birthday in May 1861. His commitment to the Southern cause was every bit as intense as his brothers'. In November, the *Daily Nashville Patriot* announced that Litton and five other Tennesseans were named Confederate Commissioners, empowered to arrest all violators of C.S.A. laws and "to examine, bail or commit them for trial by the Confederate courts." Following the unexpected fall of Fort Donelson two months later, Litton realized his situation had changed dramatically. Should Nashville fall, as seemed inevitable, his status as a Confederate Commissioner would place him in jeopardy. More than likely, Federal authorities would arrest him within days of their occupation of the city. Already, he had sent Bettie, then in her ninth month of pregnancy, and their three children south to be near her parents in Columbus, Mississippi. Bettie delivered a baby boy, named Litton for his father, on February 18, two days after the fall of Fort Donelson. The baby was born in West Point, Mississippi, eighteen miles from Columbus.

At the family gathering in Nashville, each member considered what he or she should do. Mrs. Bostick was adamant that she would remain in the city even if she could not stay in her home on the Charlotte Pike. Litton was determined to leave Nashville before the city surrendered. He planned to follow Albert Sidney Johnston's army south along the Nashville & Chattanooga Railroad and join the army when he caught up with it. He probably encouraged his sisters, Mag and Mary Anne, to follow Bettie to Mississippi. They decided to do so, and arrangements were made for them and Mary Anne's two children to stay with Percival Halbert, an uncle of Catharine's deceased husband, John Bently Halbert. The sixty-six-year-old Halbert lived on a plantation in Oktibbeha County, about twenty miles west of Columbus.[9]

As the oldest Bostick daughter, Catharine decided it was her duty to stay in Nashville with her mother, her own children, and her youngest sister, Susan. She did until the spring or early summer of 1863, when she, her mother and her children either fled the city or were expelled by Federal authorities.

The other Bostick daughter, Eliza Early, was not involved in the intense family discussion. She, her husband, John, and their baby, Hardin, may have been living near Jackson, Mississippi, when the deliberations took place. By the third week of April, Mr. Early was a member of Lt. Charles E. Fenner's[10] Louisiana Battery of Light Artillery, which was organized in Jackson earlier in the month. The battery was quickly sent to New Orleans, where Admiral Farragut's fleet threatened the city. On May 9, Eliza and her baby were living in Hinds County, Mississippi, with her husband's uncle, Orville Rives. His plantation home, Forkland, had plenty of room. A widower too old to fight himself, Mr. Rives was a Confederate patriot of the first rank. He not only gave liberally to the Confederate cause but opened his home, not only to Eliza and her baby, but to every Confederate soldier who needed shelter. On numerous occasions, every available square inch seemed filled with family members or soldiers.[11]

After the Bosticks finalized plans for each family member, Litton felt free to leave. A day or two before Nashville fell, he said good-bye to his mother and, in company with several other men, left on horseback. On the day that Federal troops occupied Edgefield, across the Cumberland River from Nashville, Litton had gotten as far as Shelbyville. In a letter to his mother from there, he mentioned the possibility that he might visit Bettie and his children in Columbus before joining the army.

Litton did not make it to Columbus as soon as he hoped because a battle was shaping up along the line of the Memphis & Charleston Railroad in north Mississippi. By early March, having followed the Confederate Army of Mississippi from Fayetteville, Tennessee, to Athens, Alabama, and then west across north Alabama, Litton caught up with them, probably at

Iuka, Mississippi. The army camped there, having taken the cars from Decatur, Alabama. Bostick joined Company C of the Twentieth Tennessee Regiment, the same regiment that Abe had briefly been a member of the previous spring. This was also the regiment where his first cousins, Bill Robinson and Jim Thomas, served and where Jim Cooper had also served until his capture at Fishing Creek. Nearly all the company members, who were either from Nashville or its vicinity, remembered Abe and welcomed Litton, whom most knew, if only by sight.

A day before the Battle of Shiloh, Litton stood on dress parade and listened to Albert Sidney Johnston's "Famous Battle Order." The Twentieth Tennessee took 380 men into the Battle at Pittsburg Landing. Of these, 158 were either killed or wounded. Although Litton's company was engaged on both days of the battle, including close range fighting for an hour and a half on the first day, Sunday, he survived. In a history of the regiment, Litton was said to have "fought gallantly" despite almost no training.[12] After falling back to Corinth, the Twentieth Tennessee was reorganized, with twenty-two-year-old Capt. Thomas Benton Smith being promoted to colonel.

From Corinth, the Twentieth Tennessee moved successively to Baldwin and then to Tupelo, Mississippi, where they camped for several weeks. In June, Gen. Braxton Bragg, then in command, having replaced Gen. Beauregard, divided his forces with Breckenridge's Division, to which the Twentieth Tennessee belonged and which was being sent to besieged Vicksburg. The balance of the army traveled by rail to East Tennessee to take part in the Kentucky campaign. At this point, Litton was granted leave to see his family in Columbus. After spending a few days with Bettie and their children there and after seeing his sisters, Mary Anne and Mag, Litton rode horseback across north Alabama to Chattanooga, a twelve-day trip. There, he was delighted to run into his close friend Randal W. McGavock at the State Bank.[13] The next month, Litton was commissioned a first lieutenant and Aide-de-camp to Brig. Gen. St. John Richardson Liddell.[14]

Shown below are transcriptions of two of Litton Bostick's letters from this period; Albert Sidney Johnston's famous Battle Order of April 3, 1862; a letter from Litton's sister, Eliza Early to their mother; and Joe Bostick's letter to his mother, written from Morristown, Tennessee, on July 7.

Shelbyville, Tenn. Feb 23rd '62

My Dear Mother

I write to let you know that I reached this place today without accident of any kind. We got to Uncle Jimmy's[15] on Thursday in time for dinner where we found Mary and the children all well. On Friday we left, Mr. Porter for Murfreesboro and the rest of us for this place, but we stopped about 16 miles from Uncle Jimmy's with an old gentleman named Ransom who entertained us very hospitably without charge. Here we staid [sic] all day yesterday on account of the rain which fell in torrents from about 3 o'clock A.M. till night. Our object in coming here is to be on the line of railroad and near the army so as to keep advised as to the movement of our forces. Mr. Porter has not yet arrived from Murfreesboro and I have not determined what will be my next move. Porter has doubtless been detained by high water as some of the bridges have been washed away.

I am considerably improved since I left, my cold having nearly left me and my appetite being excellent. I have had much anxiety about you since I left, but feel pretty well satisfied that you will not be molested by the enemy. We heard one report that the Lincolnites had reached the city and had opened fire upon it but did not believe the report. We hear tonight that they have not yet reached the city but that their pickets were on the north side of the river. I suppose they will not occupy the city in force for a week or ten days. Tell Catharine to keep a record of events on letter paper and send it to me whenever she has an opportunity. She must be certain to keep a regular journal in this way of everything that transpires as well of facts as of her doubts, fears & hopes and if she fails to find a sure hand to convey them to me, to preserve them till my return which I hope will be soon.

I met Judge Baxter[16] here today; he left for Murfreesboro. I will write by every opportunity but will have to be cautious as to what I write for fear my letters may fall into the hands of the Lincolnites. Did Hardy[17] get his gun? Let me know every time you write how you are provided with money. I will soon let you know where letters will reach me.

Give my love to Catharine and the children. Hoping that you will get along as comfortably and happily under the circumstances, I remain your affectionate son

J. L. Bostick

Shelbyville
February 25th 1862

My Dear Mother,

Mr. Herriford[18] goes to Nashville today and I avail myself of the opportunity of again writing to you. I wrote yesterday to the care of Mr. Maney[19] and hope that you will receive the letter. Uncle Ike[20] started this morning for Richmond. Porter for New Orleans. Rice[21] and myself will probably start today for Huntsville by way of Fayetteville. I think it probable that I will make the trip to Columbus before joining the army as I do not wish to join before it settles upon some permanent basis of operation. But my plans are not yet settled. If any resistance is to be made here or at Murfreesboro I will join immediately.

Tell Catharine not to forget or fail to keep a regular journal of everything that happens while I am gone. I have entirely recovered from my cold and feel in fine health and as good spirits as could be expected.

Leiper & Menifee of Murfreesboro[22] owe me a fee of $25 for which I give you an order. You can get some person to collect it when affairs become settled. I will charge them that amount and pay the court costs which are some 2 or 3 dollars. Davy Love the circuit court clerk will remember that I dismissed the case (Leiper & Menifee vrs Cook & Kidd) before the appearance time but the case has been kept on the docket by mistake and the costs have accumulated to 6 or 8 dollars, but you must only pay the amount due at the time I dismissed. Uncle Cooper[23] will attend to this for you and by showing Love this letter he will remember the case and do what is right. Understand now that I charge Leiper & Menifee $25 and out of that when collected I will pay the court costs.

With much love to Catharine and the children, I remain

your affectionate son
J. L. Bostick

HEADQUARTERS, ARMY OF MISSISSIPPI

Corinth, Miss. April 3, 1862 SOLDIERS OF THE ARMY OF MISSISSIPPI: I have put you in motion to offer battle to the invaders of your country. With the resolution and discipline and valor becoming men fighting, as you are, for all worth living or dying for, you can but march to decisive victory over the agrarian mercenaries sent to subjugate and despoil you of your liberties, your property, and your honor. Remember the precious stake involved; remember the dependence of your mothers, your wives, your sisters, and your children, on the result; remember the fair, broad, abounding land, and the happy homes that would be desolated by your defeat.

The eyes and hopes of eight millions of people rest upon you; you are expected to show yourselves worthy of your lineage, worthy of the women of the South, whose noble devotion in this war has never been exceeded in any time. With such incentive to brave deeds, and with the trust that God is with us, your generals will lead you confidently to the combat—assured of success.

A. S. Johnston, General commanding[24]

Forkland[25]
May 9th 1862

My Dear Ma,

Knowing you must feel very anxious to hear from Mr. Early and knowing that he has not had time or an opportunity to write to you, since the fall of Orleans.[26] I write this morning to tell you where and how he is. He is very well I have had only one letter from him since he left the city, and that was received on last Wednesday. He is at Camp Moore about 70 miles from the city.[27] The company succeeded in saving their battery, harness and took 30 horses to haul it out 15 miles from the city where they got on the cars and as they had the horses that far out they did not think it worth while to send them back. Mr. E took a splendid horse of Gen. [?] but while he was attending to the battery it was taken by some one but he got another. Capt. Davis says if [it] had not been for Mr. E he could have saved nothing. He has been elected 2nd Lt. since they have been in camp. There were a great many of the troops [who] remained in the city, but I suppose you have seen a full account of everything connected with the fall of the place.

The Federals are expected at Vicksburg today. The place is being well fortified and there will certainly be a fight there. The citizens say they will hold the place or burn it.

There is a great deal of excitement in the country. The Gov. has called out the Militia and they expect to go into camp soon. Uncle Fletcher[28] is busy getting ready, he thinks he will certainly go—it seems that we will be left in a dreadful state without a white man on the place and so few left around us—but I think the women will be as brave soldiers as the men before this war is over. I am willing to do anything now rather than yield and although I gave up a great deal when I gave up my husband, I should not have him back now—he is one that will always be at his post and I believe God will shield him. The time I have to be separated from him seems very long and dark. I cannot be happy while he is gone. I don't believe I could stand it but for little Hardin.[29] he is so much company. he is very much like his Pa. We all think him a beautiful baby—he is nearly six months old weighs 22 pds and has two teeth—alltogether [sic] he is a wonderful boy; (I think).

My sisters Mrs. Anderson & Mag[30] are still in Columbus, Mi. I heard from them yesterday, both very well working for and waiting on the sick soldiers. There are a great many there. My brother Litton was in both day's fight at Shiloh but was not hurt. Jimmy Thomas[31] was there also but not hurt. Uncle Henry Rives' oldest son was there also he was not hurt.

It has been two months since I received a letter from Mother. I feel very anxious to hear from her.

I was very sorry to hear of Bro Orville's[32] sickness hope he is entirely well. I wrote to Sister Mary about 2 weeks ago. It has been a long time since I heard from any of you—a letter is a treat in the country. What is Fannie doing with herself—How is Bettie—Give her my love when you write or see her—Much love to Sisters Mary & Fannie, Bro O & T. Kiss the children for me. Sarah & Aunt are very well send a great deal of love to you all. Little Orville was over the first of the week, he is very well. Mr & Mrs Parham and all their family are at Mr. Blount's all well. Accept much love from yours affectionately

Eliza B. Early

Morristown [Tenn.]
July 7th 1862

Dear Tom,[33]

I got the letter you sent me by Col. McMurray[34] last week. I had been trying to find out for some time where Abe was to get him in my company. I wanted to give him a Lieut's place in my company. There is a vacancy in the company and anyone I recommend to the Col. and Gen. could get the place. But poor fellow it is too late now. He deserved a better place. There are a great many captains and higher officers not half as deserving as he was. I think they have adopted the true policy now of examining and turning out all incompetent officers and appointing others in their places. I saw Clint Douglas today. He told me that he brought Mat out with him. What do you intend doing with yourself now? Can't you come up to see me? I am on the railroad just 40 miles above Knoxville. I got a letter from Mary[35] today. The Yankees have not injured me at home much.[36] They have taken several horses but nothing else. They keep a guard about the place and do not allow the soldiers to interrupt anything. When did you hear from Litton? If you cannot come up to see me write occasionally.

Your aff. brother
J. Bostick[37]

CHAPTER SEVEN

LIFE IN OCCUPIED NASHVILLE

fter the fall of Nashville in late February 1862, Federal authorities systematically tightened their control of the city. By early April, a roundup of prominent secessionist leaders was well underway. A few days earlier, George Washington Barrow, one of three commissioners appointed by Tennessee's Gov. Isham Harris to negotiate Tennessee's alliance with the Confederacy, was arrested. So was Gen. William G. Harding, wealthy plantation owner and a former president of the Military and Financial Board of Tennessee. Both were put in the state penitentiary on Spring Street. Others arrested the last week in March included Thomas M. and Joseph Brennan, whose foundry and machine shop had manufactured cannons for the Confederacy. Unlike Barrow and Harding, the Brennan brothers were paroled and summoned for hearings. On the following Monday, James Hamilton and Thomas Sharp, whose firm on South Spruce Street had manufactured cavalry sabers for the Confederacy, were arrested.

A week later, on April 7, Military Governor Andrew Johnson seized control of the city government from Rebel officeholders. He declared the offices of the mayor, Richard B. Cheatham, and all but three of the councilmen and aldermen vacant and put Union men in their places.

The allegiance of most of the city's protestant ministers to the Southern cause particularly annoyed Johnson. On April 10, he arrested five of them only to release them on their own recognizance. For the next ten weeks he unsuccessfully attempted to persuade them and their fellow ministers to declare their allegiance to the United States. Fed up with their intransigence, Gov. Johnson summoned Rev. C. D. Elliott of the Nashville Female Academy; R. B. C. Howell, minister of First Baptist Church; Bishop E. W. Sehon, Corresponding Secretary of the Missionary Society of the Methodist Episcopal Church, South, and a good friend of the Bosticks; and Reuben Ford of the Cherry Street Baptist Church, back to his office. They appeared and returned the following day with three more ministers and two members of the faculty at Nashville University. All were given until June 28 to sign the loyalty oath. When Howell, Ford, Sehon, W. D. F. Sawrie of the Methodist Episcopal Church, South, and S. D. Baldwin refused, they were arrested and confined in the Tennessee State Prison at Nashville.

The Federal occupation provided ample opportunities for men holding grudges against their rebel-sympathizing employers to seek revenge. One man, who had been discharged by David McGavock at Two Rivers for drunkenness, informed the Provost Marshall that McGavock was concealing arms on the plantation and had Confederate stores hidden there. Federal soldiers came out and searched the house, the servants' houses and the smokehouse, all to no avail. Nevertheless, McGavock was taken to town where he appeared before the Provost Marshall before being released.

The arrests of their fellow countrymen, often on contrived charges, and such ill-advised actions as Gen. David Hunter's General Order #11 abolishing slavery in Florida, Georgia, and South Carolina incensed Whig-Unionists in Middle Tennessee and drove them by the hundreds into the arms of the Southern Confederacy.

Young wives of Federal officers stationed in Nashville, such as the quiet and lady-like wife of Capt. C. H. Wood, wondered why, after several months in the city, no ladies other than Mrs. Harding and Mrs. Barrow had called on her. Mrs Harding wrote her husband, then imprisoned with Gen. Barrow on Mackinac Island, that she felt like telling Mrs. Wood that "no Federal officer's wife had received as many [calls], even after two months residence."[1]

Even Mrs. James K. Polk, whom Federal officers treated with utmost courtesy, was not immune from suffering. Several of her nephews were in the Confederate Army. One, Elisha Whitsett, died from a wound inflicted at Shiloh. His brother Johnny survived the war despite being wounded four times. A third nephew, Capt. Marshall T. Polk, was wounded and captured at Shiloh. After having his leg amputated, he was sent to a Northern prison. Mrs. Polk, having heard about his plight, successfully petitioned Gen. Halleck for permission to have him brought to her home. Marshall's pulse was never under 120 during his first ten days at Polk Place, and many expected him to die; nevertheless, he survived.

In July, Gen. Nathan B. Forrest's capture of Murfreesboro threw "Nashville into spasms." Confederate pickets were as close as the bridge over Mill Creek on the Nashville-Lebanon Turnpike. On the Murfreesboro Pike, Forrest's men burned three bridges on Brown's and Mill Creeks within six miles of town. Johnson responded by barricading some of the principal streets leading in the direction of Lebanon and Murfreesboro and placed cannons on Capitol Hill and College Hill. Spring Street was blocked at the depot and only the Charlotte Pike, where the Bosticks had lived until recently, gave unobstructed passage to the west and south.[2]

In the summer of 1862, Margaret Bostick, having moved the previous winter, was living in a smaller house in town with her widowed daughter, Catharine Halbert, Catharine's children, and her youngest daughter Susan, then sixteen. Mrs. Bostick no longer had the company of her sister, Elizabeth Thomas, who formerly lived next door, or her brother, Ike Litton. Elizabeth and her husband, Jesse Thomas, had been smuggled out of Nashville soon after its fall and were living at Marietta, Georgia. Ike and his family had also fled to Marietta where the two families were crowded together in a small house.

Whenever Margaret drove out to the Charlotte Pike to see her sister, Ann Cooper, whose home was across Bostick Street from hers, she must have tried not to look at or even think about her old house. To do so would have been painful as it was being used as a pesthouse for Union soldiers with contagious diseases. Soldiers' tents took up much of her back yard. Miss Jane Thomas, Jesse Thomas' sixty-one-year-old spinster sister, was staying in his house, next door to the Coopers. Miss Jane had persuaded Federal Gen. Robert S. Granger to give her protection for her brother's place.

One Sunday Miss Jane spent the night in town. The next morning Ann Cooper sent for her. When the somewhat alarmed Miss Jane got home, she found a Col. Kennett and his regiment camped on her yard. Someone told her that he planned to take possession of her house, which his soldiers referred to as "the old Rebel's house." Miss Jane went to see Kennett and showed him her papers, which he didn't know she had. He politely asked if he and his wife might stay in one room for which he offered to pay rent. He also suggested that his presence would provide protection for her. Miss Jane agreed, and the Kennetts were her renters for nine months. During that time, Col. Kennett supplied Miss Jane with "everything she wanted at government prices." She recalled years later that "he and his wife were just as nice to me as they could be." When he left, the colonel, who was from a wealthy Cincinnati family, wrote Miss

Jane a flattering letter, recommending her to the care of all soldiers, saying that she would treat them like a lady.

Meanwhile, next door at the Coopers' place, Captain Marshall's company was camped on the lawn. He and his wife also rented a room from Miss Jane. Captain Marshall, who stayed four or five months, also treated her with respect. Other Yankees were not always so nice. Once, after her brother's hunting dog stole a steak from one of the Federal cooks, someone poisoned him. Miss Jane went to the front yard, where all the officers' tents were and said: "'I want all the officers to come here. I know you are gallant fellows, and when you go home you want to carry some trophy of your gallantry, and I want you to take a lock of this poor dog's hair to take back with you to show that you killed something.' They did not say a word, but stayed in their tents."[3] Later, the Yankees confiscated "the old Rebel's house" and made Miss Jane pay ten dollars a month rent to stay in her bedroom. Federal soldiers took over the two other bedrooms. A Yankee named Heeley and his wife lived in one of them. Miss Jane described him "as the grandest thief I ever saw. He went to Mrs. John Thompson's one day, and came back with his pockets and arms full of towels and things. He also had a pair of opera-glasses that he had stolen. He stole all the clothes for his wife to wear, and she had seven stolen breastpins. They went foraging every day, and came back with all kind of things." Miss Jane felt sure that a man named Trent was using her servant's room to store stolen goods in.[4]

Meanwhile, the pressures on Margaret Bostick and Catharine Halbert were enormous. In addition to the trauma of losing their home, the emotional strain of caring for Catharine's sister, Susan, who had chronic physical and mental problems, their joint responsibilities for Catharine's children, and harassment by the Yankees, the two women had financial worries. They were dependent on Catharine's income from teaching school and whatever monies her brothers and sisters could periodically send them. They only had $40 a month in steady income, and that would end by July 1 as it seemed doubtful that school would open for the next session. Whenever Margaret or Catharine left home to go to school, to buy food, or to visit their Cooper or Robinson relatives, pickets harassed and occasionally threatened them. Although upset by this, sometimes to the point of tears, the ladies were not easily intimidated. Catharine regularly went to the city's hospitals to nurse dozens of Confederate prisoners to whom she brought "food and good cheer." At some point, Federal authorities were sufficiently annoyed that they ordered the "great little Rebel" to stop nursing Confederate prisoners unless she agreed to give Federal wounded equal attention. Catharine did so but only to those Yankees who were too badly wounded to fight again.

One day, Federal authorities found a particularly contemptuous inscription written on the shutter of a house in Nashville then used as a hospital. The inscription, written in a female hand, said:

> I hope that every officer who enters this house may depart this life in double-quick time; that they may suffer the torture of ten thousand deaths before they die. And paralyzed be the hand that would alleviate their sufferings; and may the tongue of him who would speak words of comfort cleave to the roof of his mouth. And as for the Yankee women who are hungry for the spoils, may _____ but cursed are they already. God bless the Southern cause! Curse the Northern and all that fight for it![5]

One wonders if the house was the Bostick home, which the Federals were using as a hospital, and if the unknown female was Catharine Halbert.

On one occasion late in the war, Federal soldiers came into the Bostick home and stole, among other things, a gun that Catharine's grandfather, John Bostick, had fought with in the Revolutionary War. A day or two later, a Union-sympathizing Nashville newspaper ran a story about the successful raid, saying that Union soldiers had "found a small armory" in Widow Bostick's house.[6] Still, Margaret and Catharine did not fear the Yankees and refused to be harassed out of Nashville.

Early in July 1862, Mrs. Bostick had received the horrible news that her youngest son, Abe, had been killed at Gaines Mill on the 27th. Having been widowed only sixteen months earlier and with so many family members not there to support her, Mrs. Bostick's loss of a son was an enormous trial, despite her strong Christian moorings. Margaret Litton Bostick's displaced children could only give their love and strength through correspondence.

The following letters, all written in July, give insights into the feelings of bereavement and anxieties that three Bostick children had over their mother's situation in Nashville. Also included is a letter Margaret received from Dr. Sehon, her old friend who was then occupying the same cell in the State Prison that Gen. Harding stayed in the previous spring.

July 13th [1862]

My Dear Brother[7]

For nearly two weeks we have been in a dreadful state of suspense—yesterday was much relieved when we received a letter from you but before we had finished reading it, the one I enclose to you was handed to me—Oh what a shock—although I had heard several days ago that Ed Bostick from Nash[ville] was killed & feared it might be either you or Abe. I would not—could not believe it our loss is great—but I could submit to it much better if I could forget my dear loved mother's sufferings—she has had so many trials I fear she cannot stand it—we received a note from her dated the 19th of June—a long letter was enclosed to be sent to Abe in which she expressed so much hope for her dear boy's safety—said she could not nerve herself to think of never meeting him—always banished the thought—one too dreadful to dwell on & before he had time to receive her letter he was taken—how can she stand it—if we could have her with us—it would be so much better. There is a house furnished with a large garden attached about a half mile from here—why can't mother & Catharine come & live there & if we move from here—of course arrangements will be made for them as a part of our family. They must leave Nashville. Mother says she does not fear them but I do—in her letter of the 19th she said that she and Aunt Anne[8] were going out to see Aunt S[9]—who had been very ill—& one of the villains drew a knife half as long as her arm & shook it at them—she told him to put it up—that she neither feared him or his knife—and Aunt A called him a cowardly villain—another time in going out they were stopped six times by the pickets within a few miles—they ought not to remain there—I can send for them if you can get them out of their lines—write or come immediately if you possibly can—I would start today to see you but am very uneasy about Col A[10]—I received a letter from him three weeks ago saying he would leave Granada [Miss.] and be with me in a few days—I have not heard from him since—have no idea where he is—very much fear he is sick—am afraid to leave until I hear from him—it will be better for you to come here anyhow—probably Eliza[11] will meet you here—I received a letter from her yesterday—she was well—had been up to see Mat[12] just before mother wrote—she and Kate were well—Mary Litton[13] had had a spell of sore throat but was recovering—I feel more anxious than ever to be with my dear brothers—Oh God it is so hard to feel that we have to give him up—that such a sacrifice should be made—I never could feel that any of my loved brothers should be sacrificed—do come—write the day before you start and I will meet you at Crawfordsville[14]—address to that place—care of P. P. Halbert[15]—if you can find an opportunity write & send McKenzie's letter—we have written frequently but she has never received a line from us—Bently[16] was sick when she wrote—I fear he will not live much longer—I must have them with me your fond sister

Mary A.[17]

⊂⊃═◦═⊂⊃

Jackson [Miss.] July 17th 1862

Dear Mother—

My heart is aching so much for you this morning that I can hardly write. I never heard of my precious brave brother's death until yesterday. I received a note from Tom telling me to meet him at the depot and go to Jackson with him to see Mat.[18] I never felt so happy in my life as I did at the idea of seeing Tom and Mat and expecting such a pleasant trip knowing I could hear from you all but such sad sad news did I hear. I had heard nothing from Abe and had ever since the battle felt very uneasy about him but I could not think God would send such a blow to my almost broken hearted mother—but oh my mother was it not a happy meeting between him and my dear father? Although we have given up so much, for no better or nobler hearted boy ever lived than Abe, yet we know he is safely housed with his father. I do wish so much that I could be with you and if it were not for my little baby I would go now to see you but he could not stand the trip.

My husband[19] is near Jackson as he is with me today. He sends a great deal of love to you and says that, as soon as he thinks I can with any safety go to see you, [I should].

I cannot write this morning but will write again soon and get Tom to send my letter to you. My husband's brother Abe's Dr is here and will leave for home this evening. My husband is going to get him and will write by him to his brother Tom to get Abe's body and bury it in their family burying ground. I knew you would feel better satisfied to have it there until you can have him moved. As soon as I hear anything about

[this] I am going to write to him myself and I know he will do all he can. I send you by Mat $40. Please pay Uncle Jimmy[20] $16 (sixteen) of it and take a receipt. It is money he gave my husband to buy molasses. Do you & Catharine[21] plan to write to me? Give Catharine and the dear little children much love and many kisses from me.

I will write to Catharine soon. I was sorry to hear Sue was so sick. Does she ever mention me or the baby? God bless my dear mother is the prayer of

your devoted daughter
Eliza [22]

Direct to Edward's Depot, Mi[ssissippi]
care J. F. Rives[23]

***

Chattanooga, Tenn. 21st July 1862

My Dear Mother

I have just reached this place from Columbus, Miss. which place I left about twelve days ago having come through on horseback. I found Mr. Bernard here on his way to Nashville and gladly avail myself of the opportunity to write to you. I have just heard the sad news of Abe's death in the recent fight near Richmond. Mr. Bernard tells me that you had heard it before he left. I received a letter from Tom dated the 23rd ulto. in which he stated that Abe was well. I hear now that he received a telegram after the date of his letter that Abe fell while making a charge on the 28th of June. It is some consolation to know that his life was sacrificed in defense of his country and that there is hope that his death will be amply avenged. I understand that his remains were taken care of & buried by a friend & the grave carefully marked so that it can be found hereafter. I have not seen Tom since I left Nashville but wrote to him the day before I left Columbus informing him that I would be in Chattanooga by this time. I expect to see him here in a day or two. I understand that he is at Marietta, Ga. with his wife. Until I see him, I have given you all that I have heard of Abe's death.

I have just heard from Joe. He is well. I left Bettie and the children in Columbus all very well. Bettie is looking better than I ever saw her. The little boys are as fat as they can be & the baby is the best baby in the world. Mag and Mary Anne are staying at Mr. Percival Halbert's about 20 miles from Columbus both very well. Hardie Anderson is a fine large boy. Col. Anderson was expected in Columbus when I left, having been assigned to that post.

I have frequently sent verbal messages to you by persons going in who were unwilling to undertake to carry letters.[24] Whenever I find a man willing to take a letter I write but it is very seldom that I can do so. I received your letter dated 28th May and was glad to hear you are all well and getting on with a reasonable degree of comfort. I hope you will write by every safe conveyance and write only about family matters avoiding public matters as your letters may fall into the hands of the enemy and may give them an excuse to annoy you.

I have met here Andrew Ewing, Judge Humphreys,[25] Jno Fisher and Col. Torbett[26] who are all in good health. If you see Mr. Bernard he can give you all the news which it would be improper to write in a letter.

I do not know where Joe's wife is having received no letter from Joe for several months. I will try and send another letter soon, certainly by the first opportunity. Write to me by every chance & still direct to Columbus, Miss: Bettie will forward the letters wherever I may be.

Give my love to Catharine and the children. Hoping that you may continue to get along with as little trouble as possible under the circumstances that surround you and that we may be soon reunited. I remain with the warmest love,

Your affectionate son
J. L. Bostick

"State Prison," Tennessee
August 1, 1862

Mrs. H. P. Bostick
My dear Sister,

Most deeply do I sympathize with you and your afflicted family in the death of your dear son.[27]

He was a good son—lovely and amiable and [in] every way a most useful citizen—with a bright future before him. He left all and went forth a brave and valiant soldier at the call of his suffering country—noble he bore himself—forgoing the comforts of home—enduring toil and labor he marched to his country's defense. In the unquestioned and inscrutable providence of God, he was doomed to fall but he fell at his post and fills a hero's place. His name is forever bound in the same bright volume of [the] fallen in which are preserved the names of all those who fell bravely fighting for their country's rights and liberty—and he fell too a Christian hero. He has fought the good fight—finished his course—and God has taken him home.

My dear sister in thy additional trouble and bereavement which has come upon you—you will have more need than ever before of faith in God—you shall and will have it—God will hear your prayers—he counts your tears and hears your sighs.

He is your God & your Father, in him you ever trust.

I now remember with mournful pleasure that your son was one of the very last with whom I shook hands when his regiment left. I was standing on the street as they passed—walked to him and gave him my love and on parting "God bless you." But he is gone.

Yes, forever gone from earth to heaven. We shall if faithful all join him there.

I am under great obligations to your kind family. Mrs. Halbert, Mrs. Cooper, and Mrs. Thomas[28] for their oft repeated kindnesses to me in my prison home. I am sincerely grateful to them and pray heaven's choicest blessings toward and upon each of them with their families.

Kindest regards to your family—
God bless you and yours forever.

Your friend
E. W. Sehon[29]

CHAPTER EIGHT

KENTUCKY AND TENNESSEE

uring the summer of 1862, Union forces controlled most of Middle and West Tennessee and threatened Chattanooga, a strategic railroad center in the southeast corner of the state. To relieve the pressure there and to drive Gen. Buell's forces out of Middle Tennessee, Gen. Bragg met Maj. Gen. Edmund Kirby Smith in Chattanooga to coordinate strategy. He had to talk to Kirby Smith, even though he outranked him, because he was contemplating operations in an area under Kirby Smith's jurisdiction. At that point, Bragg had no idea of launching an expedition into Kentucky. His focus was on Nashville. However, he changed his mind and decided to "strike for Lexington and Cincinnati, both of which are entirely unprotected."[1] Kirby Smith started for Kentucky from Knoxville on August 14, with two divisions; one under Brig. Gen. Thomas James Churchill and the other under Gen. Cleburne. Among Bragg's soldiers was Capt. Joe Bostick.

Two weeks later, Bragg's army crossed the Tennessee River at Chattanooga and moved up the Sequatchie Valley through Pikeville to Sparta. His destination was Glasgow, which he reached on September 13. Meanwhile, in Nashville, Buell quickly realized that Middle Tennessee was not Bragg's target. He left Gen. George Thomas in Nashville with three divisions and set out as fast as he could for Louisville with the rest of his army. By this time, Kirby Smith had gained virtual control of Central Kentucky, occupying both Lexington and Frankfort. By late October, Buell had his entire force at Louisville, having beaten Bragg there. Bragg's army was at Bardstown. Instead of combining his army with that of Kirby Smith and attacking Buell, Bragg turned his attention to staging an elaborate gubernatorial inauguration ceremony at Frankfort, where Richard Hawes was named provisional governor under the Confederacy. While Bragg was there, Buell initiated a fight. He moved his forces toward Perryville where they first clashed with Col. Joseph Wheeler's cavalry. Gen. William J. Hardee's Confederate forces quickly formed a line of battle and the fighting escalated. Bragg ordered Leonidas Polk's and B. F. Cheatham's divisions into the action which turned into a bloody battle. Among those who fought at Perryville on that parched October day were Litton Bostick, who had been commissioned a first lieutenant and aide-de-camp to Brig. Gen. Liddell only two weeks earlier. In reporting on the battle, Liddell praised Bostick and two other staff officers who "cheerfully and fearlessly assisted me in the conveyance of all necessary instructions, regardless of all exposure." Liddell said that, as he was forming his line of battle, he noticed that the Eighth Arkansas Regiment, which held the left wing, was not in place. He sent Bostick "to look after it." Having no time to lose, Liddell moved on in line of battle without support on his left wing. On reaching the front of the enemy, he was relieved to find that the Eight Arkansas had, "by a rapid right oblique movement, rejoined the brigade at the very time needed."[2]

Without Kirby Smith's troops, which included Maj. Tom Bostick, Bragg's forces were outnumbered 36,940 to 16,000. At Perryville, he lost about 20 percent of his men while Buell lost 3,696. Bragg met up with Smith's army at Harrodsburg and retreated from Kentucky via Cumberland Gap, chagrined at having failed either to successfully recruit soldiers or rid the state of the Federal presence.

Although Gen. Bragg lost the confidence of his generals during the failed Kentucky campaign, he was not relieved by President Davis. He established his headquarters at Murfreesboro and announced his determination to "occupy Middle Tennessee in force, and if possible to hold for the coming winter the country between the Cumberland and Tennessee Rivers." Buell was not so fortunate. While on his way back to Nashville, he received orders from Washington to turn his command over to Gen. W. S. Rosecrans. He had been at cross purposes with both Andrew Johnson and President Lincoln for some time.

At Murfreesboro, Bragg waited for Rosecrans to attack him. Bragg's newly christened Army of Tennessee was spread out in a rough semicircle southeast of Nashville, his left at Triune and his right at Readyville. Polk's corps occupied the center near Murfreesboro. As members of that corps, Tom and Joe Bostick were among those waiting for the inevitable battle and still confident of the South's ultimate success. Meanwhile, Litton was still aide-de-camp to Gen. Liddell, commander of the Second Brigade of Pat Cleburne's Division near Readyville. Jim Cooper, who had been exchanged the previous August, Bill Robinson, and Jim Thomas also awaited the battle. Once again, they were all in the Twentieth Tennessee, which was part of John Breckinridge's Division of Hardee's corps. When the fight opened, Jim Thomas was so sick he could hardly sit on his horse. Nevertheless, he fought and survived without mishap in a battle in which the Confederates lost 10,266 men out of a total force of 37,712. His Bostick, Cooper, and Robinson first cousins also escaped unscathed. The three-day battle, which ended on January 2, 1863, was reminiscent of the Battle of Shiloh in that both were bloody engagements in which the Confederates surprised the Yankees with devastating surprise attacks at dawn. Although technically a draw, the Battle of Stones River was, in strategic terms, a major defeat for the Confederates because it determined that the Union would continue to control Middle Tennessee's railroads and productive farms.[3]

The Confederates withdrew toward Wartrace in a driving rain on January 3. Bragg's men were exhausted and he had received an erroneous report that Rosecrans had received reinforcements. In truth, Rosecrans had also considered withdrawing. Although he did not, he felt his troops were too weary to contest the Confederate retreat.

In his official report on the battle, Confederate Gen. Liddell wrote that his adjutant-general, G. A. Williams, and his aide-de-camp, Lieut. J. L. Bostick, "not only behaved with the most undaunted bravery, but assisted me voluntarily, and with the utmost alacrity, in pushing forward the brigade, in placing the battery in positions, and in the deployment of skir-mishers in the very face of the enemy, and in the heaviest fire whenever required, oftentimes using their own judgment without waiting for orders, for the good of the service and success of the day."[4]

Following the battle, Bragg's Army of Tennessee fell back about thirty miles to the natural barriers of the Duck and Elk Rivers. He established his headquarters at Winchester. Hardee's corps moved to Tullahoma by way of Manchester, while Polk fell back to Shelbyville, twenty miles from Murfreesboro. As members of Polk's corps, Tom and Joe Bostick went into winter quarters near Shelbyville, where they shared a tent. Litton was at Wartrace where Gen. Liddell established his headquarters, while Jim

Cooper was at Tullahoma. Cooper was struck by the intemperance of many of his fellow soldiers. He recorded in his diary that "we were no sooner in camp, than the wickedness and depravity of the soldiers, began to show itself in a thousand ways. Card playing, gambling, cock fighting and drunkenness were every day amusements."[5]

Bill Robinson received a furlough in February and went home to Blue Springs Farm in Williamson County for a short rest before reporting to Company D of the Tenth Tennessee Cavalry where he was made captain.

Jim Thomas spent several months at or near Tullahoma, often side by side with Jim Cooper. In April, the Twentieth Tennessee moved to Fairfield, a cross-roads hamlet five miles east of Bell Buckle. The regiment remained there until one wet morning in June when Union Gen. J. T. Wilder's brigade made its surprise appearance at Hoover's Gap, a few miles to the north. There, in a thicket on a steep hillside, Thomas, who was in position just behind the colors, rushed to the front when he saw his regiment falter in the face of Wilder's charge. He assisted his colonel, Thomas B. Smith, in rallying the regiment for a counterattack. Shot in the chest, Thomas fell on his face. Painfully, he twisted over, raised his sword over his head, and weakly exclaimed: "Go on boys, don't stop for me. Go on and drive them back."[6] Thinking himself mortally wounded, Thomas made Jim Cooper and other friends leave him on the field which they could not hold.

Thomas was one of sixty-two men in his regiment who were either killed or wounded at Hoover's Gap. Captured and taken that night to a Federal field hospital at Murfreesboro and later to a larger one at Nashville, he was treated with the utmost kindness.

Jim Thomas' uncle, Washington Cooper, initially heard, probably from his son, that his nephew had been killed. When he learned that the boy was still alive and in Nashville, he asked Union Brig. Gen. Daniel McCook Jr. if Jim might be brought to his home to recuperate. McCook granted that request and Thomas was taken by ambulance to his uncle's house next door to his own. There, he was treated by his family physician, Dr. T. L. Maddin, and tenderly cared for by the women in the family, including his aunts, Ann Cooper and Margaret Bostick, and his first cousin, Catharine Halbert.

One day, Dr. Maddin discovered that a life-threatening aneurysm was forming on the main artery near Jim's heart. After consulting with Federal surgeons, Dr. Maddin concluded that a dangerous operation was necessary to save his life. With the family's permission and with the assistance of Federal surgeons, Dr. Maddin performed the surgery, which was successful. After three months of painful convalescence at his uncle's home, Jim was well enough to be sent to a Federal prison at Fort Delaware. He never recovered fully from the wound, however, and was exchanged late in the war. Unable to return to active duty, he was honorably discharged from Confederate service.[7]

Reprinted below are three letters written by Litton and one by Tom, along with an ordnance report written by Tom. Two letters, one each by Litton and Tom, were written in March 1863 during the six months lull between Stones River and the expulsion of Bragg's from Middle Tennessee in June. A second letter from Litton, written from Chickamauga Station, Georgia, in July, immediately after the retreat from Shelbyville, shows his frustration and indignation over the inglorious withdrawal. In the same letter, Litton voiced the hope that Jim Thomas had only been wounded and not killed at Hoover's Gap.

The final communication is a report that Tom Bostick wrote on September 1, 1863, to Col. Josiah Gorgas, Chief of Ordnance for the Confederate States of America. In his report, Tom explained the loss of ordnance and ordnance stores that occurred during the retreat from Middle Tennessee and enclosed a list of arms lost. It seems odd that a captain would communicate directly with a relatively high government official in Richmond. Tom's report also reflects the relative lack of bureaucracy in the Confederate Army of Tennessee in that Gorgas, despite the importance of his position, was only a colonel.

——————➤-◦-◄—————

Wartrace.Tenn.
March 12 '63

To Mrs. C. W. Halbert[8]
My Dear Sister,

I wrote to mother a few days since and hope she received my letter; for fear she did not I write you as I have an opportunity of sending direct to Nashville. Your letter dated some three weeks since was duly received and afterward forwarded to Bettie, and Mary Anne. I was very glad to hear that you were getting on so well at home and that you had a fair prospect of getting a school of your own. I decidedly approve your plan and have no doubt you will have much better success than as an assistant in Mrs. Holcombe's school. I hope you will find numbers of good friends in Nashville who will render you valuable assistance in your undertaking.

I frequently see Joe and Tom who are both near Shelbyville and both very well. Since I saw you, I have had the pleasure of spending a week in Columbus, having been sent there in charge of a detail from this command. Mag & Mary Anne who had been staying in Pickensville, Ala. came to Columbus the day after I got there. Tom was with me but left in a day or two with Mag for Joe's present home in Georgia, where Mag is now staying. I found Bettie and the children well, except that the baby was a little thin from teething. Bettie has since written that he is now as fat as ever. Willie and Hardy have grown a good deal since you saw them & Hardy Anderson has become quite a large fine boy. Col. Anderson is stationed in Columbus & was quite well. Mag looked better than I ever saw her; Mary Anne was also looking very well.

I received a letter a short time since from Eliza which I enclose with this to you. It will give you a better idea how she is getting along than I could. I get letters from Bettie every week or ten days. You must write to me by every opportunity as nothing gives me greater pleasure than to hear from you and know what you are doing at home. I saw Uncle Jesse[9] in Chattanooga; he was very well but I think is somewhat grayer than when you last saw him. George Litton[10] was well when I last saw him; Jimmie Cooper[11] and Jimmie Thomas I have not seen for a long time though I suppose they are well. I have enjoyed the luxury of living in a comfortable little house at this place for several weeks and have thus avoided the heavy rains which have fallen during the past month. I expect to vacate it soon however. My health is excellent; was never better.

I see Nashville people every day at this place. Young Saurie [sic] (son of Rev. Mr. Saurie)[12] is here attached to this command, is a good soldier & an excellent young man. I hope to be able to assist him in the way of promotion as he richly deserves it.

I believe I have given you all the information which it would be proper to write. Give my love to mother and kiss all the children for me. Tell Sue[13] that I will send her a little present by the first opportunity.

I hope you will let me hear from you by every opportunity. That God may protect and bless yourself, my mother and all the little ones at home is the constant prayer of your affectionate brother.

J. L. Bostick

Shelbyville
March 13th 1863

My Dear Mother,

I have a chance to write to you. I have gone regularly into the Army again. I am Commissary of the 4th Tenn. Regt.[14] Joe and I occupy the same tent and each of us has a negro so we are quite pleasantly situated. I went home on the 11th of last month and found Mat and the children well.[15] I got there at two o'clock and left at four same day. I was in Columbus [Miss.] about five weeks ago. All well down there. I brought Mag up to Joe's and left her there to stay with May. Mary A gave me one hundred & ten ($110) for you but I cannot get anything but Confederate notes to send you so I will not send it. I saw Litton about three weeks ago. He was quite well. He will write to you by the one that carries this. I cannot write anything that will interest you except that all your children out in "Dixie" are in fine health and spirits. I have not heard from Mat since I left. If you can, send her word that I am in fine health and fattening every day. I hear often from Mag through Mary's letters. As soon as I can I will send her to Nashville. I will be rather closely confined now. My pay is $140 per month. My address is Capt. T. H. Bostick, McMurray's Regt., Maney's Brigade, Cheatham's Division, Polk's Corps. Write to me. I have not heard lately from Jimmy Cooper & Jimmy Thomas. Love to all.

Your aft son
T. H. Bostick

Chickamauga, Tenn.
July 19th 1863

To Mrs. C. W. Halbert
My dear Sister;

Your letter of the 25th of June was received in the midst of our inglorious retreat from Middle Tenn. and for some time afterwards I had no opportunity of writing. I felt exceedingly mortified at giving up so much of the state with so little resistance, but all feeling on the subject was absorbed in the great disaster sustained in the fall of

Vicksburg,[16] the news of which reached us just as we finished our retreat. The loss of the Miss. River, which necessarily follows the fate of Vicksburg, is certainly the heaviest blow that we have yet received. It does not change the final result of our struggle, but it will add to our difficulties, increase the suffering of our people, open a new field for the enemy to plunder and probably prolong the contest for one or two years. For a time it will give great encouragement to the North, but when they find, as they will very soon, that it does not "break the backbone of the rebellion," a reaction will take place in public opinion in the North and they will learn at last that the subjugation of the South is an impossibility. In the meantime however they will rob and plunder the citizens throughout the country embraced in their lines and the destruction of property will be immense. Gen. Johnston has already been compelled to fall back from Jackson [Miss.] and I expect that his next base will be the Mobile & Ohio Railroad.[17] The enemy will meet with serious obstacles to his advance across the State of Mississippi and it may be that we will be able to check him at or near his present position. But I would not be surprised if the whole of Mississippi was overrun and Mobile fell into the hands of the enemy in the next few months. I do not look for this to take place with any degree of certainty, but I think it is altogether possible. I therefore think that it would not be advisable for you & mother to move to Mobile for the present. It would be decidedly better for you to remain where you are until military operations assume a more settled aspect. I consider your present location one of the safest from Yankee invasion, in the Confederacy and to move to Mobile & soon after to be forced to move again would involve considerable loss and inconvenience. I hope that you can make yourselves pretty comfortable where you are. I did think, a short time since, that I would soon be able to visit you but I cannot now say when I will have that pleasure. Gen. Liddell had a promise of a 60 days' furlough from Gen. Bragg to visit his family on the other side of the Miss. River but since the fall of Vicksburg he is doubtful whether he would be able to cross the river in safety and I fear that he will not ask for the leave of absence. If he should do so however, he will include me and I will at once visit you.

I am at present at Chickamauga, a station on the Chattanooga & Atlanta R. R. about 7 miles south of Chattanooga. Our brigade will probably remain here for some weeks though it is liable to be ordered off at any moment. Direct your letters to this place for the present. I received a note from Tom a day or two ago stating that Mary Ann [sic] would be in Chattanooga today, but I examined the train yesterday evening & she was not aboard. She may arrive this evening. Tell mother that Mary Ann [sic] sent me $20 for her nearly a month before she reached Belle Buckle. I entirely forgot it while mother was with me but will send it to her by the first opportunity.

Our brigade did some fighting at Liberty Gap on the 24th, 25th and 26th of June, our loss being 120 men killed, wounded or missing.[18] We held a greatly superior force of the enemy in check at that place until we were ordered to retire to Tullahoma. We inflicted a much heavier damage upon the enemy, their own accounts stating their loss at from three to four hundred men. The enemy have given no evidence as yet of an intention to advance & I think we will be idle here for several weeks.

I hope that you will write often. Let me know how you are getting along & tell me freely all your wants. You must consider, my dear sister, that whatever I have is yours and mother's and do not hesitate to call on me at any time for anything that I can supply. Give my love to mother and tell her to write to me often. I suppose that I will see Mary Ann [sic] in a day or two & will send this letter by her.

You have doubtless heard that Jimmy Thomas was killed at Hoover's Gap.[19] I have since heard that it is probable that he is still alive & in a hospital at Murfreesboro. I trust that this may prove true. Give my love to all the children.

Your affectionate brother
J. L. Bostick

Hd Qtrs 4th Conf Tenn. Regt.

Sept 1st 1863
Col. J. Gorgas [20]
Chief of Ord. CSA
Richmond, Va.

Sir

The loss of the subjoined list of ordnance & ordnance stores (Entered on return "lost by shipment") occurred during the retreat from Shelbyville, Tenn. The circumstances connected therewith were duly investigated by Maj. Clair of Gen. Bragg's staff & to whom I refer this for his remarks & approval.

The following are the stores lost by the 4th Conf. Ten. Regt: One thousand (1000) cartridges Cal 69 Ten (10) muskets Cal. 9 Two (2) Rifles Cal. 58 Three (3) Rifles Cal 57. Three (3) Rifles Cal. 54.

Respectfully submitted
J. Bostick Capt.
Com'dy 4th Conf. Ten. Reg.

CHAPTER NINE

CHICKAMAUGA AND MISSIONARY RIDGE

he twin blows of Gettysburg and Vicksburg were devastating to the hopes of the South. Gen. Lee's invasion of the North, envisioned as a high-water mark for the Confederacy, turned into an early obituary. With the fall of Vicksburg and that of Port Gibson two months earlier, Federal gunboats not only gained control of the Mississippi River but effectively shut off the Confederacy's supply line from Texas, an important source of food for the South's armies. To have Braxton Bragg's Army of Tennessee thrown out of Middle Tennessee in only eleven days with so little resistance that Federal casualties were less than 600 was viewed in the South as an humiliation and a disgrace. Another wave of unrest swept through the officer corp of the Army of Tennessee. Corps commanders William Hardee and Leonidas Polk demanded Bragg's ouster as an incompetent. President Davis listened but decided not to relieve him, probably because he could not think of anyone he liked who could do any better.

The target of the Army of the Cumberland was Chattanooga, a small but important industrial center and railroad gateway to the Deep South. The town of 2,500 was then occupied by Bragg's Army of Tennessee. His soldiers languished there through the heat of July and early August, bored and, at the same time, anxious to wreak revenge on the Yankees. Their time was coming. By mid-August, Rosecrans had decided to cross the Tennessee River downstream from Chattanooga, drive east across Lookout

Mountain, and cut Bragg's supply line to Atlanta. With a confidence born from having hoodwinked Bragg out of Middle Tennessee and also from exaggerated reports of morale problems in the Army of Tennessee, Rosecrans put his plan into effect.

After executing effective feints upstream of Chattanooga and at Harrison's Landing, Rosecrans divided the bulk of his army into three columns and began a wide advance across the mountainous terrain south of the city. One hundred miles to the north, Gen. Ambrose E. Burnside, the late commander of the Army of the Potomac, occupied Knoxville, much to the relief of President Lincoln, who had long waited for a chance to free East Tennessee from the yoke of Confederate rule.

Outflanked and outnumbered, Bragg did the only thing he could. He abandoned Chattanooga and pulled his army back to the vicinity of Lafayette, Georgia. There he frittered away several opportunities to pounce on isolated elements of Rosecrans' divided Army of the Cumberland. The reprieves gave Rosecrans time to get his exposed army back together. On September 17, Maj. Gens. McCook and Thomas joined forces and pushed northward along Chickamauga Creek to join Maj. Gen. Thomas Chrittenden's Twenty-first Corps at Lee and Gordon Mill. Here, they violently collided with the Army of Tennessee and fought the largest battle of the Western theater. Bragg's army, bolstered by the arrival of Gen. James "Pete" Longstreet's two infantry divisions, on September 19, were no longer at a numerical disadvantage. With numbers slightly on his side, Bragg saw an opportunity to destroy the Union army. In the heat of battle, Rosecrans believed that he had a gap in the right-center of his line. He ordered Brig. Gen. Thomas Wood's division to fill it. In fact, no gap existed until Wood's division moved and created one. Before the error could be corrected, John Bell Hood's brigades swept through it, causing pandemonium on the Northern side. Only a stubborn and valiant stand by Gen. Thomas, on a heavily wooded height known as Horseshoe Ridge, prevented a defeat from becoming a disaster.

Despite being urged by Gen. Nathan B. Forrest to pursue the demoralized Federals fleeing toward Chattanooga, Bragg demurred, citing a lack of supplies. Forrest retorted: "Gen. Bragg, we can get all the supplies our army needs in Chattanooga." When Bragg still refused, Forrest rode away in fury. Bragg's victory, the last one the South would win in the west, turned out to be a hollow one in that it did not result in the recapture of Chattanooga. Also, Bragg's losses were horrendous and irreplaceable. He suffered an estimated 18,000 casualties out of an army of 65,000. Rosecrans had losses of about 16,000 out of 62,000 engaged. No wonder, veterans thereafter nick-named Chickamauga the "river of death." Jim Cooper, who participated in a charge by Bate's brigade that struck the Federal line in mid-afternoon later said: "In five minutes all the horrors of war that a soldier ever witnessed were there."[1]

A few weeks after the battle, Gen. Liddell made an official report of the action of his division during the fight. In it, he commented that Lieut. J. L. Bostick, his aide-de-camp, and another staff officer "behaved with their usual gallantry and need no commendation at my hands."[2]

Following the battle, Gen. Rosecrans was beside himself with grief and despair. His wires from Chattanooga to Washington made it clear to Lincoln that he had a completely demoralized and paralyzed commander on his hands. The president immediately ordered massive reinforcements to the beleaguered city—20,000 troops from Mississippi under Maj. Gen. William T. Sherman and an equal number from Virginia under Brig. Gen. "Fighting Joe" Hooker.

The Confederate forces formed a semicircle around Chattanooga, occupying the heights on Missionary Ridge, Orchard Knob, and Lookout Mountain. Also, about a thousand of Longstreet's men were stationed downstream from the city at Brown's Ferry to prevent supplies from coming up the river. However, the Confederate leaders were nearly as disorganized as the Federals were. Bragg's failure to pursue the Army of the Cumberland into Chattanooga rekindled the smoldering resentment his corps commanders had for him. Longstreet, who coveted command himself, wrote the secretary of war, urging that Gen. Lee be sent to Tennessee to lead the Confederacy's largest army in the west. Of course, that did not happen. Privately, Longstreet joked about the Chattanooga siege because the Confederacy did not control the mountain passes to the west of town. Over them at least a trickle of supplies were reaching the town.

Fed up with Rosecrans, President Lincoln replaced him with the steady George Thomas. He also gave Thomas help from above by giving Ulysses S. Grant, the North's newest hero, command of all Federal forces between the Mississippi and the Appalachians. Grant wasted no time getting to Chattanooga. He arrived on September 23 and listened to Thomas' plan to lift the siege. Four days later, under cover of fog, Federal troops crossed the Tennessee by pontoon bridges and took Brown's Ferry. Later that day, a long column of men under "Fighting Joe" Hooker could be seen by Confederates on Lookout Mountain as they marched up the valley from Bridgeport. Inexplicably, Longstreet did not counterattack at once to regain control of the river. When he did so that night, it was too late and too little. The Federals had dug in and were able to throw back the assault.

When conditions quieted down after the Brown's Ferry embarrassment, Longstreet, smarting from that and anxious for an independent command, talked Bragg into letting him take two infantry divisions, two artillery battalions, and two small cavalry divisions under Gen. Joe Wheeler, and capture Knoxville. Maney's Brigade, including Joe and Tom Bostick, went with him. Even though this division of forces meant Bragg would be reducing his army to approximately half that of Grant's forces in Chattanooga, he agreed. He was glad to get rid of a man he considered a problem. His was a bad decision, however, as Longstreet not only failed to capture Knoxville but was gone when Bragg needed him at Chattanooga.

The Knoxville campaign failed primarily because the poorly equipped Confederates, not having sufficient supplies to starve Burnside out of Knoxville, miscalculated in their plans to storm Fort Sanders. Having seen Union soldiers cross the ditch surrounding the fort, but not realizing they were walking across planks, Longstreet and his staff underestimated the ditch's depth. Consequently, the three assaulting Confederate brigades were not given scaling equipment. As a result, the ditch became a "death pit." With no means to cross the ditch and scale the parapet, the attack was doomed.

Within an hour of his failure to capture Fort Sanders, Longstreet received a telegraph from Jefferson Davis, advising him that Bragg had been defeated and that he should abandon the siege of Knoxville and join Bragg in North Georgia. Longstreet did drop the siege but decided that logistics would preclude him from rejoining Bragg. Instead, he and his staff decided to go into winter quarters near Bristol, Virginia.

Longstreet did not know that Davis had finally decided to relieve Bragg of his command and replace him with Gen. William Hardee. Bragg was ordered to relinquish his command on December 2. Two nights later, Longstreet's forces abandoned Knoxville. As they marched through the night to the northeast, some of his men sang "Carry Me Back to Old Virginny."

In January, Maney's Brigade rejoined the Army of Tennessee at Dalton, Georgia. There, Joe and Tom, both of whom survived the assault at Knoxville, were reunited with Litton. He too missed the debacle at Missionary Ridge because during the second week in November he went on furlough to visit his wife Bettie and their children in Columbus, Mississippi. Jim Cooper was at Missionary Ridge where he was badly wounded.[3] After walking twenty-five miles to Dalton, Georgia, he managed to climb on the top of a freight car, which took him to Marietta, where he was nursed back to health by Dr. Setts, a local physician, and members of the Litton and Thomas families who were in exile there. At Marietta, Jim saw George S. Litton who had also been wounded.[4]

The following letters that Litton Bostick wrote between the end of August and late November give interesting accounts of the Battle at Chickamauga, the Federal capture of Brown's Ferry, life on Missionary Ridge during the siege of Chattanooga, and the refugee status of Bostick family members trying to stay out of harm's reach.

                                        Chickamauga, Ga. Aug. 31st 1863

My dear Sister:[5]

I wrote to mother two days ago, directing my letter to Marietta. As Capt. Hunt[6] leaves this evening for Joe's place, I take the opportunity to send you a little money ($50) which I thought you might need and also to acknowledge the receipt of your letter a few days ago. Capt. Hunt will be able to give you all the news. My health continues excellent. I will write to you and also to Mag in a short time. Give my love to mother and all the children. Tell Hardie[7] that if he was here now, I could take him to a hill near camp and show him the shelling which takes place nearly every day at Chattanooga.

Gen. Liddell[8] sends his regards to you and mother. I send Hardies letters by Capt. Hunt. Write to me often and do not wait for me to answer your letters before you write again. Joe says that mother has about $200 in Tenn. Bank money & that it can now be sold for near a thousand dollars. Sell it at once before we whip the Bankers & Confederate money goes up. I expect to get a furlough after our next battle & will stop a while with you.

That God may bless and protect you is the daily prayer of your affectionate Brother

                                                          J. L. Bostick

If Mag is broke, give $10 to her.

Hd. Qtrs. Liddell's Division 6 miles from
Chattanooga Sept. 22nd '63

My Dear Mother;

I write you a few lines, during a halt, to let you know that I am safe and understand that Joe is also safe after a hard fought battle of two days.[9] Tom was not in the fight & is of course safe. Our victory, from present indications is complete, the enemy being now in full retreat and we having captured 26 pieces of artillery, 15 or 20,000 stand of small arms, several thousand stand of prisoners, besides killing or wounding a large number. I do not believe that the Yankees will make a stand this side of the Tenn. River. I am expecting every moment orders to move towards Chattanooga and have no time to write a long letter, besides having to write with my papers on my knee. I will write more fully at the first opportunity.

That God may bless & protect you & all with you, is the prayer of your affectionate son

J. L. Bostick

Joe is in command of his Regt. all the field officers having been wounded.[10]

Missionary Ridge,
Oct. 14th 1863

My Dear Mother;

Your letter of 6th Inst. was duly received from which I learn that mine written immediately after the battle[11] was some two weeks in reaching you. I also wrote to Catharine after the army reached this place, giving her some account of the battle field etc. which ought to have reached you before the date of your letter. The mails seem to be conducted in the worst possible manner; the last letter that I received from Bettie was dated the 8th of last month.

Our army is motionless at the present time, no change having taken place in our position since we reached this place. The two armies are in sight of each other, their pickets standing within two hundred yards and all looks as quiet and peaceful as if they were two friendly forces. Only occasionally a gun is fired from one side or the other, to try the range or to feel for a battery. The pickets on both sides are ordered not to fire unless in case of an advance, and the Yankees became so familiar as to exchange several papers with our men and seemed quite desirous of entering into conversation on all occasions, until positive orders were issued by Gen. Bragg forbidding all intercourse of every description. I understand that one Yankee captain persisted in coming over to our pickets notwithstanding he had been warned not to leave his line and was quickly made a prisoner in spite of his earnest entreaty to be released.

The policy of our army is to annoy the enemy in the rear, interrupt his communications and force him to fall back for want of supplies. It has been raining for two days & nights and the roads over the mountains must be by this time almost impassible [sic] and I do not see how Rosecrans can subsist his army much longer in Chattanooga. He possesses great perseverance however and may be able to do so. I am of the opinion however that his defeat at Chickamauga destroyed all prospect for his making or even attempting any advance movement before next spring & that he will be compelled to fall back at least to Bridgeport [Ala.] within the next month.

I have not seen Joe or Tom for two or three weeks; I suppose however that they are both well or I should have heard from them. My health continues excellent. Camp life is exceedingly dull and monotonous here and we all anxiously wish for some movement.

Hugh Topp[12] is now at Chickamauga Station, being a member of Gen. Stevenson's Signal Corps.[13] Eugene Topp, son of Dickson Topp, was mortally wounded in a skirmish on Missionary Ridge on Monday after the Battle of Chickamauga and died about a week ago. His mother and father were with him when he died.[14]

Give my love to all. You must write frequently as your letters give me great pleasure.

Your affectionate son
J. L. Bostick

⟫•◦•⟪

Missionary Ridge,
Oct. 26th 1863

My Dear Sister;[15]

I received your last letter, without date, on yesterday. I have written to mother, since my letter to you, but it seems that she had not received it when you wrote. I am sorry that you allow yourself to have the "blues" which you complain of having, in your letter. It is a disease, which like chills, will become chronic if allowed to continue unchecked. I have, in my younger days, sometimes indulged myself in gloomy dreams and fancies but I have quit the bad habit. I have suffered more intensely from the anticipation of evils that never came to pass, than I have ever from actual, real sorrows. I have learned that real happiness has its source in the heart and not in external circumstances. There are few afflictions to which mortals are ever prepared for which a healthy, Christian nature will not find consolation. Happiness is like the sunlight, free to all, high and low, rich and poor alike, and is only denied to those who willfully shut themselves up in the darkness. Have the blues no more. Turn your thoughts more upon the blessings which you have, rather than to those which you have not; never double sorrows by anticipating them but wait till they come upon you and then, forget them as soon as possible.

These are the times, above all others, when the patriotic men and women of the South should cultivate a spirit of cheerfulness and contentment. The time will come when these will be looked back to as the heroic days of our country and it will be considered a proud privilege to have lived through the trials to which we are exposed.

You speak of getting a place for the next year where you can teach school. I doubt the policy of teaching at all. You will receive but little pay, which will be more than absorbed by the additional expense attending to the location suitable for a school. I think it would be far better to get a pleasant little place in the country where wood is plenty & where you can have a garden etc. In a town, two or three loads of wood would consume all that a school would probably pay you. On the other hand, you can easily raise in the country, many things which would cost a great deal in a town. An enterprising hen would make more clear cash for her owner than a respectable school in the existing state of society.

I have made application for a furlough and have some hope that it will be granted. If it should be, I will start about the first of next month and will be with you in about a week or ten days from the present time. We can then talk over all plans and propositions and discuss them thoroughly. It will be three or four days before I know whether my application will be granted and then about the same time before I start. If I get a furlough, I will write to inform you immediately, so that you had better send Hardie over to the post office about the 31st of this month, when you will probably receive my letter.

There is nothing new in the situation of the two armies at this place. Joe and Tom have gone with their brigade towards Knoxville. I have not seen them for several weeks. Give my love to mother, Mag, Mary and all the children. I hope that mother has received my last letter before this time.

Hoping that I may soon follow this letter and have the pleasure of seeing you all once more, I remain with much love

Your affectionate brother

J. L. Bostick

———➤◆◀———

Missionary Ridge,

Oct. 30th 1863

My Dear Mother;

I wrote to Catharine a few day ago, that I was about to apply for a leave of absence & if it was granted, that I would start about the 1st of next month. My application went up approved at all the Head Quarters through which it had to pass until it reached Gen. Bragg's where it had endorsed on it "disapproved now." This indicates some anticipated movement which prevents all furloughs being granted for the present but implies at the same time a promise that I shall get mine when matters assume a more settled condition. I look for a leave of absence sometime in the course of next month.

On the 27th the enemy made an attack on our extreme left under the command of Gen. Longstreet, and succeeded in driving our forces from their position. We had, I believe only about a regiment engaged and it suffered pretty heavily. Gen. Longstreet afterwards made a night attack upon the enemy who had fortified themselves, but was repulsed. The enemy now have possession of the valley west of Lookout Mountain and if not driven away will be able to bring up supplies on the Nashville & Chatta[nooga] rail road.[16] Gen. Longstreet is very much blamed for allowing the Yankees to get possession of the position. He ought to have had this place strongly fortified and as it was, when the enemy had driven in the regiment, he should have ordered up a sufficient force at once, to dislodge them before they had time to fortify.

I have not seen Joe or Tom for several weeks. They were ordered off with their command to East Tenn. some two weeks ago & I have not heard from them since.[17] I suppose that you get letters from them regularly.

I would like very much to be with you for a few days and consult with you as to what you had best do next year. Catharine speaks of teaching. I do not think she ought to be influenced in her selection of a home by the prospect of a school. The pay that she would receive would be so small in comparison with the present enormous rates of living, that one additional item of expense would absorb the whole of it. Can you get any comfortable place near where you now are? If so, I would prefer getting it to moving about. Write to me what your views and wishes are on the subject; let me know how you are getting along in every respect and whether you are in need of money. You must not fail to let me know all your wants and wishes.

I get letters now pretty regularly from Bettie; she was well when she last wrote but Willie & little Litton[18] had both been sick but were better. Let me know where Eliza's[19] post office is; I wish to write to her but do not know how to direct my letters.

Give my love to all. Direct letters to Chickamauga, Tenn. Hoping that I may soon be able to see you, I remain your affectionate son

J. L. Bostick

Columbus [Miss.]
Nov. 19th 1863

My Dear Mother;

I reached here last Sunday evening and found all well. I had to stop all night in Montgomery and all day in Mobile where I found Mary Anne and Major Anderson.[20] They were getting their furniture ready for moving and making arrangements to sell a portion of it. They returned to Columbus on Tuesday evening and Mary Anne has gone to Pickensville [Ala.] to put her house in order.

I think your best route is by way of Selma. Take the train which passes Hogansville [Ga.] about midnight and reaches Montgomery about 11 o'clock A.M. The boat leaves Montgomery at 4 o'clock P M. and you can go directly from the depot to the boat provided it has arrived.[21] It is due in Montgomery in the morning but does not always arrive at the proper time, but you can send down and ascertain before you leave the depot or probably you can learn from the hackman. If you take the day train at Hogansville you will reach Montgomery at 9 o'clock at night & remain there until 4 o'clock the next evening. I will meet you at Meridian [Miss.] if I can know when you will reach that place. I dislike very much for you to start on the trip without some gentleman with you and am almost tempted to return for the purpose of accompanying you. I regret exceedingly that you were not able to come when I did. If I was certain of meeting you at Montgomery I would go that far and return with you. Could you not get Uncle Ike[22] to come with you as far as Selma and see you safely on the cars at that place? You must let me know if possible by telegraph the time that you will start. I would much prefer seeing you located in a comfortable house near where you now are.

I have not been very well since I got to Columbus owing I suppose to the change in my mode of living. Bettie and the children are all well. Give my love to all.

Your affectionate son
J. L. Bostick

CHAPTER TEN

THE ATLANTA CAMPAIGN

hen directed to succeed Braxton Bragg as commander of the Army of Tennessee, Gen. Hardee said he did not want the position if it was to be permanent. Jefferson Davis realized that he had to look further. Robert E. Lee recommended Gen. Beauregard for the position. Secretary of State Seddon and Gen. Leonidas Polk both recommended Joe Johnston, although most of Davis's cabinet members initially disagreed. However, as other names came up, it gradually became clear to most cabinet officials that Johnston was the best man available. Davis reluctantly agreed and ordered him to turn the Department of Mississippi over to Gen. Polk and report to Dalton, Georgia. Johnston arrived on December 27. Soon, thousands of Confederate soldiers, who simply went home after Missionary Ridge, returned. They liked old Joe Johnston and would fight for him. In turn, he did his best to care for them and to remedy the serious shortage of blankets, rifles, shoes, and the feeble condition of his horses. He was operating in a mountainous area, already stripped of forage, during a particularly cold winter. During this time, the cautious Johnston was continually prodded by Davis to take the offensive in conjunction with Longstreet's 16,000 men in upper East Tennessee. Realizing his numerical inferiority, he refused. When Longstreet was recalled to the Army of Northern Virginia in April, everyone realized that any opportunity the Army of Tennessee had to recapture Nashville was gone. Meanwhile, Gen. Ulysses S. Grant had been named supreme commander of all Union armies. Gen. William T. Sherman succeeded him as commander of the Military Division of the Mississippi. Sherman brought together the 25,000-man Army of the Tennessee, the 60,000-man Army of the Cumberland, and the 13,000-man Army of the Ohio. With some cavalry thrown in, he soon had more than 100,000 men to deal with Johnston's 45,000. The only problem was that the wily Johnston had the advantage of operating in his own country, which, with its mountain passes, ravines, and rivers, was ideally suited for defensive warfare.

The Atlanta Campaign began on May 7 when Sherman threw the Armies of the Cumberland and the Ohio against Johnston's defenses north and west of Dalton. The Confederates were forced to withdraw to Resaca a few days later. For the next two weeks, the Confederates fought stubbornly only to fall back from one line of breastworks to another. Sherman was frustrated. He said, "It is useless to look for the flank of the enemy as he makes temporary breastworks as fast as we can travel." A fierce battle at New Hope Church the last week of the month was so intense that men on both sides were constantly under fire, giving little time to cook, much less to sleep. Sherman resumed edging left, forcing Johnston to fall back to a new position. The Army of Tennessee's new line of defense, ten miles long, included strong positions on Brush, Lost, and Pine Mountains. When Gen. Thomas' Army of the Cumberland threatened to extend their line beyond Lost Mountain, Johnston fell back again, this time to Kennesaw Mountain, which he heavily fortified. Changing tactics, Sherman decided on a frontal attack. It failed after two hours of heavy fighting, during which he lost three times as many men as did Johnston. Still, the pressure of the larger Union army was relentless, and the Confederates fell back to Smyrna Station and positions protecting ferry crossings and a railroad bridge over the Chattahoochee River. Sherman was now out of the infernal mountains and within sight of his goal—Atlanta. He also had a secure supply route back to Nashville and could replace his losses. Johnston could not replace the approximately 14,000 men he had lost.

Jefferson Davis, who had long disliked Johnston, became increasingly exasperated at his commander's unwillingness to be more aggressive. By mid-July he had waited long enough. On the eighteenth, Davis replaced the beloved and skilled Johnston with the combative, gambling John Bell Hood. Sherman was delighted. He anticipated that Hood would attack his army. Hood did so two days later at Peachtree Creek with disastrous results. Other fights occurred in quick succession in such places as Ezra Church and Jonesboro. On September 3, Sherman captured Atlanta and became a national hero. The South was despondent.

Litton, Joe, and Tom Bostick participated in almost every fight of the Atlanta Campaign from its beginning on May 7 until July 21 when Litton was fatally wounded. The previous fall, after Chickamauga, Gen. Liddell had asked him, as his aide-de-camp, to accompany him to his new assignment in the Trans-Mississippi Department. Litton turned down the opportunity because it would have put the Union-controlled Mississippi River between him and his wife, Bettie, and their children. They were still living in Columbus, Mississippi, partially dependent on him for support. After Liddell's departure, Litton became aide-de-camp to his successor, Brig. Gen. Daniel C. Govan. For a brief period that appointment seemed temporary. In March 1864, Maj. Gen. William B. Bate asked Gen. Samuel Cooper, adjutant and inspector general, that Lt. Bostick be appointed assistant adjutant general with the rank of captain and assigned him for duty. In his request, Bate said "I know him to be in every way worthy and competent. I desire and need his services." Bate added in a postscript that Gen. Govan had consented to the arrangement. He also lauded Bostick with these words: "Lieut Bostick was a lawyer of fine ability and high reputation in Nashville, Tenn. and at the out-break of the revolution, entered this army, and has honorably borne his part in all its fortunes—I trust General, you will find it consistent with the interest of the service to appoint and assign him to me with the rank of Captain." As so often happened in the Confederate Army, the request was denied and Litton continued to serve unofficially as aide-de-camp to Gen. Govan.

Gen. Govan's request of April 9, 1864, that Lt. J. L. Bostick be retro-actively appointed as his aide-de-camp is transcribed below, along with seven letters from Litton, whose optimism seems remarkable in face of the odds the Army of Tennessee faced after three years of war. His letter of June 14, 1864, gives one of the most comprehensive accounts available of the fierce fight at New Hope Church.

Periodically, during the Atlanta Campaign, Litton saw his brothers, Joe and Tom. He also occasionally crossed paths with his cousins, Jim Cooper and George Litton, both of whom had recovered from their wounds, and with his brother-in-law, John Early.[1]

On May 14, Jim Cooper was wounded again, this time in the throat by a minié ball, which miraculously missed his spinal cord and jugular vein before emerging from the back of his neck. Initially taken to an Atlanta hospital for treatment, he soon went to Marietta, which by then he almost considered home. Jim remained there for a week, cared for by Eliza and

Elizabeth Early. Pressured by the inexorable Union advance, Jim Cooper and his Early kinswomen took a train to Atlanta with some other young women. There, he, Eliza, Elizabeth, and the other girls stayed in the Athenaeum Theater for several weeks. He wrote in his diary that "we had a merry crowd and had nothing to do but to amuse ourselves, and of course we took advantage of the opportunity."[2]

On July 21, soon after Jim Cooper returned to his unit, Litton was shot through the right arm and body. His brother Tom reached his side at Griffin, Georgia, three days later. On the twenty-fifth, Tom wrote Bettie that Litton had been badly wounded. Six days later, Tom telegraphed her that Litton died on the twenty-ninth. The same day, he wrote his mother giving her the devastating news that the second of her sons had died in the service of his country. Transcriptions of those letters are also shown below, as are copies of the telegraph Tom sent his sister-in-law, Bettie Bostick, on August 1, and letters of condolence written Mrs. Bostick,[3] by her brother, Ike Litton, and by Nathan Green Jr., aide to Confederate Gen. A. P. Stewart, and Mat Bostick's brother-in-law.

Tunnel Hill, Ga.
Jany. 20th 1864

My Dear Sister;

I write again, although I mailed a letter to you on yesterday, to let you know that I intend making my application for leave of absence on next Saturday & in case it is granted, I will start for Columbus next Tuesday. I will therefore probably reach Columbus in a few days after this & the other letters that I have written in relation to the socks, reach you. If you have not already started the socks, I will undertake to bring them to the army for you. As I wrote in my last letter, Gen. Govan[4] will ask for a leave of absence to visit his family at Macon, Miss. and will certainly have his application granted. He expects to start Tuesday and if my application should be refused on account of my recently having had a leave of absence, the delay caused by retaining the socks will be but short. I am very anxious to get these socks for this brigade and hope that you will use every exertion to accomplish that object. I intend to state in my application that "I expect to procure for the brigade a large lot of socks" and I have no doubt it will add considerably to my chance of success. You must not let my expectations be disappointed.

I have just written a letter to Aunt Ann Cooper[5] at Nashville which I will send through a flag of truce which will leave here tomorrow morning. The letter has to go unsealed and I could say but little except to tell her how Jimmy[6] and the relatives were.

Give my love to all.

Your affectionate brother
J. L. Bostick

———•◦•———

Hd. Qtrs Govan's Brigade
near Dalton, Ga. Ap. 9, 1864

General,

I have the honor to recommend for appointment as Aide-de-Camp, J. L. Bostick, a citizen of Nashville, Tenn.

This gentleman was appointed in this capacity in Sept. 1862 for Brig. Gen. John R. Liddell, former commander of this Brigade, with whom he served until about the 1st Dec. 1863, when that officer was transferred to the Trans-Mississippi Department. His family being on this side of the Mississippi River, Lieut. Bostick, with Gen. L's consent remained here, and has since been acting as my Aide-de-Camp. I request that his new commission may date from December 29, 64,[7] which is the day of my appointment.

I have the honor to be, General, your obd't servant.

D. C. Govan

Brig. Genl. Gen. S. Cooper At. I. Genl
Richmond

———•◦•———

In the field near New Hope Church
May 31st 1864

My Dear Bettie;

My last letter was written on last Friday (27th last) in which I stated that we had just finished a line of breastworks, after having made a reconnaissance to the front and ascertained that the enemy was in force before us. Soon after starting my letter, we became engaged in one of the sharpest and most successful little fights in the campaign. When we made the reconnaissance the brigade was on the extreme right of the infantry lines of the army with a force of cavalry protecting our right. Information had been received and it was generally believed by our generals that there was no force or at least a very small force of the enemy in front of our position & it was under this belief that our brigade was ordered to go forward and develop the Yankees. Even after our report was made, Gen. Cleburne did not believe that there was any considerable force confronting us. It was only on the urgent request of Gen. Govan that our brigade was allowed to fall back to the lines & put up breastworks at the time we did so. Granbury's brigade was ordered into position on our right in a pretty thick woods and had just formed when the enemy appeared in heavy force on their front and opened fire on them. In our front was an open field & from my position which was near the right of the brigade I could see distinctly the movements of the enemy. The newspapers say that Gen. Cleburne ambushed the enemy. This is not true; Gen. Cleburne did not know of the approach of them, nor did Granbury's brigade, until a moment before they opened fire. We afterwards ascertained that the Yankees advanced in six lines of battle with the intention of turning our right by storm. If any but the very best troops in the army had opposed them, they would have been successful. The woods seemed alive with Yankees and the first line advanced to within fifteen or twenty paces of Granbury's brigade and called on them to surrender. These brave Texans did not understand the meaning of those words but taking them to be an offer of surrender on the part of the enemy, replied "Then lay down your arms" and at the same time the order passed along our line to "cease firing." For a moment or two there was a perfect cessation of the fire and our brigade thought that either the Yankees were giving themselves up or that the Texans were preparing to charge. I saw the lines of the Yankees steadily advancing however and felt that we had ceased firing under some mistake. I took a gun from one of the men and fired at the nearest Yankee about 125 yards distant and had the extreme pleasure of seeing him fall to rise no more. This caused the firing to open again along the right of our brigade and probably, for two hours, a heavy and constant fire was kept up between the opposing lines. Granbury's brigade never wavered for one moment but was in great danger of being turned by the enemy on the right. In order to meet this movement, Gen. Govan sent a regiment of our brigade, the 8th Ark. rapidly around to the right of the Texas brigade and Lowery's brigade was sent still further to the right. The 8th Ark. met the enemy and drove them back with a loss to the Regt. of about 100 men. The fight lasted until after dark, the lines in front of Granbury's brigade not being more than thirty paces apart. There was no attack in front of our brigade but one or two regts. on the right had an enfilading fire on the enemy and killed a great many of them. I fired 30 or 40 shots and think that I must have killed or wounded a good number of the Yankees. My duties would not allow me to spend much time, however, in firing. Soon after dark the firing ceased, and Gens. Govan and Granbury requested Gen. Cleburne to allow them to charge the enemy, our brigade on the flank and the Texans from the front. He would not consent but about 10 o'clock at night agreed that a heavy line of skirmishers might be thrown forward. This was done & the enemy was driven in a panic from the woods leaving their dead & many of their wounded and about 200 unhurt prisoners in our hands. The battle-field was in our possession & the next day it was visited by hundreds of officers, including Gens. Johnston, Polk, Hardee & all agreed that they had never seen dead Yankees piled more thickly on any battlefield. Along Granbury's front the dead lay in almost a perfect line of battle and such terrible wounds I never saw before. Some of the Yankees are pierced with twenty or thirty bullets and great numbers of them were shot in the head, their skulls being broken to pieces as if shot by artillery. I think the enemy left at least 500 dead on the field, which making a moderate allowance for wounded, would make their loss in the field between three and four thousand.[8] Granbury's loss was 150. Our brigade lost about 115 of which the 8th Ark. lost 107, the balance of the brigade being behind breastworks only lost about 14 men killed & wounded, though our right was under pretty heavy fire.

The mail carrier is waiting and I must close. Gen. Govan is very well. I will write more in a day or two.

Give my love to all. I received two letters from you on yesterday; continue to write often. Kiss the little boys for me. May God bless you, my darling wife. With assurances of the warmest and most constant love, I remain your affectionate husband

J. L. Bostick

I have written every three or four days since the commencement of active operations. You must let my sisters at Pickensville hear from me every time I write. I have not seen Joe, Tom, Hugh or Mr. Early for a week. Mr. Ridley of 8th Ark. was not hurt.[9]

⟨≫–◦–≪⟩

Hd. Qrs. Govan's Brigade in the field
near Gilgath Church, Ga. June 13th 1864

My Dear Mother;

I received your letter dated 9th Inst. on yesterday and was glad to hear that you were all well. You express much anxiety to know how I stand the fatigues of the campaign since the commencement of active hostilities. Just now, I have had so long a rest, that I wish I had more to do & feel heartily tired of the inactive life which I am now leading. For a portion of the time after the army left Dalton, our brigade did some very hard marching and endured considerable hardship but never so much as not to be in good condition for meeting the enemy. We would sometimes march and maneuver so as to be almost without sleep for two or three days and nights but then we would get a chance to rest for a day or two and by sleeping about twenty four hours, we would revive & be as fresh as when we began the campaign. More than a week ago, we moved to a position a few hundred yards to the right of where we are now and since that time we have been in a state of perfect inaction except to shift from that position to this which was accomplished in a few moments. We are in line of battle in the trenches but this does not prevent our eating, sleeping and enjoying ourselves with about the same regularity as we could in camp. The enemy are at least a mile off and I have not even heard a bullet whistle, since we have been here, except when I choose to ride forward to the outposts in front where they keep up a pretty steady skirmishing on a small scale by day and night. We hear the report of the small arms and occasionally the heavy boom of artillery but this does not disturb us in the least as the balls do not pass anywhere in our vicinity. The greatest drawback to our enjoyment since we came here, has been the incessant rains which have fallen putting the road in the worst possible condition and compelling us to remain almost constantly in a small leaky tent which we occupy as Head Quarters. As long as we are stationary officers and men generally manage to keep dry, by means of a few tents and flys but principally with little "dog houses" as the soldiers term them and bark shelters which the men build out of bark taken from the chestnut trees in the vicinity. The "dog houses" are constructed by stretching a blanket or bed quilt or piece of cloth of any kind over a ridge pole resting on two forked sticks about two feet & a half high & pinning the end to the ground on each side in the shape of a tent. The men have to crawl into these little establishments and lie pretty close while they are under them. Though very lowly and humble shelters they keep the rain off. I found Joe fast asleep in one of them today, when I rode up the lines to see him, about a mile on our right. He is very well & informed me that Tom had gone to Atlanta & would probably visit you before he returned.

It would be a great pleasure to me to see you and my sisters, before you return to Pickensville, but it will not be possible for me to leave at the present time. Though we are at present so quiet, the proximity of the army to the enemy renders a battle possible any hour of the day and I cannot leave the command for even a short time. I have no idea when an engagement will take place, but think it probable that it will be delayed some days, on account of the late rains which have rendered the roads and ground generally too muddy for moving artillery with any ease. We have had nothing as yet, like a general engagement, though we have had several sharp fights, amounting altogether to the magnitude of a battle. One of the heaviest of these partial engagements, was the one of 27th of May in which our brigade took a prominent part.[10] I feel certain that the enemy lost in that affair 5000 men in killed, wounded and missing, while our loss was not one tenth of that number.

I had the pleasure of killing one or more Yankees myself in that fight and will try and give you a full description of the whole affair as soon as I have an opportunity of doing so. My facilities for writing have been very limited during this campaign and that is my reason for not writing to you before. Joe told me that Tom promised to let you hear every day or two from us, and keep you advised of our movements etc. I have managed to write to Bettie every few days but most of my letters have been extremely short.

I have not written to you since the death of Sue, as we commenced the campaign soon after.[11] Death could bring no terrors to her, but came as a rest from her troubles, bringing peace, health and happiness, in place of the sickness and pain which she endured during life. While I know you cannot but grieve for the loss of a dear child whom you nursed and watched over with so much patient and tender love for so many years, you should certainly find consolation in the thought of how much she has gained by the change from a life of unceasing sickness on earth, to one of never ending happiness in Heaven. I have often thought of Sue's consciousness of her hopeless condition, of her sorrows that she could not learn & improve as the other children and of her wishing to die, and I have thought that death, so terrible to most persons, came to her as a gentle Deliverer and no doubt her pure spirit welcomed him with a happy smile.

I will write to you as often as I can. Give my love to Catharine, Eliza, Mary and the children. What is the little stranger named? I received Eliza's letter several days ago. You must write as often as you can. With much love your affectionate son

J. L. Bostick

————⇒»-◦-«⇐————

In the Field near Gilgath Church, Ga.
June 14th 1864

Mrs. C. W. Halbert Hogansville, Ga.
My Dear Sister;

I wrote to mother on yesterday and promised to give her an account of the fight between a portion of Cleburne's division and the enemy, on the evening of the 27th May, and as I have nothing to do today, I have concluded to spend an hour in giving you a correct description of that brilliant little battle, so far as the facts came under my observation, or came to my knowledge through reliable sources. I have seen no account published in the newspapers which gives an accurate idea of it, or that does full justice to the troops engaged, though some of the letters describing it, have abounded in that overstrained and extravagant language, so popular with army correspondents. A simple narrative of the facts in this case, is the highest praise that can be bestowed on the men engaged.

On the morning of the 27th of May, Brig. Gen. Govan received an order from Gen. Cleburne, originating I think from Gen. Hood, to make a reconnaissance, with his brigade in front of the extreme right of the lines occupied by our infantry. He was directed not to bring on an engagement but to feel the enemy and ascertain what force there was in this front. For some reason, it was believed the enemy had withdrawn from this position leaving probably a body of cavalry or a line of skirmishers. It was to ascertain positively whether this impression was true or not, that the reconnaissance was ordered.

Govan having moved his column to the right of Polk's brigade, which was then at work building breastworks on the extreme right of our infantry lines, and having formed on the prolongation of his line, deployed a heavy line of skirmishers in advance, and moved his command in line of battle, to the front. After marching some three hundred yards, across an open field, we passed into woods, the ground being broken and hilly, and covered with pretty thick undergrowth. The line of skirmishers, which had been ordered to precede the brigade about three hundred yards, had encountered the skirmishers of the enemy, soon after entering the woods, and had driven them back without difficulty. After passing through the woods, a half mile or more, our skirmishers again came to some open fields on the far side of which the enemy was found in force behind breastworks. Some pretty sharp skirmishing took place here and it became evident that a further advance on our part would meet with decided resistance and would probably bring on an engagement. The command was accordingly halted. A force of cavalry under Gen. Kelly[12] had cooperated with our brigade in making the reconnaissance and had protected our right flank. Soon after we halted, a staff officer reported to Gen. Govan that the enemy were passing to the right and rear of our cavalry and that Gen. Kelly had sent to inform him that it had become necessary to

withdraw the cavalry from our right, and form in a new direction to
meet this movement of the enemy. It subsequently appeared that the
staff officer had not understood the message of Gen. Kelly who only
wished to inform Gen. Govan of the movement of the enemy & that
the right of the cavalry would be retired leaving the left in connection
with us, but not that the cavalry would be withdrawn. The staff officer
(Lieut. Mason of Gen. Kelly's staff) was very positive however in his
communication and Gen. Govan, acting promptly upon the information, determined at once to withdraw his brigade from its isolated
position to the edge of the field in front of our intrenched [sic] lines.
The skirmishers were withdrawn at the same time, but kept deployed
some three hundred yards in front of the new position of the brigade. It
was very fortunate, as subsequent events proved, that the command was
moved to the rear as soon as it was.

Gen. Govan, having retired his brigade without orders, went at
once to report the facts to Gen. Cleburne, myself accompanying him.
On reaching Gen. Govan's Hd. Qrs., which were at a house about a
third of a mile in rear of Polk's line, Gen. Govan explained everything that had taken place. Gen. Cleburne objected to nothing that
had been done, except the withdrawal of the skirmishers whom he
directed to be advanced to the position which they had occupied previous to their withdrawal. Gen. Govan had already ordered this
advance of the line of skirmishers in accordance with instructions
given him by Major Benham of Gen. Cleburne's staff, whom we had
met on our way to Division Hd. Qrs. Gen. Govan then urged Gen.
Cleburne to allow him to form his brigade in the position it was
expected to occupy in case of an engagement and throw up breastworks as the brigade could be of no further possible service in the
woods where it had halted. Gen. Cleburne consented to this, and the
brigade was at once moved to the right of Gen. Polk and commenced
building rifle pits. Notwithstanding the report of Gen. Govan that
the enemy was in force in our front, Gen. Cleburne still held to his
original impression that they had retired, leaving but a line of skirmishers, or at least but an insignificant force and he wrote a note to
Gen. Hood some time after this stating that he believed that there
were but few Yankees in our front or that they were not massing on
our right. When Col. Brasier of the 2nd Ark. Regt., some hour or two
afterwards, reported to him in person that the skirmishers reported
the enemy massing in force on our right, he turned away and

observed that he "believed nothing that he heard now."

In the meantime Govan's brigade, having received a good supply of shovels, picks and axes from the engineer department, were rapidly completing a formidable line of breastworks. Our line of skirmishers, which had been left some three quarters of a mile in front, was attacked by a heavy force of the enemy and escaped capture by moving quickly to the rear by the left flank. They came into our line some distance to the left of Polk's brigade. The sharpshooters of the enemy swarmed along the edge of the woods across the field in our front and made it dangerous for anyone to show his head over the breastworks. Key's battery of howitzers[13] had been placed in position on the right centre of our brigade. Swett's Battery of Parrott guns, under command of the gallant Lieut. Shannon, occupied a high point on the right of Polk's brigade. Brig. Gen. Granbury, with his brigade of Texans, had been ordered to form on our right and on the prolongation of our line. Our brigade occupied the crest of a ridge with an open field, before spoken of, in front, our right resting on the termination of the open ground at the strip of woods across which Granbury's brigade had been ordered to take position. Granbury had hardly formed his line and had not had time to throw forward skirmishers when the cavalry which had been on our right were rapidly driven in and the enemy appeared swarming over the hill in his front, line after line passing in quick succession into a ravine, the rocky slope of which protected them from the fire of the Texans. The ravine was at the foot of the hill on which the Texans were formed and not quite a hundred yards distant. The Yankees, evidently ignorant of the reception which awaited them, and thinking there was nothing before them but the retreating cavalry, halted but a moment in the ravine and pushed forward their lines of battle up the hill. As we afterwards learned, they had six lines of battle, following in close succession, and expected to carry the position with ease, by the mere weight of overwhelming numbers. On they came, giving and receiving a pretty heavy fire, until their picket line suddenly stood within twenty five paces of Granbury's brigade and called on them to surrender. These brave Texans could not understand the meaning of that word when applied to them, but at once mistook the enemy as offering to surrender themselves, and immediately passed the word on down the line to "cease firing." The firing on both sides ceased for a few moments by common consent and there was a perfect lull in the storm which had raged but an instant before. The 6th and 7th Ark.

Regts., under command of Col. Sam Smith, formerly of Nashville, was on the right of our brigade and had been firing upon the flank of the enemy but, as the cry to "cease firing," came down the line, had at once silenced their fire under the impression either that the enemy was about to surrender or that the Texans were about to charge. I was in the trenches on the left of the 6th and 7th Ark. Regts. and, during these few seconds of silence, saw the rear lines of the enemy pushing steadily forward with arms trailed and with no appearance of surrendering. I felt that there was some mistake in the order to cease firing and called upon one of the men to give me a gun. I fired at a Yankee on the right of the enemy's line not more than one hundred and twenty five yards distant and had the pleasure of seeing him reel & fall. This was a signal for a renewal of the firing by the 6th and 7th Ark. Regts. and Granbury's brigade, having learned, that the enemy did not mean to surrender, about the same time, the firing was renewed along the whole line. The first line of the enemy fell where they stood, almost in perfect line of battle. The brave Texans never yielded an inch before the overwhelming force opposed to them, but fired with all the steadiness and coolness that they could have exhibited if firing at game. The answer they gave to the demand to surrender, when it was understood, was a shower of bullets, each of which went crashing through the brain or heart of the insolent foe. The rear lines of the enemy were appalled by the sudden and unexpected check which had been given to their advance and sought shelter behind trees, rocks or anything that could save them from the terrible storm in front. But the shelter, which shielded them from Granbury's fire, afforded them no protection from the deadly aim of the Arkansas brigade which poured a galling fire into their right flank. They gave up all idea of advancing and, being afraid to retreat on account of the heavy fire of this brigade and the batteries of Shannon and Key, which swept with canister and shell, the ravine and exposed hillside in their rear, they sought safety in lying flat upon the ground behind trees, logs, rocks, or any shelter that was nearest.[14] In this position, they managed to maintain the contest for several hours.

In the meantime, the front of the enemy, being much greater than that of Granbury, overlapped him on the right and finding nothing to oppose them but a weak line of cavalry, had passed his right flank and had actually pushed a line of skirmishers to the rear of his right. He at once notified Gen. Govan of this fact and the latter general ordered the

8th and 19th Ark. Regts. under Col. Baucum[15] to move as quickly as possible to his support. Some of Granbury's regiment, seeing the enemy to their rear, sent word to him that they would be compelled to fall back, but the general told them that the Arkansans were coming to their support, & they replied that they would hold their ground while there was a man remaining. Baucum came into position just in time, met and gallantly charged the enemy and drove him back across a field and, continuing the pursuit too far, became exposed to a fire from the front and left flank that caused him the loss of one hundred men in the short space of about thirty minutes. His charge however effectively checked the enemy on the right and Lowrey's brigade,[16] coming up soon after on his right, with Quarles' brigade[17] supporting, made matters very secure in that quarter. A portion of Gen. Kelly's cavalry and the 33rd Alabama Regt. of Lowrey's brigade made the charge at the same time that Col. Baucum did.

During all this time, heavy firing was kept up between the enemy and Granbury's & Govan's brigades & Key's and Shannon's batteries kept up an incessant shower of canister & shells until dark, when the contest ceased. I think the fight began about 4 o'clock in the evening and lasted between three & four hours. Soon after the engagement commenced, Gen. Cleburne came up to the lines & took position a few feet in rear of the 6th & 7th Ark. Regts., where he remained until after dark.

About sundown or a little after, Gens. Govan and Granbury suggested to Gen. Cleburne to make a charge on the enemy in front & flank, and asked his consent to the movement, thinking that they could capture a large number of prisoners. He objected however on the ground that he had no troops in reserve to hold the works and he did not consider the taking of prisoners worth the risk of losing the position occupied by his troops. The firing having ceased on both sides soon after dark, everything remained pretty quiet until about 10 o'clock. The enemy occupied this time in removing their wounded, [and] keeping their lines in the same position they held at the close of the fight.

Gen. Cleburne at length agreed that Granbury might charge upon the enemy in front while Govan should send out a force on the flank. The dispositions were all made and between 10 and 11 o'clock at night, at the sound of the bugle, the Texans rushed upon the enemy with loud & ringing yells, while the Arkansans fired from the flank. The Yankees were seized with a panic and, after firing one volley, without doing the slightest damage, fled in the utmost confusion, leaving their dead, such of their wounded as had not been removed, and near two hundred prisoners besides in our hands. This panic was not confined to the enemy who were in front of Granbury, but extended to the right & left. For a front of nearly a mile, they ran off in perfect terror, leaving the battlefield & its spoils in our possession.

The prisoners captured, among whom was a Lieut. Col., informed us that we had fought the 4th Army corps, commanded by Gen. Howard,[18] and that they had advanced against Granbury's brigade with six lines of battle. On the next day, the battlefield in front of the Texas brigade presented a scene such as I have never before witnessed. I have never seen such a number of dead on any ground of the same extent and I have never before seen such terrible wounds. The heads of many of them were struck with from ten to twenty bullets and one body was said to have forty wounds. The heads of many of them were torn to pieces, the balls tearing holes through the skulls as large as a man's fist. Behind every tree from which the Yankees had sought shelter, groups of three, four and five dead lay, shot from every direction. While they protected themselves from Granbury's brigade, Govan's regiments peppered them from their right. During all the day succeeding the battle, numbers of officers, including Gens. Johnston, Hardee & Polk visited the field and all agreed that seldom, if ever, had they seen the dead so thickly strewn on the ground.

The loss of the enemy must have been near 5000 men in killed, wounded and missing. I do not know that any accurate count was made of the dead, as they were buried by details from different commands. In the immediate front of Granbury's brigade and ours, and near the lines, we buried 280. Still further out, and across the ravine, 30 more dead were found, making over 300 dead, left in Granbury's front which were counted. On his right, where Baucum's Regt. and Lowrey's brigade fought, assisted by the cavalry still further to their right, there was heavy firing and hard fighting and, I am told, many Yankees were killed. I have heard that over seven hundred dead were counted by the different burying parties, and have no doubt that many were carried off by the enemy before the night charge as very few officers were found among the dead, and none, I think, over the rank of lieutenant.

Our loss was small. Granbury's brigade lost in killed and wounded about 150. Our brigade lost about 140 which includes the losses by the skirmishers in the reconnaissance of the morning. Of this, the 8th and 19th Ark. Regts. lost 101 in their charge against the enemy across an open field. I do not know the loss in Lowrey's brigade, but understood that it was about the same as ours. Our total casualties did not reach 500 men.

I never saw a more beautiful fight. I occupied a position during the greater portion of the time on the left of the 6th and 7th Ark. Regts. from which I had a fair view of the enemy's movements and, at the same time, an opportunity of participating in the engagement. After my first shot, I left two or three men loading for me while I fired at the Yankees, who presented a fair mark at the short range of 125 yards. I fired thirty or more rounds when Gen. Govan called me to attend to some order, after which time I was at various points along our line watching the effects of the artillery and conveying orders to different portions of the command. In the early part of the engagement, when the firing had ceased, under the impression that the enemy was about to surrender, & when I saw the blue lines pushing forward one after another upon Granbury's single line, I trembled least [sic] the Texans should be overpowered by numbers & either captured or driven from their position. But they stood firm as a rock and, after ten minutes, I felt that all was safe.

Our brigade performed an important part in the engagement. The 8th and 19th Ark Regts., by their gallant charge, prevented the enemy getting in the rear of the Texas brigade, while our other regiments, by their well directed fire on the enemy's right flank, killed & wounded great numbers and drew off, from the main attack, a heavy & continued fire. But the greatest praise is due to the brave men of Granbury's brigade, who stood with an undaunted and unflinching front, against the heavy masses of the foe, which were hurled suddenly and unexpectedly against them. They had no works of consequence, but were somewhat protected by a few logs and chunks which the cavalry had hastily thrown together. If they had been anything but the very best of troops, the sudden & vigorous attack of the enemy would have driven them in disorder from the field.

I have given you as complete an account of the fight of the 27th Ulto. as I can, under present circumstances, and, as heavy firing has been going on upon our right for some time, and [as] the artillery is now opening in our immediate front, I will close my letter. A message from our line of skirmishers has just been received to the effect that Lowrey's brigade, which is on outpost in our front, is falling back, and the enemy may be advancing to attack us. The artillery is booming on the right and in front with a continuous roar. If the Yankees will attack us in our present position, we will end this campaign in a few hours. Give my love to mother, Eliza, Mary and the children. I will send this letter by the same mail that takes the one I wrote to mother. Write often. With much love I remain

Your affectionate brother
J. L Bostick

I just received a letter from Bettie dated the 8th Inst., all were well. I have concluded this letter, from the ninth page to the fifteenth last, having been obliged to stop at that point on yesterday. I suppose that you have heard that Gen. Polk[19] was killed yesterday. He was shot, while I was writing this letter, about a mile to our right. The enemy fired a battery of four guns at him while he was reconnoitering the lines, and the shell passed through his body, tearing off both arms. There was not a more gallant man in the army and his death is universally regretted.

J. L. Bostick

━━━━━━━━━━━━

Hd. Qrs. Govan's Brigade in the field
near Marietta, Ga. June 26th 1864

Mrs. C. W. Halbert Hogansville, Ga.
My Dear Sister,
I have nothing of interest to communicate but as everything is quiet this evening and I have nothing to interrupt me, I have concluded that I could not spend any time better than in writing a few lines to you. Uncle Ike and Tom were here on a short visit about two hours ago. It is the first time I have seen Tom for several weeks or Uncle Ike[20] since last Feb. Both are very well. Tom told me that Henry Ramage[21] was killed in a charge on last Thursday. It had been but a short time since he returned to his Regt. from East Tenn. and I had no opportunity of giving him the bundle of socks which you sent to him but I had sent word to him that I had such a bundle. We have been separated from our baggage wagons during the campaign except for a few days, about a month ago, when we had ours with us. I am sorry that I was not able to give the socks to him before he was killed. I will dispose of them in any way you wish.

Tom told me that Joe was very well although I have not seen him for several weeks. The enemy are now so close to us that they may attack us at any moment and I consequently very seldom leave our position. I do not think, however, that there will be an engagement for some time and in fact see no end to the present style of campaigning during the entire summer. Our lines are within a few hundred yards of those of the enemy and each side has a line of skirmishers thrown out in front, and they are continually popping away at each other, usually with very little loss, as they are protected by little breastworks. Our brigade has one hundred and twenty five men all the time on duty as skirmishers, and they are relieved every twelve hours, so that it is not very hard on the men. I was out at the skirmish line this morning and saw quite a number of Yankees sitting in front of their works and moving about in perfect unconcern though not over one hundred yards distant. The cause of this was that the two lines just at that point had agreed to cease firing on each other for the time, and both sides were showing themselves without any fear. Usually, however, the skirmishers are fighting day and night and the trees in our front are as much marked by bullets as if a great battle had been fought there.

I send you a Yankee account of the fight of the 27th May of which I wrote you a description a short time since. I cut it from the Memphis Appeal of the 18th last. You notice that it states that we were "nearly two Rebel Divisions in strong entrenchments fighting against seven thousand men (Yankees)." The only forces that we had engaged were the whole of Granbury's brigade, about half of Govan's, a small part of Lowrey's and probably a small part of Quarles', a part of Key's and Shannon or Swett's batteries and a little cavalry, making altogether not more than two brigades and amounting not to 2500 men. More than half the fighting on our side was done without breastworks of any kind. The account further states that they succeeded in bringing in their dead and that they, with the wounded, were collected in a little valley. The valley referred to was a considerable distance in rear of the enemy's position during the fight and, as the enemy held possession of it, we never had a chance of witnessing this portion of the dead and wounded. The dead, referred to in my letter, and buried by us, were too near our lines to be removed and are entirely ignored in this Yankee account, and very likely the writer was ignorant of the great slaughter on this part of the battlefield.

I also send you an acknowledgment, which you probably have seen, of the donation of socks to the 4th Confederate Tennessee Regt. by Lt. Col. Bradshaw commanding, which I clip from the Mem. Appeal of the 8th Inst.

You must write to me as often as possible. I regret very much that I did not learn that mother was in Marietta until a week or two after she was gone. I am only two and one half miles from that place and it would have been a great pleasure to me to have seen her and Eliza. Your letter, which was received two days ago, was the first that I had heard of their visit to Marietta.

My health is excellent. We now have very warm and dry weather, having had no rain for three or four days.

Give my love to all. I hear from Bettie pretty regularly though I have not received a letter for the past week. With much love I remain

Your affectionate brother

J. L. Bostick

—————◦—————

Hd. Qtr. Govans Brigade in the field,
near Marietta, Ga. June 28th 1864

My Dear Mother;

I received today, your letter of the 26th Inst. and hasten to reply as our mail carrier will start back this evening or tomorrow morning. I wrote to Catharine on Sunday and stated that I saw no prospect of a general engagement for some time to come. Some accidental occurrence may bring on a battle at any time or the enemy may change their tactics and risk all, on a desperate assault on our works, and hence no one can predict with any great degree of certainty that a decisive battle will not be fought even today or tomorrow. The two armies are now so close together, that by either marching a few paces to the front, they would be brought in conflict. I think it probable however that we will not have an engagement of that character. I feel certain that Gen. Johnston will not make any serious attack upon the enemy, unless they should make some move or commit some blunder, which would give us, immensely, the advantage over them. On the other hand, the enemy will not be so rash as to make an attack on our works which will involve the safety of their army, but will continue to make assaults at particular points with a division or two, hoping finally to break our lines, at some weak place. They made a pretty heavy attack on yesterday against Gen. Cheatham and two brigades of Cleburne's division and were repulsed with heavy loss.[22] Gen.

Cleburne estimates the loss of the Yankees in front of his brigades, at 1000, while his own loss was only 8 men killed and wounded. Cheatham's Division, I am told, inflicted a proportionately heavy loss on the Yankees and lost hardly any men. In their front, the ground was strewn with the Yankee dead and wounded, some of whom were burned up by the brush which formed the abattis [sic] taking fire from the explosion of the guns. Our men proposed to cease firing, after the Yankees had been driven back, until their wounded could be moved, but it was not agreed to, and consequently some of the enemy who were too badly hurt to move out of the way of the fire, were burned to death.[23] Our brigade was not in the fight at all, the attack having been made some distance to our left. The enemy, however, shelled us a little, at the same time, wounding two of our men slightly in the foot.

It is expected that Gen. Johnston will finally fall back across the Chattahoochie River, where, I understand, he has a fine system of fortifications, and where he will make a stand from which there is to be no retreat. Atlanta will be held, and, until the enemy get possession of it, there is no danger of raids in the direction of Joe's place. I consider Hogansville [Ga.] as safe from the Yankees as any place in the Confederacy, a little more so than Pickensville [Ala.]. Sherman needs all his cavalry to protect his flanks and rear, and is not likely to send off any force to attempt to cut our communications. If he can keep his own intact, and can supply his army in our immediate front, he will be doing remarkably well.

I enclose $100. I suppose it will go safely by mail but I will send it by private hands, if I can find anybody going to Hogansville. It does not put me to the slightest inconvenience & affords me much pleasure to send it. I have rec'd the shoes which fit very well & am much obliged to you for having them made & Mary Anne for the nice socks which accompanied them. Give my love to all. Tell Mary[24] not to let Joe frighten her about the Yankees taking Hogansville.

With much love your affectionate son
J. L. Bostick

Let me know whether this comes safely to hand. J. L. B.

Griffin, Georgia
July 25th 1864

Mrs. J. L. Bostick
Dear Betty[25]

Litton is at this place badly wounded. He is shot through the right arm, the ball passing into his body. It was cut out at his left shoulder blade. He was wounded July 21st. I have telegraphed to you. I got him here yesterday. He is comfortably situated. You and mother come up.

Yours & etc.
T. H. Bostick

Hogansville, Ga.
July 31st 1864

Mrs. J. L. Bostick
Dear Betty

I would have telegraphed you of Litton's death but the wires were cut. He died last Friday 29th at five minutes of eleven in the day. I was with him all the time and buried him in the grave yard at Griffin where none but officers from Tenn. are buried. He suffered but little considering the way he was wounded. He was conscious all the time and told me early in the morning he had to die. About ten minutes before he died, he called me to him and told me what disposition he wanted made of his property. His only regret at dying seemed to be the leaving of his "wife and little orphan boys." He said "I feel I have done my duty. Oh God have mercy on my wife and little boys." I asked him if he felt prepared to die. He could not speak but his countenance showed very plainly that he was. He lived about two or three minutes after this but never spoke. I was with him when he died. He had every attention both medical and nursing. He had a very comfortable room and was waited on by Mrs. M. V. Callaway[26] of Griffin. He was at Mrs. Mitchell's house. She is Mrs. Callaway's mother and was very kind and attentive to him. Mrs. Callaway was as kind and attentive to him as you or mother could have been. He had a great many friends in Griffin all of whom were very kind. Mrs. Ellis & Mrs. Dr. Buchanan[27] of Nashville were kind to him. Capt. Rice,[28] John Thompson and Uncle

Ike assisted me in nursing him. He was buried Friday evening about dark. The enemy were reported within six miles of the place so I had to leave that night and made my way to this rail road. I will go to the front today. I regretted exceedingly that I could not wait at Griffin and see you and mother but I was there without leave and could not run any risk of being captured. I will write to you more freely when I get to my quarters. His watch and pocket book I left with Mary Hunt for you. His clothes and bedding are at Mrs. Callaway's, but when the road is rebuilt to Griffin, I will have them sent to Mary A.

My dear Betty you have my sympathy, but few things could have pained me more than seeing that noble brother breathing his last, but I believe he is better off today than any of us for I am satisfied he is with his God. God bless and shield you and the children.

Affectionately and etc.

T. H. Bostick

Hogansville, Ga.

July 31st 1864

My Dear Mother

Another one of the family is gone. Litton died Friday last at 5 minutes of 11 o'clock. My dear Mother I was so sorry you could not get to Griffin before he died. He lived just one week from the time he was shot. I regretted too that I could not stay in Griffin to see you, but while I was burying him the enemy were reported within six miles of the place advancing on the town. I was there without leave and could not be captured, so as soon as he was buried, Joe and I started for this place on foot fifty-five miles. It was dark before we finished burying him. Joe got to Griffin the night before he died. I was with him all the time. He suffered but little considering the nature of his wound. Just before he died he told me what he wanted done with his property. He said, "I feel that I have done my duty." He was conscious all the time. He was staying at Mrs. Mitchell's house and was waited on by Mrs. Callaway. I give you her address that you may write to her for a kinder, better and more attentive woman doesn't live. Mrs. M. V. Callaway, Griffin, Ga. I love her better than any woman I ever saw that is no kin. Night and day all the time she was trying to do something for

Litton. Mrs. Mitchell the mother of Mrs. Callaway was also very kind and attentive. Mrs. Ellis and Mrs. Dr. Buchanan[29] of Nashville were very kind. All of my women friends as well as his in Griffin were kind to him and me. [Capt.] Rice, John Thompson, and Uncle Ike helped me to nurse him. I have not been able to telegraph on account of the wires being cut. I got to Griffin Sunday evening and telegraphed you Monday morning. This was the first dispatch sent over the wires after they were fixed. The wires are cut again. Will write more fully when I get to my quarters. Joe and I will leave at daylight in the morning for Atlanta. Joe and I are all the boys you have left but we will love you the more, and God grant we may be spared to comfort and protect you in your old age. Mother I hope you will hear of his death before you get to Griffin. Oh how I hated to leave before you got there but it could not be avoided. I was there without leave and could not run any risk of being captured. I will write again soon. I leave with Mary Hurt, letters, watch and pocket book. In the pocket book you will find two bundles marked for you and one for Betty. They contain Litton's hair. He gave Catharine[30] his Haley tract of land and a horse he captured. He gave me his spyglass. Everything else he gave to his wife. Good bye my dear mother. God bless and protect and comfort you.

Your affectionate son,
T. H. Bostick

I wrote Betty today.

———▸•◂———

Griffin, Ga.
[early] August, 1864

Dear Margaret,

I received Eliza's dispatch in Eatonton and started on the first train for this place where I arrived today. I regret that I could not see Litton, but suppose it is all for the best. I was with your boy most of the time after he was wounded, had no idea the wound would prove fatal; he never complained and it was terrible to think that such a man should fall victim to Yankee villainy, but his mother and relatives have the consolation of knowing that he died as he would have wished in defense of all that was dear and precious. It is I know a terrible loss to his family but God who rules does not willingly afflict us, and although it seems hard for us to lose such a son and nephew yet he will sometime satisfy us that it is right, and we can only trust him for grace to bear and understand such a loss. May he in his mercy sustain us under this crushing blow and at least save us all in Heaven is the prayer of Yours affectionately,

Isaac Litton

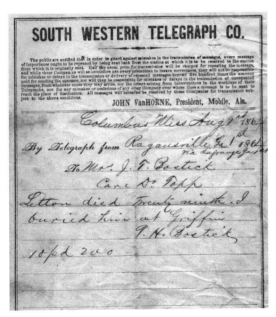

Columbus Miss August 1st
1864
By Telegraph from Ragansville,
Ga 1st 1864
via Lagrange Ga 1st

To Mrs. J. T. [sic] Bostick
Care Dr. Topp[31]
Litton died twenty-ninth. I
buried him at Griffin
T. H. Bostick

Macon, Ga.
August 30th 1864

Mrs. H. P. Bostick
My Dear Madam

I just rec'd a letter from your son, Capt. Tom Bostick, the day before yesterday giving me your address, which I had forgotten, and for which I had written to him. I did not hear for a long time after I saw you here of the fate of Capt. Litton Bostick. No one wrote to me, and I happened to miss the Daily which announced his death.

I cannot think any words of mine could assuage a mother's grief or cause her for a moment to forget so great a loss. I only ask the privilege of dropping a tear for the brave, the noble man who has offered up his life so freely for his country.

To you, and especially to those other dear ones of his, the loss is irreparable. We cannot bring him back, and we will not see his like again. We can only indulge the mournful pleasure of suffering over his grave, while our hearts account all the sweet moments his life gave to our lives. As a parent, I know something of the indescribably strong affection that exists in the human heart towards a child; and experience has taught me that nothing short of the grace of God can ever dry up our grief when one has been torn from us and laid in the grave. We feel like we could lie down with them in the grave, and be willing to be shut out of this world of sorrow, just so we could be very near them.

I got a letter from Col. John L. House[32] a few days since referring to the loss of your son, and speaking of the high points in his character he very affectionately remarked that it seemed we were likely to lose all our promising young men from Tennessee. I have thought much of that myself. When we get peace and independence, Oh, how dear a price we will have paid for it! How ought we to prize the liberties which have cost the richest, noblest blood of the land! I sometimes think the most worthy and the bravest men have been sacrificed, and those of us who remain to enjoy the rich harvest of their labors and lives are utterly undeserving. We can never do enough honor to the memories of our noble dead.

Allow me to say that among the officers of the army, I met none who combined more fully the high qualities of the soldier, scholar and gentleman than Capt. Litton Bostick. I admired him while living, and being dead I honor him. I expect to speak of his virtue and his courage and his fate to my children. Sweet be his rest among the sons of glory who have fallen in this struggle!

My dear Madam, you have made great sacrifices for our country. You have suffered much, and you are, doubtless, ready to suffer more. If all the mothers and all the sons were like you and yours, tyrants might try to subdue us in vain. May God help you! May God comfort your heart amid all your afflictions! And may we all at last meet our lost and our loved ones in that happy land where parting and sorrows are no more!

Ever your Friend,
N. Green, Jr.[33]

CHAPTER ELEVEN

HOME TO TENNESSEE

fter the fall of Atlanta, there was a scramble for safety. With the help of a detail of enlisted men, Lt. John F. Early of Fenner's Louisiana Battery, worked hard to move forty-seven horses and thirty-five mules from Griffin, Georgia, to Bear Creek Station. When his animals became entangled with the wagon train and troops from a Georgia militia unit, two of the animals became separated and were lost. While looking for the stray mule and horse, three other mules were stolen from a pen hastily built that evening.[1]

On a higher level, one of Gen. Hood's priorities was to remove the Federal prisoners from Andersonville Prison so that he would have freedom to maneuver without having to keep his army between Sherman and the prison. By September 21, the prisoners had been taken to Florida. This freed Hood to move twenty-five miles west of Atlanta to Palmetto on the Atlanta & West Point Railroad. There, he did what he could to restore the morale in his army, which had been badly shaken by the loss of Atlanta. President Jefferson Davis got a good whiff of the dissatisfaction when Gen. S. G. French wrote him about "a feeling of depression more or less apparent in parts of this army." Davis, who was despondent himself over Atlanta's loss, decided to visit the Army of Tennessee. Accompanied by two of his aides, he arrived at Palmetto on September 25. Gov. Isham Harris of Tennessee and Gen. Howell Cobb of Georgia visited at the same time.[2] Despite fervent speeches by the three men, rank and file soldiers remained dissatisfied. At one review of the troops, a few soldiers were brazen enough to cry out, "Give us back General Johnston," or words to that effect.[3] Davis' conversations with Hood's Corps commanders, Steven D. Lee, Alexander P. Stewart, and William J. Hardee revealed that Johnston and Beauregard were their choices to succeed Hood. Had the people of the South been given a vote, they would have chosen similarly. A few weeks before Atlanta fell, Dr. Alexander Jackson, of Jackson, Tennessee, wrote his son, Brig. Gen. William H. "Billy" Jackson, one of Hood's Division commanders, that there was "much regret" in West Tennessee at the removal of Johnston.[4] Davis was not receptive to the suggestions of Hood's corp commanders as he hated both Johnston and Beauregard. Just as had been the situation with Bragg after Missionary Ridge, he knew public opinion demanded that he do something. Swallowing his pride, he asked Gen. Beauregard to assume command of a new "Military Division of the West" with Gens. Richard Taylor and Hood reporting to him. Beauregard accepted. The president then instructed Gen. Hood to relieve Gen. Hardee of his command[5] and replace him with Gen. B. F. Cheatham, a hard-drinking and hard-fighting Tennessean. Davis knew that Hardee had long been a thorn in Hood's side.

With the high-level reorganization of the army in place, Davis, Beauregard and Hood agreed on a strategy of placing the Army of Tennessee on the Western & Atlantic Railroad to disrupt Sherman's "Cracker line" to Chattanooga and Nashville. Gen. French put it this way, "General Hood conceived that in the enemy's rear we would feed upon their rations, destroy their communication, and at the same time draw back much more force than that sent on this duty."[6] During October, Hood diligently set about the task of tearing up the railroad. Sherman, who seemed as uncertain as Hood concerning his own moves, followed desultorily. At Allatoona, he telegraphed Grant that "Hood, Forrest, Wheeler and the whole batch of devils were loose" and that with them on the prowl, he could not protect his supply line to Tennessee. By the end of the month, Sherman concluded that his best option might be to leave Gen. Thomas to contend with Hood while he backtracked to Atlanta and cut across Georgia to Savannah. Sherman was tired of chasing the erratic Hood and guessing what his intentions were. Unlike his earlier foe, Joe Johnston, whose moves were logical and predictable, Hood might do anything. Confederate cavalry Gen. Joseph Wheeler got wind of Sherman's plans through various means and advised Hood daily by telegraph of Sherman's movements. Meanwhile, Hood actually had come up with a daring but plausible plan of his own. It was to cross the Tennessee River near Guntersville, overwhelm Federal positions at Bridgeport and Stevenson, and destroy Schofield and Thomas' armies before they could scurry north to heavily fortified but undermanned Nashville. Once he captured Nashville, Hood could resupply his army from the great military warehouses there, gather recruits, move on Kentucky and Cincinnati, and even cross the mountains to help Lee whip Grant. Beauregard approved the plan but was sufficiently leery of its success that he decided not to accompany Hood. The soldiers overwhelmingly approved the idea, particularly the Middle Tennesseans who had not seen their girlfriends and loved ones for what seemed like an age. When the Tennessee regiments heard about the plan, they let go with their famous Rebel yell.[7]

Hood did not cross the Tennessee at Guntersville. The river was dangerously high and, being temporarily without a cavalry arm, he was reluctant to do so. Earlier, he had dispatched Joe Wheeler's cavalry to keep Sherman's communications cut and to prevent him from stockpiling supplies in Atlanta. Hood did not realize that, because of the bumper crops in the rich counties of Georgia through which Sherman would soon pass, the Federals could supply their army even with no supply line to Tennessee.

Rather than cross at Guntersville, Hood moved west along the Memphis & Charleston Railroad. His purpose was to join with Nathan Bedford Forrest's cavalry force, which had been ordered from West Tennessee to take Wheeler's place as the eyes and ears of his army. At Decatur, Alabama, on the twenty-sixth, the Federals were too strong to be taken by a quick frontal assault, so Hood simply bypassed them and moved on to Tuscumbia. By then, Sherman had turned back to Atlanta, where he would burn the city on November 16 and set out on his celebrated "March to the Sea."[8]

As soon as Hood decided on Tuscumbia as a destination, he ordered that the Memphis & Charleston Railroad be repaired between there and Corinth so that he could bring shoes and other supplies over the road from north Mississippi. When he arrived, however, he found that a ten-mile gap still existed between Cherokee, Alabama, and Tuscumbia. This forced him to waste three valuable weeks waiting for its completion. The rain-swollen Tennessee's continued rise was another obstacle and frustration. After part of Lee's corps crossed the river on a pontoon bridge to Florence, the operation had to be scratched because the river partially submerged the bridge and the roads leading to it were quagmires. On November 13, Hood and his command crossed the river and set up headquarters at Florence. Forrest and his

James Litton Cooper.   *James W. Thomas.*

cavalry reported the next day. The balance of Lee's corps crossed on the fifteenth while a resumption of heavy rains delayed the crossing of Stewart's and Cheatham's corps for another week.[9] Beauregard decided not to cross at all. On the twentieth, he was at West Point, Mississippi, in communication by telegraph with Bragg and Davis in Richmond, Hood at Florence, and Wheeler in Georgia, where he was dogging Sherman.

Among the members of the Army of Tennessee who crossed the rainswollen river at Florence that November were Tom and Joe Bostick; three first cousins, James Litton "Jim" Cooper, Jacob "Jake" Thomas, and George Litton; and the Bosticks' brother-in-law, John F. Early. Below is a transcription of a letter which one of the first cousins, Jim Cooper, wrote his first cousin, Kitty Litton Robinson. Jim was acting brigade inspector for Gen. Thomas B. Smith's Brigade while Kitty was helping manage her family's Blue Springs Farm in Williamson County, Tennessee.

Florence, Ala.
November 18th 1864

Dear Kitty[10]

I have at last an opportunity to send you a letter. A friend has promised to carry it to you, and you will perhaps have an opportunity to answer it through the same source. If so, do not fail to write.

We have been in Florence some time. George Litton[11] is here in this, Tyler's Brigade. Jacob Thomas[12] is with Major Bransford[13] at Cherokee Station, sixteen miles from this place. Tom Bostick is brigade commissary for George Gordon's brigade. Joe Bostick is acting inspector for our Corps. All are in excellent health.

I suppose that you have heard that Jimmy Thomas had been paroled. He is now at Eatonton.[14] I received a letter from him yesterday. He did not say how he was. Nearly all the Thomas' and Littons' have been sick. Eatonton does not appear to be a healthy place. Cousin Catharine Halbert had been sick the last time I heard from Pickensville, but was convalescent.

You have heard before this that I had been promoted. Gen. Tyler has not returned to the army yet,[15] and Gen. Tom Smith commands his brigade.[16] I was ordered up on duty with him, by Gen. Tyler and am now acting brigade inspector. It is not such an easy place as an Aid's [sic], but I succeed very well in my new capacity.

I find that I have been very much mistaken in one particular. I once thought that "staff officers" dressed finer, looked better every way than other men, but I find myself about as rough looking as before. Tell Ma that I will be in Nashville before long and I want her to "lay up a stock" of good clothes for me. If I am not in Nashville I think I will be very close to the city in a short time.

Kitty, your old admirer Wm. Shy is commanding six consolidated Tennessee regiments in our brigade, with the rank of Lt. Col. He will be Colonel of the Twentieth before long.[17] He says he is determined to marry, the first chance he has in Williamson County. Probably you have concluded that the other Colonel is the better bargain.[18] Probably, you are right.

Clay Lucas is now Major of the regiment.[19] Will Ewin will be major when Smith receives his commission as Brigadier. Ewin is now on leave, in Georgia.[20] He says that he will not leave the service because he has lost one leg. More patriotic than I am.

I have seen Anderson Ray several times recently. He gave me the first news I had heard from you, for a long time. I also saw George Hill, who gave me a letter from you.

Anderson Ray told me that you still had "Satin" at home, and wanted to send him south. I wish you would send him to me. I will promise never to ride him into a fight, but will keep him for reviews and special occasions. I have got one pretty good horse, but want another. The horse I have now is one Litton Bostick had. He has been wounded twice since I had him, pretty severely. He has as bad luck as his master.

The ladies of Florence seem to be very devoted to the Southern cause. When our army first crossed, the advance guard was almost overwhelmed by kisses from the "fair females." One poor Colonel was kissed by every lady in Florence. It was caused by one of his cousins saluting him when he landed from the boat. This act was supposed by the other ladies there assembled, to be prompted by patriotism, and all followed suit. Delightful mistake.

Kitty, I am so anxious to see you all at home. It seems an age since I saw you. I wish I had my embryotype [sic] to send you. I think it would be a fine thing to scare Yankees with. I am a hard looking case. I bid fair to rival pa in size. Oh! I will astonish you when I see you. It would amuse you to see the respect with which I am treated some times, and the regard paid to my opinions. You would think me a person of importance were you to hear me called "Lieutenant," and see me bridle up my head, and look wise. Oh it's jolly.

We are all in good spirits, and expect to be in Tennessee ere long. We know we have prayers of thousands of loved ones at home, and with the right on our side we must succeed. God grant that we may soon end this war. This may fall into the wrong hands so I will close.

Give my love to all at home. I will write whenever I have an opportunity. God shield you all from danger and soon unite us all in peace is the sincere prayer of yours affectionately

Jas. L. Cooper

I hear nothing but unceasing roar of cannon. Can't you come out & make up. Tom Sneed is mortally wounded.

⇒➤-◉-◅⇐

Hood's Army of Tennessee began moving northeast toward Columbia, Tennessee, on November 21, 1864.[21] His three corps, totaling about 30,000 men, utilized three different roads to reach their destination. As the weather continued wretched, their progress was slow as their wagons churned the dirt roads into quagmires. Rain, sleet and snow added to the discomfort of the men, many of whom were poorly clothed. Hood's goal was to reach Columbia before the arrival of Federal Brig. Gen. John Schofield, his West Point classmate, with his approximately 23,000 men. Schofield had been at Pulaski, where his job was to delay Hood's advance long enough for Gen. Thomas to concentrate all the available forces hurriedly being sent him at Nashville to smash Hood. Schofield won the race because he had slightly less distance to travel and because he marched his men day and night. He reached Columbia at sunrise on the twenty-fourth, barely ahead of Confederate cavalry thus preventing Forrest from seizing the rail-road and wagon road bridges over the Duck River and cutting off Schofield's line of retreat to Nashville. Hood's forces arrived on the twenty-seventh. Hood declined to assault Schofield but decided to turn his right flank and cut him off by gaining control of the main road at Spring Hill, eleven miles north of Columbia.

With carefully laid plans, the trap seemed to be set. The weather cooper-ated by clearing up and the men were in fine spirits. Hood's main body got within plain view of the road from Columbia at Spring Hill ahead of the Federals. What happened next has been argued about ever since. Somehow, Schofield was able to march his soldiers through Spring Hill during the night of the twenty-ninth without being seriously contested. Hood's account of what happened and Cheatham's account of the same events were com-pletely at odds. According to Cheatham, one of his staff officers, Maj. Joe Bostick, returned to his headquarters after placing Gen. Edward Johnson's division in position near the turnpike. Maj. Bostick reported to Gen. Cheatham that he had heard "straggling troops passing northward" on the turnpike. Cheatham, Bostick, and other staff officers were discussing this about midnight when a courier arrived with a note from Maj. A. P. Mason, Hood's assistant adjutant general. The note said that Gen. Hood had just heard about the stragglers and said that "you had better order your picket line to fire on them." Cheatham then sent Bostick to tell Johnson to take his division or a brigade thereof "and go on to the pike and cut off anything that might be passing." Later that night, Bostick came back and reported that he and Gen. Johnson had ridden "closeup to the pike, where they found everything quiet and no one passing." Accordingly, Johnson's division did not move. The next day, Hood was furious at Cheatham for "his failure to make a night attack." He told Governor Harris that the blame was squarely on his newest corp commander. Mason, hearing Hood's angry tirade against Cheatham, confessed to Harris that "General Cheatham is not to blame for that. I never sent him the order . . . I fell asleep again before writing it." Harris told Mason to tell Gen. Hood what he told him, and Mason said he would, but apparently never did.[22]

These stories only add to the mystery. If Mason never sent a courier to warn Cheatham, why did Cheatham say he sent Joe Bostick to investigate? We will never know. The important consequence was that the Army of Tennessee lost one of the best opportunities it ever had to destroy a Union army.

In assessing the situation, Schofield knew that there was no wagon bridge over the Harpeth at Franklin. Consequently, he ordered a pontoon bridge to be sent down from Nashville as soon as possible. Putting aside his disappointment, he ordered planks to be hurriedly put down across the rails of the railroad bridge over the Harpeth so that it might be used as a wagon road bridge. Concurrently, another wagon bridge was being built by an engineering battalion.[23]

The head of Schofield's column reached Franklin unscathed about dawn the following morning. The last of his army arrived by noon. Soon, the men were entrenched in strong earthworks which formed a crescent around the southern and western edges of the town.

That morning, Hood was beside himself with rage. He lashed out at his subordinates, particularly Cheatham and Cleburne, blaming them and his soldiers. "The best move in my career as a soldier I was thus destined to behold come to naught," he later said.[24] Determined to salvage victory from a missed opportunity, he decided to punish Schofield. He said he would "make that same afternoon another and final effort to overtake and rout him, and drive him in the Big Harpeth River at Franklin." So, he ordered his three corps to press on toward Franklin as soon as they had a pre-dawn breakfast. In the vanguard, Forrest's cavalry occasionally got close enough to Schofield's rear guard to burn a few wagons.

As they marched north with their troops, Cheatham and Cleburne reflected angrily about what happened the night before and about the unfair criticism Hood had levied on them. They were both determined to clear their names. By three in the afternoon, the head of Cheatham's corps came to the crest of Winstead Hill. There, spread out before them on a warm, bright fall afternoon was a beautiful panorama of Franklin, the Harpeth Valley, and, in the background, the high hills which separated the town from Nashville. As Hood and his generals studied the Federal position with their field glasses it was obvious that the works were well built and well manned. Nevertheless, Hood snapped shut his glass case and announced: "We will make the fight."[25] Several of his commanders, including Cheatham and Forrest, were sufficiently outspoken to openly disagree with him. Forrest, who had made a personal reconnaissance of the Federal position before Hood reached the field, told his impetuous commander that the Federal position was too strong to be taken by frontal assault without excessive loss of life. When Hood disagreed, Forrest said, "If you will give me one strong division of infantry with my cavalry, I will . . . flank the Federals from their works within two hours' time."[26] Cheatham also realized the strength of the Federal position. He said to Hood: "I do not like the looks of this fight."[27] Hood countered that he would rather fight the Federals at Franklin where they had only a few hours to fortify themselves than at Nashville where they had three years to prepare. Having failed to convince the unbending Hood not to make a frontal assault over two miles of open ground, his corps commanders returned to their posts and gave the necessary commands. As soon as Stewart and Cheatham announced that their lines had been formed, and without any preliminary artillery fire to soften the Union position, Hood gave the order to launch the assault. It was nearly four o'clock when the entrenched Federals saw the Army of Tennessee forming in heavy columns all across their front. As the masses of Confederate veterans in their yellowish-brown uniforms came forward, it looked as if every company bore tattered red and white battle flags showing the emblem of St. Andrew's Cross. When the great, seething mass came within range of the Federal guns, the disciplined charge changed into a ghastly nightmare of blood and gore. During the five-hour battle, Hood's casualties were catastrophic. He lost about 7000 men, including 1,750 killed on the field, about 4,500 wounded and 700 captured.

Among those who survived the assault at Franklin was Maj. Gen. Cheatham's staff officer, Maj. Joe Bostick. Despite having scaled the Federal breastworks and fought hand-to-hand in the Federal trenches, Joe made it through the battle unscathed.[28] Tom, who went into the fight as brigade commissary for Brig. Gen. George Washington Gordon's Brigade in John Brown's Division, also survived as did their cousin, Jim Cooper, and their brother-in-law, John F. Early. Jim Cooper did so despite suffering his fourth wound of the war. He spent the night before the battle with a friend, Capt. Theodrick "Tod" Carter, also of the Twentieth Tennessee. While sharing the same ragged blanket, the two young men made a "pact." If one was

John Fletcher Early (1830–1894).

killed, he would try to get in touch with the other on the anniversary of the battle they knew was forthcoming. The next evening, Tod Carter was fatally wounded within a few hundred yards of his boyhood home in Franklin. In later years, Jim Cooper's children said that, on every anniversary of the battle, their father would get very nervous, pull his boots on, and walk around the outside of their house, saying to himself, "I wonder if he will make himself known to me." Tod Carter never did.

John F. Early went into the battle practically barefooted. When Hood's Army of Tennessee followed Schofield to Nashville after the fiasco, John walked, carrying a pair of shoes that were too small for him in hopes that he could later exchange them for some that fit. He never got any during the balance of the campaign. As a result, his feet were badly frostbitten during the frigid weather that hit the scantily clad Confederate soldiers on the night of December 8, 1864.[29]

One or more of Joe and Tom Bosticks' first cousins probably fought in the vicinity of Everbright, the palatial home of Rebecca Letitia Bostick on Carter's Creek Pike. Both Bosticks, as well as their Cooper, Litton, and Thomas cousins, were very much aware that Rebecca, the widow of their cousin, Richard W. H. Bostick, was living there. During the battle, part of which took place at Everbright's doorstep, the Widow Bostick's wounded son, Cannon, slipped into the house and was successfully hidden by his mother. Another of her sons, John Bostick, lived through the battle as a member of Bell's Brigade in William H. "Red" Jackson's Division of Cavalry. John did not see his home until after the fight because his brigade was fighting east of town near McGavock's Ford. For forty or fifty years after the war, Richard and Rebecca Bostick's grandchildren and great-grandchildren would pick up minié balls by the handful at Everbright.[30]

Joe and Tom Bostick, John Bostick, John Early, George Litton, and Jake Thomas also survived the decisive Battle of Nashville fought on December 15 and 16 a few miles south of the city. Jim Cooper[31] was not in it because of his wound at Franklin. During the battle, Joe and Tom's mother, Margaret Bostick, grew so distraught about her sons' safety that her daughter, Catharine, volunteered to personally find out how they were. She slipped through the Federal lines and into the ranks of the Confederates. Finding Joe and Tom unhurt, she retraced her steps only to be caught and taken to the State Capitol where she was reprimanded.

On January 23, 1865, after the debacles at Franklin and Nashville, Gen. John Bell Hood surrendered command of the once-proud Army of Tennessee, then consisting of approximately 5000 troops, only a remnant of its original number. He was replaced by Gen. Joe Johnston, whom he had replaced seven months earlier. Johnston reorganized the soldiers he had left, putting all the Tennesseans together in Gen. Joseph B. Palmer's brigade.

When Gen. Sherman's army invaded South Carolina, Palmer's men, then in North Mississippi, were ordered to the defense of the Palmetto State. Largely unarmed, they arrived in Augusta, Georgia, on February 5. From there they crossed into South Carolina and fought a delaying action against Sherman as he moved north from Savannah. Their last battle was near Bentonville, North Carolina, on March 19, 1865. There, they acquitted themselves well against a numerically superior foe, regaining a measure of confidence lost at Franklin and Nashville.[32]

Everbright.

The bitter end for the Army of Tennessee came on April 26, 1865, near Durham Station, North Carolina, when Gen. Johnston accepted Gen. Sherman's conditions for surrender. At that time Joe Bostick's Thirty-fourth Infantry was part of the First Consolidated Tennessee Infantry Regiment, commanded by Lt. Col. Oliver A. Bradshaw and part of Gen. Palmer's brigade.

Joe and Tom Bostick were among the 1,312 Tennesseans paroled at Greensboro, North Carolina, on May 1, 1865. Both men returned to Tennessee, via Asheville, North Carolina, and Greeneville, Tennessee, to find their families and reassume their roles as husbands and fathers.[33]

Among those who did not return were the brothers, Abe and Litton Bostick; and their first cousin, Jim Robinson Jr., who died at home after becoming ill while serving in a Confederate unit in Alabama. Jim's sister, Kitty Litton Robinson, never married her fiancee, Col. Bill Demoss. She survived the war only to die in October 1865 of typhoid fever. Her admirer, Col. William M. Shy, also never married. He died on a hill near Nashville in December 1864, with a minié ball through his brain. The hill would be named for him. Kitty's brother, Bill Robinson, never swore allegiance to the United States after the war. In January 1866 he married Sallie N. Newsom, daughter of Col. James E. Newsom of Newsom Station, Tennessee. A member of the Klu Klux Klan, Robinson lived until October 22, 1902. Another cousin, Jim Thomas, was released from prison near the end of the war. After leaving Fort Delaware Prison, he was too ill to return to active duty. His brother, Jake, also survived and returned to Tennessee as did still another cousin, George Litton. Jim Cooper recovered from his fourth wound and was paroled at Greensboro, North Carolina, in May 1865. His brigade commander at Franklin, Gen. Thomas B. Smith, was captured at the Battle of Nashville. While an unarmed prisoner being escorted from the field of battle, Smith was viciously struck three times in the head with a saber by a Federal officer. Although Smith survived the disgraceful assault, he spent the last thirty years of his life as an inmate of the Central Hospital for the Insane in Nashville. Finally, Eliza Bostick Early's husband, John F. Early, suffered from his frostbitten feet until his death in 1894.

LIFE GOES ON

Maj. Joseph Bostick, aide-de-camp on the staff of Maj. Gen. Benjamin F. Cheatham, was paroled on May 1, 1865, at Greensboro, North Carolina. As soon as arrangements could be made by Federal military authorities for him and other paroled Confederate soldiers to return home, they were allowed to do so under the command of Gen. Palmer.

The 1,312 Tennesseans in the Army of Tennessee walked or, if they were lucky, rode horseback across the Appalachian Mountains to Greeneville, Tennessee, where railroad transportation was arranged for those who lived in more distant parts of the state. Joe and Tom Bostick and their cousin Jim Cooper made this march of over two hundred miles through a hostile section of country, which had been greatly agitated by the news of the assassination of President Lincoln on April 14. The men, only two hundred of whom were allowed to retain their rifles, traveled with a small wagon train of provisions. On several occasions, there were close calls when Union home guards and Federal troops were encountered.[1]

Upon reaching Greeneville, a town on the East Tennessee & Virginia Railroad, the Tennesseans found racial tensions high. One Confederate soldier, Hampton Cheney,[2] described his stay in Greeneville as "two days and nights of hell during which Negro soldiers . . . taunted us [on] our loss of Southern rights."[3] Because Gen. Tillson, the Union commander at Greeneville, refused to allow more than one boxcar for horses, wagons and personal belongings, most of the soldiers had to leave everything they could

Maj. Joseph Bostick, M.D. (1832–1886).

not carry in their hands or on their backs in Greeneville.[4] From there, Palmer's brigade was taken by rail to Chattanooga and from there to Middle Tennessee. Along the way, men left the train at various points nearest their homes.[5]

Joe Bostick probably left the train at Stevenson, Alabama, a stop on the Memphis & Charleston Railroad only eight miles from home. As he approached his farm, he was prepared for what was in store for him. His house and out-buildings had been destroyed, his crops were in bad shape, his live-stock stolen, and his silver gone. When he last saw Bub (Mary Louisa) following the birth of their son Joseph Jr. on May 3, 1864, near Hogansville, Georgia, she had brought him up to date on the wretched conditions at home. Thankfully, she, the older children, and the baby were unharmed, and a number of their slaves were still at the home place trying to hold together what little remained. Even though conditions would never be the same and even though Bub was still mourning for her brother Will, who was killed at Cedar Creek, Virginia, the previous fall, she was eager to help her husband rebuild their home and lives.

Hard work was not new to Mary, even though she had grown up accus-tomed to luxuries in a privileged Columbus, Mississippi, home. Before the war, Joe had taught her to ride bareback. During his four-year absence, she had grown accustomed to strenuous work. "With hands unused to blisters," she learned to examine fields for the growth of corn and to use the hoe and shovel. She also learned to remain stoic when marauding Federals plundered her springhouse, tore down her farm fences for firewood, and stole her family silver when five-year-old Will told them where it was hidden. The graciousness that signified the Bosticks' lives in the ante-bellum years was gone, but by relying on each other for emotional support, Joe and Bub methodically rebuilt their river-bottom farm, which, through annual winter floods, retained its richness.

Dr. Bostick took pleasure in playing with his namesake, Joe Jr., now more than a year old, and in reacquainting himself with his three older children, Margaret "Maggie," William "Willie," and Mary Hunt. Early in 1866, Mary became pregnant with their fifth and last child. When a baby daughter was born in 1866, they named her Catharine Warren for Joe's sister, Catharine Halbert, and for his grandmother, Catharine Litton, the baby's great grandmother. To simplify matters, they called the baby "Kate."

Tragedy struck in 1871 when seven-year-old Joe Jr. drowned in the Tennessee River. The sadness of his senseless death was replaced by excitement two years later when Dr. Bostick brought home the news that their neighbors, Woodrow

Mary Louisa Hunt Bostick (1835-1915).

Wilson and Erasmus Alley,[6] had sold 3000 acres of their land, known to be rich in coal and iron, to the Old English Company, a syndicate that intended to transform the sleepy Battle Creek farming community into the Pittsburg of the South. James Bowron, an English iron-master, was in charge of local operations. The name of the hamlet was changed to South Pittsburg, two blast furnaces were quickly put in operation, fine houses were built for company officers, and numerous cottages were built on the remaining acreage, which had been subdivided into lots, streets, and alleys.[7]

With the arrival of managers and workers for the blast furnaces, Dr. Bostick, the town's first physician, saw his practice flourish. His financial situation, wretched in 1865, was so improved by 1873 that he and Mary could afford to send Mary Hunt to Nashville to attend Dr. Blackie's School for Girls and Young Ladies. Mary graduated from the finishing school in June 1877.

By 1880, the Bosticks' son, Willie, was twenty-two years old and farming along the Tennessee River. Within a year or two, his yearning to move further west got the best of him. Sometime in the early 1880s, he moved to Ozark, Arkansas, where he met and married Cora Annie Wish on September 4, 1884. She would bring him ten children, the first six born in Arkansas,[8] and the last four in Texas,[9] where they would move by wagon train about 1897.

On December 9, 1885, Dr. and Mrs. Bosticks' second oldest daughter, Mary Hunt, married. Her husband was Eugene Henry Lowman. He and his brothers owned the Lowman Stove Works in neighboring Bridgeport. Initially, Eugene and Mary lived in South Pittsburg, where their two oldest daughters, Mary Louise and Kate, were born in 1886 and 1888. Later, they moved to Bridgeport, where Annie was born in 1894. Soon after Eugene Lowman died, five months before Annie's birth, Mary returned to South Pittsburg, to open a boarding house, the Lowman Inn.[10] She owned this establishment for sixteen years.

After the war ended, Confederate veterans in the South Pittsburg and Bridgeport areas often spoke of Dr. Bostick's worth as a man, a physician, and an officer. His reconstruction-period reputation was that of a generous country doctor who helped people by treating their illnesses, often without pay, and by lending them money. The only criticism he is known to have received was for sometimes drinking too much, understandable for a Confederate veteran who had gone through enormous tribulation. A few days before Christmas 1886, Dr. Joseph Bostick died. He was only fifty-four.

A few months earlier, Dr. Bostick had sold to the South Pittsburg City Company, which had just been granted a charter of incorporation, 700 acres at the town's southern boundary. Following his death, his remains were buried beside those of his son, Joe Jr., in the City Cemetery on the side of the hill overlooking his Tennessee River farm, and the prosperous new town. In 1897, eleven years later, a Confederate veteran who fought under Maj. Bostick paid him tribute in an article published in the *Nashville Sun*. In it, the old soldier said Maj. Bostick "was a stranger to fear, but kind as a woman."

Dr. Bostick's widow, Mary, remained in South Pittsburg where she and her daughters, Maggie, Mary, and Kate, were supporters of a successful effort to establish an Episcopal Church. Mrs. Bostick was confirmed as a communicant in 1886, the same year Dr. Bostick died.[11] Eight years later, she pitched in to look after Mary Lowman's children when her widowed daughter moved back from Bridgeport. Mrs. Bostick did so with the help of Maggie Dickens, the daughter of Becky, one of her freed slaves.

When daughter Kate Bostick married Henry "Harry" Blacklock on December 17, 1890, the ceremony was held at Christ Episcopal Church. Harry's father, the Reverend Joseph H. Blacklock, an Englishman and the church's founding rector, performed the ceremony.[12] Harry and Kate Blacklock set up housekeeping in South Pittsburg, where he was superintendent of the Blacklock Foundry.[13] Later, the foundry encountered financial problems and he left to manage the Lowman Inn owned by his sister-in-law.[14] During the nearly two decades that the Blacklocks lived in South Pittsburg, they were active at Christ Episcopal Church where Harry served as a vestryman. He also enjoyed the distinction of owning the first automobile in town.

Unfortunately for Dr. Bostick's daughters, South Pittsburg did not become the Pittsburg of the South. By 1887, Birmingham, suddenly Alabama's largest and wealthiest city, had serious aspirations to that title. The explosion of growth there was accelerated by the arrival of Tennessee Coal, Iron & Railroad, which moved much of its capital from southeast Tennessee to the "Magic City" the previous December. From then on, the Tennessee mines, coke ovens, and furnaces, including those in South Pittsburg, continued to operate but at reduced levels.

After the depression of the 1890s, Birmingham experienced a new boom period, beginning in 1899 when the first steel in commercial quantities was made there from local raw materials. The first carload of Birmingham steel was shipped on the first day of the twentieth century. In 1904, Tennessee Coal, Iron & Railroad Company closed most of its operations in southeast Tennessee and moved some of its employees and equipment to Birmingham. In South Pittsburg, the South Pittsburg City Company went bankrupt. Three years later, U.S. Steel came to Birmingham and acquired the holdings of Tennessee, Coal, Iron & Railroad, the company which had brought such excitement and prosperity to Tennessee's Sequatchie Valley.[15]

About 1909, Harry and Kate Blacklock moved to Birmingham, only 150 miles away, where Harry saw far greater opportunities than in South Pittsburg. There, he sold automobiles, hoping to capitalize on a booming market of mostly young adults. This effort may not have been too successful as, later, he and Kate ran a boarding house for girls. In 1923, Kate became supervisor of the "Catharine Inn," a home for young working girls. Harry Blacklock died in 1941. Kate retired in 1947 which gave her time to devote to her long-time interests in the Daughters of the Confederacy and St. Andrews Episcopal Church. She died seven years later at age eighty-nine.

By 1894, the Bosticks' oldest daughter, Margaret, was also married. Her husband, John Wilson, was a native of Stocton on Tees, England. Following their marriage, Margaret, whose nickname was "Maggie," and John stayed in South Pittsburg long enough to have her married name registered on the rolls of Christ Episcopal Church. At some point they too moved to Birmingham, where she lived until her death on June 24, 1925.

Mary (Bostick) Lowman followed her sisters to Birmingham around 1910. The Lowman Inn, which she had owned since 1894, had catered to traveling salesmen, called "drummers," who arrived in town by rail, usually from Nashville or Atlanta, to call on the local merchants. With business somewhat diminished by the less-than-robust economy, Mary decided to open a boarding house in Birmingham, where business conditions seemed so much brighter. All three of her daughters, Annie Litton, Mary Louise, and Kate, also moved to Birmingham. Mrs. Lowman died there January 4, 1949.

Dr. Bostick's widow, Mary (Hunt) Bostick, left South Pittsburg when, or soon after, her children did. She too moved to Birmingham to spend the the last years of her life with her daughter, Catharine Blacklock. Following Mrs. Bostick's death there on June 4, 1915, her remains were brought by train to South Pittsburg where her funeral service was held at Christ Episcopal Church, where she had been "a true and tried member." At her request, she was buried in South Pittsburg's City Cemetery beside the graves of her husband and her son, Joseph Bostick Jr.

When Maj. Joe Bostick's younger brother Tom returned to Lebanon, Tennessee, from Greensboro, North Carolina, after receiving his parole, his daughters, Mary Litton and Kate, had not seen him since his visit more than two years earlier. Nevertheless, time and a father's affection soon cured whatever problems were caused by their prolonged separation. Tom, Mat and the girls continued living with the McClains while he resumed his law practice[16] and enjoyed his associations with other members of Lebanon's Magnolia Lodge No. 30 Independent Order of Odd Fellows.

In 1866, Tom Bostick demonstrated his affection for his former commanding officer, Gen. Robert Hatton, whose remains he had buried in East Tennessee nearly four years earlier. Tom went to East Tennessee where he supervised the exhumation of Gen. Hatton's remains and escorted them to Nashville by railroad, arriving on March 22. The next day, Tom was part of a delegation of men from several lodges of Odd Fellows, who escorted Gen. Hatton's remains to Lebanon, where funeral services were held in the Methodist Church and burial was at the cemetery one mile from town. In the procession to the cemetery, Jerry, Gen. Hatton's faithful servant during the war, led a little black mare that Gen. Hatton had ridden during those stirring times. As a final tribute to "the most popular man who ever lived in Wilson County," Tom Bostick and two other members of Magnolia Lodge No. 30 prepared a suitable testimonial to Gen. Hatton, who had been a member of the lodge.[17]

Tom Bostick had only a few more years of life himself. He died in 1871 at age thirty-seven. Mat, having once before assumed sole responsibility for rearing her daughters, was forced to fulfill that sad duty again. The girls grew to womanhood and married promising husbands.

Mary fell in love with State Sen. Samuel F. Wilson of Gallatin, Tennessee. They married in Lebanon on August 19, 1880, during his Tennessee gubernatorial campaign as the candidate of the Low-Tax wing of the Democratic party. The wedding was a quiet one only witnessed by relatives and close personal friends of the twenty-two-year-old bride and her groom.[18] The *Memphis Public Ledger*, the only daily newspaper supporting Wilson in the campaign, said that "his marriage would not lessen his energy or industry." It may not have. He did not win, however, as Republican candidate Alvin Hawkins swept the four-man field. Wilson received 57,080 votes, coming in third behind John V. Wright, a State-Tax Democrat. Sen. Wilson later became judge of the Court of Chancery Appeals in Nashville. At one time, he and Mary lived at 2511 West End Avenue, which was perhaps Nashville's most fashionable neighborhood.[19] When Mary died in 1920, her remains were buried beside those of her father and other family members in the Nashville City Cemetery.[20] Judge Wilson died three years later and was buried in his hometown of Gallatin.

Tom and Mat Bosticks' daughter, Catharine "Kate" Bostick, married Edward R. Pennybaker, a local farmer. During their first years as a married couple, the Pennybakers lived with Mat. Some years later, the Pennybakers moved to West Nashville where he worked as a salesman. They had two children, Frank and Edwin. Kate outlived her older sister, Mary Wilson, although the date of her death is unknown.[21]

After the Civil War, Joe and Tom Bosticks' sister, Catharine Halbert, faced the adversity and loneliness so typically endured by Southern widows. With children grown or nearly so when the war ended, she devoted much of her time after 1865 to taking care of her mother, who lived with her on Church Street in Nashville. In 1870, Elizabeth "Ann" Anderson, a step daughter of Catharine's sister, Mary Anne Anderson, was also living there, along with Catharine's sons, Hardin and Bently Halbert. Both boys were clerking in Nashville stores, which provided crucial sources of family income. Hardin later moved to Flora City, Florida, where he was still living in 1916. Bently Jr. also lived in Florida. He married Margaret Webb Moore in 1876 and died in 1907. Their sister, Mary Halbert, married a man named Lewis and lived in Nashville.[22]

On Sunday mornings during the 1870s, the Halberts could usually be found at McKendree Methodist Church, where five generations of Catharine's family were married. Beginning about 1896, she made her summer home at Monteagle, Tennessee, possibly on land which had been in the family since her grandfather, John Bostick, bought it circa. 1830. There, she traditionally celebrated her birthday with children and friends. Although Hardin and Bently were not able to come to the mountain frequently, their sister Mary did. When Catharine Halbert died in 1916 at age eighty-eight, she was also survived by six grandchildren[23] and eight great-grandchildren. In her obituary, she was described as "a refined Southern woman of the highest type" and an angel of mercy during the Civil War.[24]

Mary Anne Anderson and her sister Margaret Rebecca "Mag" Davis also lived in Nashville after the war. Mary Anne's husband, William J. Anderson, who was in his early seventies in 1880, was a book agent. Their sons, Hardie and Willie, were living with them. Hardie was employed as a railroad clerk, while twelve-year-old Willie was in school. By 1900, Mary Anne Anderson was a widow living in St. Louis.

Mag's husband, John A. Davis, ran a transfer line company named John A. Davis and Company on South Market Street.[25] In 1877, he and Mag were living on Asylum Street with their children, Kittie Litton and Margie. Around 1878, a third daughter, Mary, was born. A year or two later, Mr. Davis' mother, Kittie Davis, moved in with her son and daughter-in-law. By the mid-1880s, John was superintendent for the Empire Coal Company. A few years later, he and his family moved to California, where he died in 1899 and Mag in 1911.[26]

After the end of the war, Bettie C. Bostick, Litton's widow, remained in Columbus, Mississippi, where she and her four sons, William "Willie," Hardin, Joseph and Litton, lived with her parents, Dr. William and Kezia G. Topp.[27] Also living there were Bettie's recently widowed sister, Anne Lacy Witherspoon, and Anne's two children. In August 1865, three-year-old Litton Bostick died of bilious fever. A few years later, Bettie's three surviving children, Willie, Hardin Perkins, and Joseph, were all attending school. In the spring of 1889, Dr. Topp died. As Mrs. Topp had died in 1877, Bettie's ties to Columbus were lessened. The following December, her oldest son, Willie, married Susie Smith, of Lowndes County.[28] By 1900, and possibly somewhat earlier, Bettie moved to San Rafael, California, to live with her son, Hardin, his wife, Linnie, and a niece.[29] Ten years later, she was still living, presumably in California.

After the death of Dr. Topp's daughter, Anne Lacy Witherspoon, their home "Rosedale" was owned by Anne and Bettie's sister and brother-in-law, Ozella and J. T. Champneys. In 1904, the Italianate-style two-story house, with a tower, arched windows, low-pitched roof, and piazzas, passed out of the Topp family. It was recently restored by its present owners, Mr. and Mrs. Terry Stubblefield.[30]

Four years after the Civil War ended, Eliza Jane and John F. Early were living in Nashville with their four children, Hardin, John, Margaret, and Lila. For the next half-dozen years, John worked as a clerk, usually for the Nashville & Decatur Railroad. During that period, he and his family moved frequently. During the late 1870s and early 1880s, John worked both as a bookkeeper and as a salesman. If his frequent job changes did not bring economic stability, he and his family did settle down to one address, 40 Williams Ave.[31]

In 1885, the Earlys moved to Sanford, Florida, to be near their unmarried daughter Lila, who was teaching school there. Mr. Early get a job with the South Florida Railroad. He died in Florida on September 28, 1894.[32] Following his death, his widow, Eliza Jane Early, moved back to Nashville to help share responsibility for her aged mother, Margaret Bostick, and to devote time to Christian work at McKendree Methodist Church. In 1897, Mrs. Bostick died at Eliza's West End home. She was ninety-three years old.[33]

In 1902, Eliza and John F. Early's son, John Early, married Willie Fall, daughter of J. Horton Fall, a very successful hardware merchant in

Rosedale, W. W. Topp house, Columbus, Mississippi, c. 1855. (Courtesy, Library of Congress.)

Nashville. John and Willie lived three-and-one-half miles from the public square in East Nashville. Their house, named Pontotoc, had been owned by Willie's father since she was ten years old, originally as a summer home. Each work day, John Early would drive his buggy from Pontotoc to Nashville, where he was president of the Early-Mack Company, manufacturers and importers of fine harnesses, saddles, bridles, and horse goods at 315 North Market Street. John and Willie reared three daughters and two sons. Margaret,[34] the oldest, was born in 1903. John Early Jr.[35] was born two years later at the home of his Fall grandparents at 303 North Vine Street. Katherine "Kay" Wyche Early,[36] the second daughter, was born in 1909, while Joseph Horton Fall Early, the second son, was born in 1913. The youngest daughter, Elizabeth "Lib" Drennon Early,[37] was born in 1916.

In addition to managing his own business, John Early took an active interest in education, much as his great-grandfather John Bostick did. Mr. Early was a member of the School Board for the City of Nashville and served for seven years as president of the Board of Trustees of Montgomery Bell Academy.[38]

The same year that John Early and Willie Fall married, his only brother, Hardin Bostick Early, died. Hardin was killed by robbers while working on a railroad mail car in Memphis. Following his death, his widow, Hattie Early, and their son, Hardin Early, moved to Muir, Kentucky, to live with her brothers. Hattie later lived in Harrodsburg.

John Early's sister, Margaret Early, married Granbery Jackson, a civil engineer and inventor who was for several years associate professor of engineering at Vanderbilt University. While Margaret and Granbery were living on the Vanderbilt campus, her mother, Eliza Jane (Bostick) Early, who made her home with them, died. When Mrs. Early succumbed on October 22, 1905, she was two months short of her sixty-ninth birthday. Her remains were taken to Sanford, Florida, for burial beside those of her husband.[39]

In later years, Granbery Jackson was in private practice in Nashville as a consulting engineer. He then worked as chief engineer for the International Agricultural Corporation of New York. During his period with the New York firm, he lived in Mt. Pleasant, Tennessee, where he owned a farm and where, with his brother, Charles S. Jackson, he formed the Jackson Phosphate Company. Granbery and Margaret had two sons, John Early Jackson, born in 1902, and Granbery Jackson Jr. born in 1906. Granbery Jr. married Henriette Weaver of Nashville in 1937. Their daughter Irene Jackson Wills married the author.

ENDNOTES

Preface and Acknowledgments

1. James Alfred Bostick was a younger brother of Hardin P. Bostick. Born in 1806, he married Nancy Woolsey King in 1826.

2. The Bostick Female Academy was a boarding school which began in about 1885. It was built with funds from a bequest left by Dr. Jonathan Bostick, a wealthy Mississippian and native of Triune. About the turn of the century, the school's trustees gave the school to Williamson County. It then operated as a public school until the mid-1950s. (Virginia McDaniel Bowman, *Historic Williamson County, Old Homes and Sites* [Nashville: Blue & Gray Press, 1971]: 16).

Prologue: An Ill-fated Generation

1. George Washington Wright served as a California congressman from 1849–1851. A native of Massachusetts, he returned to the East following his one term in office.

2. These cities are on either side of the isthmus. Litton Bostick to Hardin P. Bostick, May 25, 1850, Hardin P. Bostick Collection, Tennessee State Library and Archives, Nashville.

3. Litton Bostick to Hardin P. Bostick, August 8, 1850, Hardin P. Bostick Collection, Tennessee State Library and Archives, Nashville.

4. Litton Bostick to Margaret "Mag" Bostick, June 29, 1853, Hardin P. Bostick Collection, Tennessee State Library and Archives, Nashville.

5. Ibid.

6. Litton Bostick to Bently Halbert, August 12, 1853, Hardin P. Bostick Collection, Tennessee State Library and Archives, Nashville.

7. Litton had already bought out his business partner.

8. Litton Bostick to Bently Halbert, August 12, 1853, Hardin P. Bostick Collection, Tennessee State Library and Archives, Nashville.

9. Ibid.

10. Dr. Topp came to Columbus from Davidson County, Tennessee, in the early 1830s to manage the property of his brother-in-law, Thomas Martin. He soon became a prominent member of the Columbus community, helping to organize the Columbus Female Institute. The Topp home, Rosedale, which Dr. Topp built in 1855, was a Columbus showplace. A villa with a distinctive central tower, it was the first house in town to be stuccoed. Skilled workmen were brought from New Orleans to complete it. Holly trees, which Dr. Topp planted, still adorn the grounds (Carl Butler, "Rosedale: Past and Present" [Columbus: Mississippi School for Mathematics and Science, 1993–94]: 2).

11. Lowndes County, Mississippi, Marriage License, book 4, p. 154.

12. Randal W. McGavock was Nashville's mayor from October 1, 1858 through September 30, 1859.

13. Jack Allen and Herschel Gower, eds., *Pen and Sword, The Life and Journals of Randal W. McGavock, Colonel, C.S.A.* (Nashville: Tennessee Historical Commission, 1959): 449.

14. Davidson County Deed, book 26, 79.

15. Thomas H. Bostick and Martha D. McClain were married September 16, 1856, by Wilson County Justice of the Peace D. Lowry (Thomas E. Parlow, comp., *Wilson County, Tennessee Marriages 1851–1865* [Lebanon, Tenn., 1980]: 56).

16. Josiah S. McClain (1797–1876) was the first white child born in Wilson County. He later served as Wilson County clerk for over forty years (*History of Tennessee* [Nashville: The Goodspeed Publishing Co., 1886]: 844).

17. Litton Bostick to Margaret Litton Bostick, June 29, 1853, Hardin P. Bostick Collection, Tennessee State Library and Archives, Nashville.

18. Lowndes County, Mississippi, Marriage License, book 3, p. 92.

19. Marion County, Tennessee, Deed, book H, p. 332.

20. *Catalogue of the Literary and Medical Departments of the University of Nashville 1858–9* (Nashville: John T. S. Fall, Book and Job Printer, 1859).

21. Agatheridan Debate Society record book in the collection of Henriette Jackson, Nashville.

22. A fifth brother, Manoah James Bostick, died before 1850.

23. John Bently Halbert, a native Mississippian, was an 1846 graduate of the University of Nashville. His parents were Arthur and Parmelia Arnold Halbert of Oktibbeha County, Mississippi.

24. When Randal McGavock learned of Bently Halbert's death on June 3, 1858, he recorded deep feelings in his diary. McGavock wrote of Halbert: "He was a gentleman of the highest acceptation of the word, and I know of no one whose death I regret so much" (Allen and Gower, *Pen and Sword*, 473).

25. Eliza and John Fletcher Early were married on October 18, 1860, in Nashville. John's father, Bishop John Early, of the Methodist Episcopal Church, South, officiated. (*Christian Advocate*, November 8, 1894).

26. Mag and Susan were both born in Nashville, Mag in 1842 and Susan four years later.

Chapter One: Who Are Their People?

1. In 1948, the Washington B. Cooper home (now gone) still stood on the corner of Pearl Street and 20th Avenue North (*Nashville Tennessean Magazine*, April 25, 1948).

2 Washington B. Cooper's portrait of his wife, Ann Litton Cooper, is in the collection of the Tennessee Botanical Gardens and Fine Arts Center at Cheekwood.

3. Miss Jane Thomas, *Old Days in Nashville, Tenn.* (Nashville: Publishing House Methodist Episcopal Church, South, 1897): 131.

4. The Littons arrived in Philadelphia on October 10, 1817, on the ship *Sally* (*Passenger Arrivals at the Port of Philadelphia, 1800–1815* [General Publishing Co., 1986]: 422).

5. *Southwestern Christian Advocate*, Nashville, July 3, 1846.

6. Robinson purchased Blue Springs Farm from the Joshua Pearre family. In 1985, the house still stood at 1849 Moran Road.

7. Isaac Litton High School existed for forty years before closing in 1970. It was located on Gallatin Road near Mr. Litton's home, which stood where the East Nashville Family YMCA is located today.

8. Edwin Mims, *History of Vanderbilt University* (Nashville: Vanderbilt Univ. Press, 1946): 40.

9. James D. Richardson, *Tennessee Templars, A Register of Names with Biographical Sketches of the Knights Templar of Tennessee* (Nashville: Robert H. Howell & Co., 1883): 17.

10. John Bostick (1765–1850) was born June 18, 1765, in Halifax County, Virginia. In 1767, when Pittsylvania County was created, the Bostick home was in the new county.

11. John Bostick, a Revolutionary War veteran and a farmer on Arrington Creek in Williamson County, died on September 20, 1850, at age eighty-five. His remains were buried in a graveyard off the Nolensville-College Grove Road where his wife was buried when she died seventeen years earlier.

12. In a letter from Washington, Hardin wrote his wife that Tennessee Congressman Meredith Gentry had promised to present his case to Daniel Webster, but that Tennessee's Whig Congressman John Bell might oppose his nomination (Hardin Bostick to Margaret Bostick, March 2, 1841, Hardin P. Bostick Collection, Tennessee State Library and Archives, Nashville).

13. The deed was for 148 acres on Stones River for which Bostick paid $1,700 (Davidson County Deed, book 5, 237).

14. Ibid., book 6, 75.

15. Bostick became a Royal Arch Mason on November 11, 1846, and a Knight Templar, Nashville Commandery 1, January 28, 1848. His brother, James Alfred Bostick, followed in his footsteps several years later (Richardson, *Tennessee Templars*, 17).

16. *Daily Nashville Patriot*, November 30, 1858.

17. Jack Allen and Herschel Gower, *Pen and Sword: The Life and Journals of Randal W. McGavock*, 521.

18. Hardin P. Bostick's remains were buried in Nashville's City Cemetery on February 24, 1861.

19. *Daily Nashville Patriot*, February 24, 1861.

Chapter Two: On To Virginia!

1. The Twentieth Tennessee Infantry Regiment was organized June 12, 1861. *Tennesseans in the Civil War, A Military History of Confederate and Union Units*, Part 1 (Nashville: Civil War Centennial Commission, 1964): 216.

2. Rufus P. "Rufe" McClain survived the war to return to Lebanon where he died in 1913.

3. Robert Hatton (1827–1862) was nominated for gov. of Tennessee in 1857. When he was defeated, he was sent to Congress, where he served until the beginning of the Civil War. (G. R. McGee, *A History of Tennessee from 1663 to 1900*. [New York: American Book Company, 1899]: 180).

4. *Tennesseans in the Civil War, A Military History of Confederate and Union Units*, Part 1, 188.

5. *History of Tennessee from the Earliest Time to the Present; Together with an Historical and a Biographical Sketch of Maury, Williamson, Rutherford, Wilson, Bedford and Marshall Counties* (Nashville: Goodspeed Publishing Company, 1886): 851.

6. Hatton acquired Mississippi rifles for the entire regiment in Nashville. (James Vaulx Drake, *Life of Robert Hatton* [Nashville: Marshall & Bruce, 1867]: 355).

7. W. J. McMurray, *History of the Twentieth Tennessee Regiment* (Nashville: Privately printed, 1904): 117.

8. E. W. Sehon to Mrs. Hardin Perkins Bostick, August 1, 1862, Hardin P. Bostick Collection, Tennessee State Library and Archives, Nashville.

9. Martha "Mat" (McClain) Bostick.

10. During the Civil War, Johnson City was known as Haynesville. When the town was incorporated in 1869, its name was changed to Johnson City. During their stop at Bristol, the Seventh Tennessee Regiment learned of the Confederate victory at Manassas.

11. Col. George Maney's First Regiment Tennessee Volunteers, consisting of three Nashville companies known as the Rock City Guards, and seven other companies from Davidson, Giles, Maury, Rutherford, and Williamson Counties, arrived in Haynesville on July 14 and left by rail for Lynchburg, Charlottesville, and Staunton on July 21 (John Berrien Lindsley, M.D., D.D., *Military Annals of Tennessee Confederate* [*MAOTC*] [Nashville: J. M. Lindsley and Co., 1886]: 156).

12. Frances "Fannie" Early was a sister of John Fletcher Early, who was married to Abe's sister, Eliza Jane.

13. Seventh Tennessee Infantry Regiment.

14. Eliza Jane Early.

15. The first Battle of Bull Run (First Manassas) occurred five days before this letter was written. The wounded Confederate soldiers had been brought to Charlottesville for treatment and care.

16. Lt. Newnan Toliver, Company K, Seventh Tennessee Infantry.

17. Maj. Gen. George B. McClellan, U.S.A. (1826–1885) was commander of the Department of the Ohio in the early summer of 1861. In July, he was named commander of the District of the Potomac.

Chapter Three: Western Virginia— Lee's First Campaign

1. Samuel Carter III, *The Siege of Atlanta, 1864* (New York: Bonanza Books, 1973): 62.

2. Margaret "Mag" Bostick was living in Nashville with her mother and other family members when Abe wrote this letter.

3. Huntersville was "a wretched and filthy town" on Knapp Creek about 25 miles from Monterey, Virginia. Robert E. Lee arrived there in early August 1861, to coordinate Confederate activities in Western Virginia (Douglas Southall Freeman, *Robert E. Lee*, vol. 1 [New York: Charles Scribner's Sons, 1934]: 550).

4. Triune was Abe's birthplace in Williamson County, Tennessee.

5. First Regiment Tennessee Volunteers.

6. Col. W. A. Forbes' Fourteenth Tennessee Infantry was organized at Clarksville, Tennessee, in May 1861 (John Berrien Lindsley, M.D., D.D., *MAOTC* [Nashville: J. M. Lindsley and Co., 1886]: 323).

7. William Wing "Old Blizzards" Loring was a brigadier general whose headquarters was at Huntersville when this letter was written. A few months later, Loring clashed violently with Stonewall Jackson over the conduct of the Romney campaign and was relieved from duty and reassigned to Southwestern Virginia (Ezra J. Warner, *Generals in Gray* [Baton Rouge: Louisiana State University Press, 1959]: 194).

8. Abe's widowed sister, Catharine, was teaching school in Nashville and living with her four children; her sisters, Mag and Susan; and her mother at the Bostick family home on the Charlotte Turnpike.

9. Abe's sister, Eliza Jane Early, was a recent bride. Her husband, John Fletcher Early (1830–1894), was a member of Fenner's Louisiana Battery, a New Orleans company.

10. Catharine Halbert.

11. Brig. Gen. Samuel R. Anderson, a brigadier general in the Provisional Army of the Confederate States, participated in the Western Virginia campaign under Gen. Robert E. Lee (Warner, *Generals in Gray*, 10).

12. Jacob "Jake" Thomas, Abe's first cousin.

13. When this letter was written, Dr. Joseph "Joe" Bostick was in the process of organizing a company of soldiers, known as the Davis Guards, from the Bridgeport, Alabama, area.

14. At Big Spring, Gen. Anderson's Brigade spent several weeks resting from the fatigues of a hard march and "indulged in hunting and fishing in the mountains" of western Virginia (Lindsley, M.D., D.D., *MAOTC*, 228).

15. The 11th New York or "The First Fire Zouaves" was organized in New York City by Col. E. Elmer Ellsworth. On May 24, 1861, the twenty-four-year-old Ellsworth was killed by James T. Jackson, a hotel keeper in Alexandria, Virginia. His death greatly aroused the war feeling in the North. Subsequently, the 11th New York became known as Ellsworth's Zouaves. (Robert Underwood Johnson and Clarence Clough Buel, eds., *Battles and Leaders of the Civil War*, vol. 1 [Secaucus, N. J.: Book Sales, Inc.]: 179).

16. Catharine Halbert.

17. Capt. William H. Williamson commanded Company H, Seventh Tennessee Infantry.

18. On August 4, 1861, the day this letter was written, Abe had witnessed seventeen consecutive days of rain (Freeman, *Robert E. Lee*, vol. 1, 555).

19. Col. W. A. Forbes of the Fourteenth Tennessee Infantry Regiment was killed at the Battle of Manassas, August 31, 1862 (Lindsley, M.D., D.D., *MAOTC*, 329).

20. A few days after this letter was written, Anderson's brigade, including the Seventh Tennessee Infantry, participated in an exhausting and abortive movement against Union forces on Cheat Mountain.

21. Alexander W. "Rex" Vick (1834–1901), Quartermaster of the Seventh Tennessee Infantry, was an 1853 graduate of Cumberland University.

22. Lt. B. D. Powell, Company K, Seventh Tennessee Infantry.

23. Col. Joel A. Battle.

24. This report was incorrect. The Twentieth Tennessee Infantry Regiment, familiarly known as Battle's regiment for its commander Col. Joel A. Battle, was organized at Camp Trousdale. By September, 1861, however, the regiment was part of Gen. Felix K. Zollicoffer's Brigade at Fort Buckner or Cumberland Ford, Ky. Abe and Joe's first cousin, Jim Cooper, who served in Company C, would be wounded and captured at Fishing Creek, Ky. the following January.

25. Bettie C. (Topp) Bostick, Litton's wife.

26. Catharine Halbert.

27. Henry A. Wise (1806–1876) was a Democratic governor of Virginia from 1856 to 1860. Although without military training, he was appointed a brigadier general in June 1861 and fought in the West Virginia campaign under Robert E. Lee. Wise's wife, the former Ann E. Jennings, had a Nashville connection. Her father, Rev. Obadiah Jennings, was minister of Nashville's First Presbyterian Church from 1828 until his death in 1832.

28. Margaret "Mag" Bostick.

Chapter Four: Winter Campaign

1. Benson J. Lossing LLD, *A History of the Civil War* (New York: War Memorial Association, 1895): 64.

2. James Vaulx Drake, *Life of General Robert Hatton* (Nashville: Marshall & Bruce, 1867): 397.

3. Ibid., 411.

4. Catharine Halbert.

5. A counterpin, sometimes spelled counterpane, was a bedspread.

6. Lt. M. V. Baird, Company G, Seventh Tennessee Infantry.

7. Hardie, Mary and Bently Halbert.

8. On November 6, 1861, Jefferson Davis and Alexander H. Stephens were elected to full six-year terms as Confederate president and vice president.

9. Jacob "Jake" Thomas.

10. Lt. B. D. Powell, Company K, Seventh Tennessee Infantry.

11. Lt. Newnan Toliver and Second Lt. B. J. Tarver.

12. Col. George Maney, First Tennessee Infantry, and Col. W. A. Forbes, Fourteenth Tennessee Infantry.

13. Mrs. Bostick planned to move out of her home on the Charlotte Turnpike. Probably, she felt it necessary to live more economically since she was a widow with a dependent child and limited funds.

14. This letter was probably written to Abe's sister, Eliza Jane Early.

15. In 1861, the newly organized Confederate regiments had extremely high rates of camp diseases, primarily due to the failure of line officers to insist upon proper hygienic procedures. The shortage of hospital beds in Nashville became increasingly acute following the Confederate defeat at Fishing Creek, Kentucky, on January 19, 1862. A few weeks later, Confederate authorities requested the use of the buildings of the University of Nashville for use as a hospital. (John E. Windrow, ed. *Peabody and Alfred Leland Crabb* [Nashville: Williams Press, 1956]: 97).

16. Rev. Thomas Early, a brother of Abe's brother-in-law, John F. Early, was at Staunton. He was a Methodist minister who also served congregations in Petersburg, Rappahannock, and Charlottesville, Virginia. (James Rives Childs, *Reliques of the Rives* [Lynchburg, Va.: J. P. Bell Co., Inc., 1929]: 261).

17. Probably a reference to Abe's oldest nephew, Hardin Bostick Halbert.

18. W. H. Armstrong was chaplain of the Seventh Tennessee Infantry Regiment in September 1861, and presumably when this letter was written three months later. (John Berrien Lindsley, M.D., D.D., *MAOTC* [Nashville: J. M.Lindsley and Co., 1886]: 261).

19. Brig. Gen. Daniel Smith Donelson, an 1825 West Point graduate, served under Gen. Loring in western Virginia before his transfer to Charleston, South Carolina. He joined Gen. Bragg at Tupelo, Mississippi, and commanded a brigade of Gen. B. F. Cheatham's Division at the Battle of Stones River. Donelson, who was a brother of Andrew Jackson Donelson, Andrew Jackson's private secretary, died on April 17, 1863, at Montvale Springs, Tennessee. (Ezra J. Warner, *Generals in Gray* [Baton Rouge: Louisiana State University Press, 1959]: 74–75).

20. Brig. Gen. Samuel R. Anderson's Brigade consisted of the First, Seventh, and Fourteenth Tennessee Infantry Regiments.

21. The "cars" was a reference to cars on a train.

22. Woodstock is in the Shenandoah Valley, thirteen miles south of Strasburg, Virginia.

23. Brig. Gen. Thomas J. "Stonewall" Jackson.

24. In this fight at Dranesville, in Fairfax County, Virginia, the First, Sixth, Ninth, Tenth, and Twelfth Pennsylvania Infantry Regiments, supported by artillery and cavalry, engaged the smaller Confederate force. Union casualties included 7 dead and 61 wounded. Confederate losses were 42 killed and 143 wounded. (Benson J. Lossing LLD, *A History of the Civil War* [New York: War Memorial Association, 1912]: 64).

25. Capt. D. C. Douglas, Company E, Seventh Tennessee Infantry Regiment.

26. Clack Harrison was the son of Mr. and Mrs. Ainsworth Harrison, who lived in the Green Hill community of Wilson County, Tennessee.

27. Panthea "Panth" McClain was Mat (McClain) Bostick's youngest brother.

28. Catharine Halbert.

29. Gen. Stonewall Jackson's army, including the Seventh Tennessee Regiment, moved from Bath to Romney, Virginia. On Jackson's approach, the Federals who had occupied the town, retreated across the Potomac River.

30. Brig. Gen. Samuel R. Anderson (1804–1883).

31. Ann Thomas was Abe's first cousin.

32. Hardie Halbert was Abe's nephew, the son of his sister, Catharine Halbert.

33. Abe's nephew, Hardin "Hardie" Halbert, was about twelve years old.

34. Uncle Ed was a Bostick family slave.

35. The Commercial Hotel was in Nashville.

36. Abe had, at this point, served a little more than eight months of his original period of service, which was for one year, beginning May 20, 1861.

Chapter Five: The Peninsula Defense

1. Gen. McClellan, with 90,000 men, was convinced that he was confronted with a superior Confederate force behind the Yorktown defenses. In actuality, he was facing only about 15,000 men.

2. Gen. Hatton was thirty-six years old when he died. He left a widow and three children. In 1912, a statue of Gen. Hatton was erected on the public square in Lebanon, Tennessee, by the S. G. Shepard Camp, United Confederate Veterans.

3. Abe was referring to the successive Confederate defeats at Fort Henry and Fort Donelson and the fall of Nashville, all of which occurred in February 1862.

4. Mrs. Bostick had moved from her home on the Charlotte Pike to a smaller place in Nashville.

5. James C. Robinson.

6. Ann Thomas was then living in Marietta, Georgia, having fled Nashville with other family members earlier in the year.

7. Col. Robert H. Hatton, a former Tennessee Congressman and unsuccessful gubernatorial candidate, was promoted to brigadier general on May 23, 1862, the day this letter was written. He was killed eight days later while attacking Union forces during the Battle of Seven Pines (Ezra J. Warner, *Generals in Gray* [Baton Rouge: Louisiana State University Press, 1959]: 128).

8. Capt. Archibald D. Norris, Company K, Seventh Tennessee Infantry.

9. The bloody but inconclusive Battle of Seven Pines was fought on May 31–June 1, 1862.

10. Capt. Joseph Bostick, Thirty-fourth Tennessee Infantry, was stationed at Cumberland Gap when he wrote Abe.

11. Litton was with the Twentieth Tennessee Infantry in Mississippi.

12. John S. Peyton, Company K, Seventh Tennessee Infantry, was killed at the Battle of Seven Pines on May 31, 1862 (John Berrien Lindsley, M.D., D.D., *MAOTC* [Nashville: J. M. Lindsley and Co, 1886]: 264).

13. Capt. Tom Bostick, who had been Brig. Gen. Robert H. Hatton's aide-de-camp, was assigned responsibility for escorting Hatton's body to Lebanon, Tennessee, for burial. Because of a powerful Federal presence in Middle Tennessee, Tom was unable to get any closer than Knoxville. He temporarily buried Gen. Hatton's body there.

14. Col. James Jay Archer, a Mexican War veteran, was promoted to brigadier general on June 3, 1862, to succeed Gen. Hatton in command of the Tennessee brigade in Gen. A. P. Hill's Division. Archer and a large part of his command were captured at Gettysburg on July 1, 1863. During his year-long confinement on Johnson's Island, Archer's health failed. He died in Richmond on October 24, 1864, only a few months after his exchange (Warner, *Generals in Gray*, 11).

15. Col. John F. Goodner, Seventh Tennessee Infantry.

16. Abe's uncles, James C. Robinson and Isaac "Ike" Litton.

17. George A. Howard, Adjutant, Seventh Tennessee Infantry.

18. Abe was referring to the two-day Battle of Seven Pines.

19. Jesse Thomas and his family were living in exile in Marietta, Georgia.

20. The First, Seventh and Fourteenth Tennessee Infantry Regiments.

21. Maj. Gen. Edmund Kirby Smith was in command of the District of East Tennessee at the time this letter was written.

22. Andrew Ewing (1813–1864) was a moderate Nashville Democrat who had earlier served two terms in the U.S. House of Representatives. During the war, he served under Gens. Bragg and Johnston on a permanent court-martial body (W. W. Clayton. *History of Davidson County, Tennessee* [Philadelphia: J. W. Lewis & Co., 1880]: 121).

23. Capt. William Barry "Will" Hunt, Company K, Sixth Alabama Infantry, was Joe Bostick's brother-in-law. He recuperated from his wounds at Seven Pines and returned to service only to be killed October 16, 1864, at Cedar Creek, Virginia.

24. Capt. John Allen, Company B, Seventh Tennessee Infantry.

25. Capt. Jonathan S. Dowell, Company A.

26. Alfred P. McClain, Company I.

27. Col. John K. Howard had been Captain of Company H, Seventh Tennessee Infantry.

28. Capt. William H. Williamson, Company H.

29. Mary Anne "May" (Bostick) Anderson.

30. Abe was killed when the Seventh Tennessee and other regiments under divisions commanded by Gens. A. P. Hill and James Longstreet made direct assaults against a strong Federal position near Gaines Mill. On their third assault, shortly after Abe's death, the Confederates, encouraged by receiving reinforcements and hearing Stonewall Jackson's guns, carried the position and routed the Federals (John Berrien Lindsley, M.D., D.D., *MAOTC*, 233).

31. Ephraim L. McKenzie, Company K, Seventh Tennessee Infantry, was killed at Second Manassas the following August.

32. Capt. John D. Frye, Company C.

33. Capt. Marcus L. Walsh, Company D.

34. Capt. W. E. Curd, Company I.

35. Rufus P. "Rufe" McClain, Assistant Quartermaster, Seventh Tennessee Infantry, was Tom Bostick's brother-in-law. Before the war, Rufe had been a clerk in Lebanon, Tennessee.

36. Tom's wife Mat was then living with her children and parents in Lebanon, Tennessee.

37. Bailie Peyton Jr. had been one of the organizers of the Hickory Guards, a volunteer Nashville Infantry Company in which he was elected first lieutenant. Tom Bostick was unaware that Bailie was killed at the Battle of Fishing Creek on January 19, 1862.

38. Tom Bostick's first cousins, Catharine "Kate" and Ann Thomas, were the two oldest daughters of Tom's aunt, Elizabeth (Litton) Thomas, and her husband, Jesse Thomas.

39. Gen. George B. McClellan, U.S.A.

40. The loss of the Seventh Tennessee Infantry at Gaines Mill was particularly severe. Lieut. Col. John K. Howard was mortally wounded in the first charge while Maj. W. H. Williamson was severely wounded. Many other officers and men fell in the three charges (John Berrien Lindsley, M.D., D.D., *MAOTC*, 233).

41. Capt. John D. Frye, Company C, Seventh Tennessee Infantry.

42. Jesse Thomas.

43. Margaret Rebecca Bostick.

44. Catharine Halbert.

45. Kate was referring to Gen. Lee's victory at Gaines Mill on June 27, 1862, the battle in which Abe was killed.

46. Sgt. Jimmy Thomas, Company C, Twentieth Tennessee Infantry.

47. While at Camp Trousdale, Tennessee, in May 1861, Abe Bostick transferred to the Seventh Tennessee to serve under his brother, Tom, who was Captain of Company K.

48. "Mat" arrived in Chattanooga two days after this letter was written, having come from Lebanon with another lady in a buggy pulled by a mule.

49. The Twentieth Tennessee, Jimmy Thomas' regiment, was in the Vicksburg area when this letter was written.

50. Ann Thomas.

51. This was a reference to the death of Brig. Gen. Robert H. Hatton, who was killed on May 31, 1862.

52. Tom was referring to the Seven Days' Battles which ended on July 1, 1862.

53. Tom grossly overestimated Federal losses and underestimated Confederate losses during the Seven Days' Battles. Of a total of 105,445 Federal soldiers present on June 20,

McClellan lost 15,849 men to death, wounds, or capture. Lee's losses were higher at 20,141 in a smaller army of between 80,000 and 90,000 men. Despite suffering heavy casualties, Lee had successfully raised the siege of Richmond, and forced a larger, better-equipped army to retreat (John Macdonald, *Great Battles of the Civil War* [New York: Macmillan Publishing House, 1988]: 47).

54. Jesse Thomas.

55. Kate and Anna Thomas were daughters of Elizabeth (Litton) and Jesse Thomas.

Chapter Six: Joe and Litton Join the Fight

1. When Will enlisted on May 1, 1861, his sister-in-law, Catharine Halbert, gave him a Bible to take with him.

2. Company A, the Davis Guards, was initially identified as Company H.

3. *Tennesseans in the Civil War, A Military History of Confederate and Union Units*, Part 1: 246.

4. Ibid., 247.

5. William T. Alderson, "The Civil War Diary of Captain James Litton Cooper, September 30, 1861 to January, 1865," *Tennessee Historical Quarterly*, vol. 15, June 1956: 142.

6. Jim Cooper was confined in Camp Chase, Ohio, until he was exchanged in August 1862. He then rejoined his regiment at Jackson, Mississippi (W. J. McMurray, M.D., *History of the Twentieth Tennessee Volunteer Infantry, C.S.A.* [Nashville: Publication Committee, 1904]: 424–25).

7. Jim Cooper to Washington B. Cooper, August 17, 1862, copy in collection of the author.

8. *Tennesseans in the Civil War, A Military History of Confederate and Union Units*, Part 1, 247.

9. Percival P. Halbert (1796–1864) was a son of John and Margaret Harper Halbert, early settlers of Oktibbeha County, Mississippi.

10. Charles Erasmus Fenner (1834–1911) was a lieutenant and later a captain in the Confederate Army. He served with his battery until 1865 when he surrendered at Meridian, Mississippi. Later that year, he served as a member of the Louisiana legislature. In later life, he was a member of the Louisiana Supreme Court.

11. James Rives Childs, *Reliques of the Rives*, (Lynchburg, Va.: J. P. Bell Co., 1929), 2: 514.

12. W. J. McMurray, M.D., *History of the Twentieth Tennessee Volunteer Infantry, C.S.A.* (Nashville: The Publication Committee, 1904): 425.

13. Hershel Gower and Jack Allen, *Pen and Sword: The Life and Journals of Randal W. McGavock* (Nashville: Tennessee Historical Commission, 1959): 663.

14. Litton received the promotion on September 24, 1862.

15. Possibly James Clark Robinson, Litton's uncle, who lived at Blue Springs Farm in the Sixth District of Williamson County, Tennessee.

16. Judge Nathaniel Baxter had served both as a circuit judge and in the State Legislature before the war. Although he sided with the South, he took no active role in the war and spent most of his time in Confederate-held territory south of Tennessee. Four of his sons were in the Confederate service (W. W. Clayton, *History of Davidson County, Tennessee* [Philadelphia: J. W. Lewis and Co., 1880]: 394).

17. Hardy [usually spelled Hardie] Halbert.

18. John Herriford was a Nashville banker. The following spring, he was arrested for refusing to take the Federal oath.

19. Probably Maj. Lewis Meredith Maney who lived in Murfreesboro which was not occupied by the Federals until March 1862.

20. Isaac "Ike" Litton.

21. James L. Rice later became Captain of Company C, Twentieth Tennessee Infantry.

22. Leiper & Menifee were Commission merchants and dealers in produce. Legal clients of Litton's, the firm had a reputation as first-class merchants.

23. Washington B. Cooper.

24. William Preston Johnston, *The Life of Gen. Albert Sidney Johnston* (New York: D. Appleton and Company, 1878): 566.

25. Forkland Plantation was the home of Orville C. Rives, an uncle of Eliza's husband, John Fletcher Early. The plantation was located in Hinds County, Mississippi. There, Eliza and their baby were waited on by Louisa Langley, a devoted house slave and cook (Childs, 2: 513–14).

26. After successfully running by Forts Jackson and St. Philip, Admiral Farragut's Union fleet approached New Orleans on April 25, 1862. Confederate Maj. Gen. Mansfield Lovell and his troops fled after applying torches to the cotton on the levy. Fifteen thousand cotton bales, a dozen large ships, a number of steamboats, and unfinished gunboats were burnt. The flames extended for miles along the riverfront.

27. Camp Moore was 78 miles north of New Orleans on the New Orleans, Jackson & Great Northern Railroad.

28. John Fletcher Rives was an uncle of Eliza Early's husband, John Fletcher Early. Mr. Rives owned 59 acres in Hinds County, Mississippi, in 1861.

29. Hardin Bostick Early, son of Eliza and John F. Early.

30. Mary Anne Anderson and Margaret "Mag" Rebecca Bostick.

31. Jimmy Thomas, Company C, Twentieth Tennessee Regiment.

32. Maj. Orville Rives Early was John F. Early's brother. A physician, he was dean of a Medical College in Memphis before the war. During the conflict, he had charge of Confederate hospitals in Richmond and Lynchburg (Childs, 2: 531).

33. Capt. Tom Bostick, Company C, Thirty-fourth Tennessee Infantry.

34. Lt. Col. James A. McMurray, Fourth Tennessee (Provisional Army) Infantry.

35. Mary Louisa (Hunt) Bostick.

36. Capt. Joseph "Joe" Bostick's home was in Marion County, Tennessee. In June, 1862, Federal Gen. Don Carlos Buell made his headquarters there.

37. Capt. Joseph "Joe" Bostick.

Chapter Seven: Life in Occupied Nashville
1. Elizabeth Harding to William G. Harding, May 26, 1862, Harding Family Papers, Jean and Alexander Heard Library, Vanderbilt University, Nashville.

2. Margaret "Maggie" Harding to William G. Harding, July 22, 1863, Harding Family Papers, Jean and Alexander Heard Library, Vanderbilt University, Nashville.

3. Miss Jane Thomas, *Old Days in Nashville, Tenn.* (Nashville: Publishing House Methodist Episcopal Church, South, 1897): 132.

4. Ibid., 134.

5. John Fitch, *Annals of the Army of the Cumberland* (Philadelphia: J. B. Lippincott, 1864): 103.

6. Catharine Halbert to Mary Louise (Hunt) Bostick, February 21, 1908, Hardin P. Bostick Collection, Tennessee State Library and Archives, Nashville.

7. Capt. Thomas H. Bostick was with Bragg's forces near Chattanooga when this letter was written.

8. Anne (Litton) Cooper.

9. Susan (Litton) Robinson.

10. Col. William J. Anderson, husband of Mary Anne (Bostick) Anderson.

11. Eliza Jane Early.

12. Martha "Mat" (McClain) Bostick, Tom's wife, was then living with her parents in Lebanon, Tennessee.

13. Mary Litton was a first cousin.

14. Crawfordsville was a village in Taliaferro County, Georgia.

15. Percival P. Halbert (1796–1864).

16. Bently was Mary Ann's nephew, the son of Catharine and John Bently Halbert.

17. Mary Anne "May" Anderson.

18. Martha "Mat" McClain Bostick was Tom's wife.

19. John F. Early.

20. James Clark Robinson.

21. Catharine Halbert.

22. At some point during the war, Bishop John Early, Eliza's father-in-law, was eager for her and his grandson, Hardin, to come to Lynchburg, Virginia, and live with him. With great difficulty, he booked passage for them on a hospital train full of sick and wounded soldiers. As the train passed through towns occupied by the Yankees, Federal officials supposedly ordered each coach to stop under a water tank so that water could be poured over the cars. This made every one on the train sick. Eliza Early's granddaughter, Margaret Early Wyatt, heard her father, John Early, and his sister, Aunt Margaret (Early) Jackson, say that the ordeal was so debilitating to their mother that she had a persistent pain in her side the remainder of her life.

23. John Fletcher Rives was an uncle of and the man for whom Eliza's husband, John Fletcher Early, was named. Edward's

Depot was a station on the Southern & Mississippi Railroad thirteen miles northwest of Raymond. The town was named for R. O. Edwards, who later founded the Edwards House Hotel in Jackson.

24. Mrs. Hardin P. Bostick was living in occupied Nashville when this letter was written, possibly on Summer Street.

25. West H. Humphreys.

26. Col. G. C. Torbett died in 1872. Before the Civil War, he served in the state legislature and was an editor of the *Nashville American* (W. W. Clayton, *History of Davidson County, Tennessee* [Philadelphia: J. W. Lewis & Co., 1880]: 211, 240.

27. Abram "Abe" Bostick.

28. Catharine Halbert, Anne (Litton) Cooper, and Elizabeth (Litton) Thomas.

29. When Nashville fell to Union forces in February, 1862, Dr. E. W. Sehon was corresponding secretary of the Missionary Society of the Methodist Episcopal Church, South. After this letter was written, Dr. Sehon and three other ministers being held prisoner were transferred to Camp Chase, Ohio (Walter T. Durham, *Nashville The Occupied City* [Nashville: Tennessee Historical Society, 1985]: 154–56). After the war, Sehon was elected secretary of the Foreign Mission Board of the Methodist Episcopal Church, South (John J. Tigert, *Bishop Holland Nimmons McTyeire* [Nashville: Vanderbilt University Press, 1955]: 142).

Chapter Eight: Kentucky and Tennessee

1. *War of the Rebellion, Official Records of the Union and Confederate Armies*, prepared under the direction of the secretary of war by Lt. Col. Robert N. Scott, Third U.S. Artillery (Washington: Government Printing Office, 1886), series I, vol. 16, part II, 800.

2. Ibid., part 1, 1160.

3. During the battle, Rosecrans lost a total of 13,249 men out of his 43,400-strong Federal army (John Macdonald, *Great Battles of the Civil War* [New York: Macmillan Publishing Company, 1988]: 87).

4. *War of the Rebellion, Official Records of the Union and Confederate Armies*, series I, vol. 20, part I, 859.

5. "The Civil War Diary of Captain James Litton Cooper, September 30, 1861 to January 1865," *Tennessee Historical Quarterly*, vol. XV, June 1956, No. 2, 154.

6. W. J. McMurray, *History of the Twentieth Tennessee Regiment Volunteer Infantry, C.S.A.* (Nashville: The Publications Committee, 1904): 424.

7. Ibid., 425; Thomas, *Old Days in Nashville*, 134–35.

8. Catharine and her children were living in Nashville with her mother and her sister, Sue, when this letter was written.

9. Jesse Thomas.

10. George Litton was Litton Bostick's first cousin. George's father was Isaac "Ike" Litton.

11. Capt. James Litton Cooper was in Preston's Brigade, Breckenridge's division and Hardee's corps in March 1863. He spent the months of February, March and April "fortifying, drilling and reviewing" near Tullahoma, Tennessee ("The Civil War Diary of Captain James Litton Cooper," 154–55).

12. Rev. W. D. F. Sawrie, of Nashville, was a minister in the Methodist Episcopal Church, South.

13. Susan "Sue" Bostick, Litton's sister, was nearing her seventeenth birthday when this letter was written.

14. Notice that Tom did not refer to his regiment by its official name, the Thirty-fourth Tennessee Regiment. Like nearly everyone else, he used the old name under which the regiment was organized.

15. Mat and the children were living with her parents in Lebanon, Tennessee.

16. The fall of Vicksburg on July 4, 1863, came after a long siege which began in late May. Long on courage and patience, the Confederate defenders finally yielded because their food supply ran out.

17. Gen. Joe Johnston fell back to Morton in the pine woods of East Mississippi after evacuating Jackson in the face of Gen. Sherman's more powerful force.

18. The fight at Liberty Gap, between Murfreesboro and Tullahoma, occurred during Gen. Rosecrans' successful campaign to push Gen. Bragg's Army of Tennessee out of Middle Tennessee.

19. Jim Cooper was also in the fight at Hoover's Gap on June 24, 1863.

20. Josiah Gorgas (1818–1883) had served in the Ordnance Department of the U.S. Army before the war. Because of his experience, President Davis appointed him Chief of Ordnance of the Confederate States in 1861, initially with the rank of major. He was later promoted to colonel and finally brigadier general. Gorgas deserved great credit for the Confederacy's attempt to break the stranglehold of the blockade.

Chapter Nine: Chickamauga and Missionary Ridge

1. James Litton Cooper memoirs, 36, Tennessee State Library and Archives (TSLA.)

2. *War of the Rebellion, Official Records of the Union and Confederate Armies*, series I, vol. 30, part II, 255.

3. Jim recovered in time to rejoin his regiment at Dalton on January 21 (J. W. McMurray, M.D., *History of the Twentieth Tennessee Regiment Volunteer Infantry*, [Nashville: Publication Committee, 1904]: 425).

4. "The Civil War Diary of Captain James Litton Cooper, September 30, 1861 to January, 1865," 160–61.

5. Mary Anne Anderson.

6. Capt. William Barry "Will" Hunt was trying to get to his home in Marion County, which would have been difficult as Federals controlled the country between there and Bridgeport, Alabama. Captain Hunt was killed on Oct 19, 1864, at the Battle of Cedar Creek, Virginia.

7. Hardie Anderson was Litton's nephew, the son of his sister, Mary Anne Anderson.

8. Capt. Litton Bostick was aide-de-camp to Brig. Gen. St. John Richardson Liddell.

9. The Battle of Chickamauga, Georgia, was fought on September 19 and 20, 1863.

10. After Col. James A. McMurray was killed and Lt. Col. Lewis and Maj. Bradshaw wounded, Captain Joe Bostick assumed command of the Thirty-fourth Tennessee Infantry, a position he held for some weeks. One of his men complimented him when he said: "The command of the regiment could not have fallen into any more competent hands."

11. Battle of Chickamauga.

12. Hugh C. Topp was Litton Bostick's brother-in-law. Three years younger than his sister, Bettie C. (Topp) Bostick, Hugh had enlisted as a private in the Columbus Riflemen early in the war.

13. Maj. Gen. Carter L. Stevenson had recently been exchanged when Litton wrote this letter. Carter had been captured at the fall of Vicksburg. He served for the remainder of the war with the Army of Tennessee. (Ezra J. Warner, *Generals in Gray* [Baton Rouge: Louisiana State University Press, 1959]: 293).

14. Mary and Dickson Topp, Eugene's parents, lived in Davidson County, Tennessee.

15. Catharine Halbert.

16. On October 27, 1863, Brig. Gen. W. F. Smith opened the "cracker line" supply route into Chattanooga from Nashville by taking Brown's Ferry.

17. Capt. Joe and Tom Bostick were with Longstreet's troops who had been detached from the main body of Bragg's Army of Tennessee to attack Federal Gen. Burnside at Knoxville.

18. William "Willie" and nineteen-month-old Litton Bostick were two of Litton and Bettie Bosticks' four children.

19. Eliza Jane Early.

20. Litton's sister Mary Anne and her husband, Maj. William J. Anderson, C.S.A., had lived in Mobile before the Civil War. Only in 1863 did they make arrangements to move their furniture.

21. Litton intended for his mother to travel from Hogansville, Georgia, to Montgomery by rail, from Montgomery to Selma by steamboat on the Alabama River, and from Selma to Meridian, Mississippi, by rail.

22. Litton's uncle by marriage, Isaac "Ike" Litton was still living in Georgia.

Chapter Ten: The Atlanta Campaign

1. John F. Early was still with Charles Fenner's Battery by then part of S. D. Lee's Corp in the Army of Tennessee.

2. "The Civil War Diary of Captain James Litton Cooper, September 30, 1861 to January, 1865," 163.

3. Margaret Rebecca (Litton) Bostick.

4. Gen. Daniel C. Govan was a lieutenant colonel in the Second Arkansas Infantry early in the war. He was promoted to brigadier general on February 29, 1863, and was captured at the Battle of Jonesboro during the Atlanta campaign (Ezra J. Warner, *Generals in Gray* [Baton Rouge: Louisiana State University, 1959]: 112).

5. Mrs. Washington Bogart Cooper.

6. Litton's first cousin, Jim Cooper, was then in Marietta, Ga., recuperating from a wound he received during the Federal assault on Missionary Ridge the previous November. While in Marietta, Jim stayed with his uncles Ike Litton and Jesse Thomas. Jim rejoined his regiment at Dalton, Ga., a day after this letter was written. He was wounded for the third time at Resaca in May (Cooper, "An Account of the principal events that occurred under my observation during the late war September 1861–April 1865," 46–47).

7. Gen. Govan meant to say December 29, 1863.

8. In this fight at New Hope Church (also known as Pickett's Mill), Gen. Hooker estimated his loss at 1,665 dead and wounded. The Confederates estimated Union losses to be much higher. Maj. Gen. Alexander P. Stewart, C.S.A., said in his official report that "no more persistent attack or determined resistance was anywhere made" (Stanley F. Horn, *The Army of Tennessee* [Norman: University of Oklahoma Press, 1941]: 330).

9. There were two privates/musicians in the Eighth Ark. Infantry. One was John Ridley, Company E. The other was M. V. Ridley, Company A.

10. Between May 25, and June 4, 1864, Federal troops under Maj. Gens. Thomas, Schofield, McPherson, and Sherman fought Confederate forces in the Army of Tennessee. Union reports gave Federal casualties at 2,400 killed, wounded, and missing and Confederate losses at 3,000 killed, wounded, and missing. The Confederate figures were probably exaggerated (Benson J. Lossing, LLD, *A History of the Civil War* [New York: War Memorial Association,

1895]: 352). For example, the fights at New Hope Church and Pickett's Mill cost Gen. Sherman 3,000 men against Confederate losses of 300 (Samuel Carter III, *The Siege of Atlanta, 1864* [New York: Bonanza Books, 1973]: 138).

11. Litton's sister, Susan "Sue" Bostick, died earlier in 1864.

12. Brig. Gen. John H. Kelly was the youngest general officer in the Confederate Army at the time of his appointment. He enhanced his reputation while commanding a division of cavalry in Wheeler's Corps during the Atlanta campaign. He was mortally wounded in an engagement at Thompson's Station, Tennessee, on September 2, 1864 (Warner, *Generals in Gray*, 168–69).

13. Capt. Thomas Key, C.S.A.

14. A significant outcome of this Southern victory was to convince both sides of the advantage of fighting behind breastworks. For the balance of the Atlanta campaign, this method of fighting was employed whenever possible (Horn, *The Army of Tennessee*, 331).

15. "Col. George F. Baucum, Company K., Eighth Arkansas Infantry."

16. Brig. Gen. Mark P. Lowrey's Brigade was attached to the corps of Gen. Hardee in Pat Cleburne's division.

17. Brig. Gen. William A. Quarles.

18. Maj. Gen. Oliver O. Howard commanded the IV Corps in the Atlanta campaign. His Civil War career constituted a great paradox in that "no officer entrusted with the field direction of troops has ever equaled Howard's record for surviving so many tactical errors of judgement and disregard of orders, emerging later not only with increased rank but on one occasion (Gettysburg) with the thanks of Congress" (Ezra J. Warner, *Generals in Blue* [Baton Rouge: Louisiana State University Press, 1964]: 337).

19. Lt. Gen. Leonidas Polk, C.S.A., was killed at Pine Mountain, Georgia, on June 14, 1864.

20. Isaac Litton.

21. Pvt. Henry L. C. Ramage, First Tennessee, was killed at Kennesaw Mountain, June 23, 1864.

22. In a bold attempt to break the Confederate line, Gen. Sherman ordered a sudden attack by Gens. Schofield, Thomas, and McPherson on the Confederate center. Thomas' troops delivered the main assault against Cheatham's and Cleburne's divisions of Hardee's corps. The slaughter of Union troops, who had to cross an exposed area covered by fallen timber, was so great that it was called the "Dead Angle." Sherman minimized the significance of the defeat. In his report he said that he lost 3000 men to a Confederate loss of 650. Critics called the assault "an utterly needless move and an inexcusable slaughter" (Horn, *The Army of Tennessee*, 335–37).

23. Appalled at the sight of Federal wounded being burned alive, Col. W. H. Martin of the First Arkansas, Cleburne's division, tied a handkerchief to the ramrod of his gun and, jumping on the parapet, yelled, "We won't fire a gun until you get them away, but be quick." The Federals accepted the truce and saved some of their wounded from the fire. Afterward, a Federal major presented Martin with a brace of fine pistols as a salute to his humanitarian gesture (Horn, *The Army of Tennessee*, 336).

24. Capt. Joe Bostick's wife, Mary Louise (Hunt) Bostick.

25. Elizabeth (Topp) Bostick's nickname was sometimes spelled "Betty." Her husband, Litton Bostick, always spelled it "Bettie."

26. Mrs. Margarette Virginia Calloway was the widowed daughter of Mr. and Mrs. Lewis Mitchell of Griffin (1870 Spalding county, Georgia, census).

27. Dr. A. H. Buchanan had his office at 8 South Cherry Street in 1857.

28. Capt. James L. Rice, Company C, Twentieth Tennessee Infantry.

29. Probably this was a reference to the widow of Dr. A. H. Buchanan of Nashville. Dr. Buchanan, a professor at the University of Nashville and a Southern sympathizer, had been ordered south when Nashville was occupied by the Federals. He died at Stone Mountain, Georgia, on June 20, 1863 (W. W. Clayton, *History of Davidson County, Tennessee* [Philadelphia: J. W. Lewis and Co., 1880]: 282).

30. Catharine Halbert.

31. Dr. William W. Topp (1799–1889), of Columbus, Mississippi.

32. Col. House was a lieutenant in the Williamson Grays, Company D, First Tennessee Infantry. He was promoted to major after the Battle of Shiloh, and subsequently to colonel (John Berrien Lindsley, M.D., D.D., *Military Annals of Tennessee Confederate* [Nashville: J. M. Lindsley & Co., 1886]: 159).

33. Nathan Green Jr. was married to Mat (McClain) Bostick's sister, Bettie (McClain) Green. Nathan Green Jr. was a member of the first graduating class of Cumberland Law School in 1849. During the Civil War, he served as an aide to Gen. A. P. Stewart. When he returned home in 1865, wearing a coarse gray uniform and riding a horse given him by a Union sergeant in Chattanooga, he was so thin and his beard so gray that his children did not recognize him. He became Cumberland University's first chancellor in 1873 (Ben M. Barrus, Milton L. Baughn, and Thomas H. Campbell, *A People Called Cumberland Presbyterians* [Memphis: Frontier Press, 1972]: 224); (G. Frank Burns, *Phoenix Rising! The Sesquicentennial History of Cumberland University 1842–1992* [Lebanon: Cumberland University, 1992]: 70–71).

Chapter Eleven: Home to Tennessee

1. Virginia Military Institute Archives Records for John Fletcher Early, Lexington, Virginia.

2. Howell Cobb (1815–1868) was an antebellum governor of Georgia and a strong candidate for president of the Confederacy. He presided at the Montgomery convention which brought the Confederate States of America into being. In 1864, he was a major general and commander of the District of Georgia.

3. Stanley F. Horn, *The Army of Tennessee* (New York: The Bobbs-Merrill Company, 1941): 372.

4. Dr. Alexander Jackson to W. H. Jackson, July 27, 1864, William Hicks Jackson Papers, Tennessee State Library and Archives, Nashville.

5. Gen. Hardee was assigned command of Confederate forces in the Charleston, South Carolina, area.

6. Dr. Edwin L. Drake, *Annals of the Army of Tennessee and Early Western History* (Nashville: A. D. Hayes, 1878): 347.

7. Horn, *The Army of Tennessee*, 380.

8. Ibid., 380–81.

9. John Bell Hood, *Advance and Retreat: Personal Experiences in the United States and Confederate Armies* (New Orleans: G. T. Beauregard, 1879): 275.

10. During the Civil War, Kitty Litton Robinson managed her family's Blue Springs Farm in the Grassland area of Williamson County. Part of the time, she wore a Confederate regimental flag under her petticoats to safeguard it from Federals who occasionally plundered her farm.

11. George was a son of Isaac "Ike" Litton.

12. Jacob "Jake" Thomas was a son of Jesse Thomas. His regiment was at Cherokee, Alabama, then the eastern terminus of the Memphis & Charleston Railroad.

13. Maj. John S. Bransford of Nashville.

14. Eatonton is in Putnam County, Georgia, thirty-eight miles northeast of Macon.

15. Col. Robert Charles Tyler had been so badly wounded at Missionary Ridge that he lost a leg by amputation. During his convalescence the following spring, he was promoted to brigadier general. Too ill to return to the Army of Tennessee, he spent most of the winter of 1864–65 at West Point, Georgia. There, on April 16, 1865, with a handful of men, he defended a small earthwork against a brigade of Federal cavalry. As the position was being stormed, he was shot and killed by a sharpshooter.

16. Thomas Benton Smith had been promoted to brigadier general as of July 29, 1864.

17. William M. Shy, a modest twenty-six-year-old Williamson Countian, who was always calm and collected in battle, was promoted to colonel after Col. Thomas Benton Smith received his promotion to brigadier general.

18. Kitty was in love with Col. William Demoss, C.S.A.

19. Clay Lucas, a Nashvillian who graduated from the Cumberland Law School and who had a special love for literature, had been promoted to major when Maj. John Guthrie was killed at Jonesboro, Georgia.

20. Capt. William G. Ewin lost a leg to amputation after being severely wounded at the Battle of Kennesaw Mountain. Although incapacitated for service, he refused to be discharged and stayed in the army.

21. John Bell Hood, *Advance and Retreat*, 281.

22. Southern Historical Society Papers, IX, 526.

23. The wagon bridge on the Nashville Turnpike had been burned earlier.

24. John Bell Hood, *Advance and Retreat*, 290.

25. James Lee McDonough and Thomas L. Connelly, *Five Tragic Hours: The Battle of Franklin* (Knoxville: Univ. of Tennessee Press, 1983): 63.

26. John Allan Wyeth, *That Devil Forrest* (New York: Harper & Brothers, 1959): 480.

27. Irving A. Buck, *Cleburne and his Command* (New York: Neale Publishing Company, 1908): 327.

28. *Nashville Sun*, 1897.

29. Margaret Early Wyatt, *Nothing Happens by Chance* (Franklin, Tenn.: privately published, 1992): 204.

30. Virginia McDaniel Bowman, *Historic Williamson County: Old Homes and Sites* (Blue & Gray Press, 1971): 142.

31. James Litton Cooper was paroled at Griffin, Georgia, on May 18, 1865. After returning to Nashville, he was employed by Fife, Tisle, Porter & Company from 1865 until 1880. In 1880, he married Sarah Vaughn, daughter of Hiram and Martha Johnson Vaughn. Around 1881, he and Sarah moved to a farm in the Eighteenth District of Davidson County where he became one of Middle Tennessee's best-known breeders of Jersey cattle. He died on September 7, 1924 (William T. Alderson, ed., "The Civil War Diary of Captain James Litton Cooper, September 30, 1861 to January, 1865," *Tennessee Historical Quarterly*, vol. XV, June 1956, No. 2: 141).

32. Joseph E. Johnston, *Narrative of Military Operations, Directed During the Late War Between the States, by Joseph E. Johnston, General C.S.A.* (New York: D. Appleton and Company, 1874): 389.

33. Robert O. Neff, *Tennessee's Battered Brigade* (Nashville: Historic Travellers' Rest, 1988): 158.

Epilogue: Life Goes On

1. Robert O. Neff, *Tennessee's Battered Brigade* (Nashville: Historic Travellers' Rest, 1988): 158.

2. Capt. Hampton J. Cheney Jr. was the son of Mary E. and Hampton J. Cheney of Louisiana.

3. Fred Arthur Bailey, *Class and Tennessee's Confederate Generation* (Chapel Hill: University of North Carolina Press, 1987): 108.

4. Neff, *Tennessee's Battered Brigade*, 162.

5. Ibid., 163.

6. Erasmus Alley's son, Levan Alley, fought under Capt. Bostick during the war. When Joe was promoted to major in October 1863, Levan succeeded him as captain.

7. Martelia Cameron Kelly, *History of South Pittsburg, Tennessee* (South Pittsburg: Hustler Printing Co., 1973): 5–6.

8. The children born in Arkansas were Elva Lelan, 1884; Mary Ann, 1886; Joseph Litton, 1888; Margaret Litton 1890; Catharine Belle, 1893; and Andrew Jackson, 1895.

9. The children born in Texas were William Claud, 1898; Alta Ann, 1900; John Franklin, 1903; and Wilson, 1906.

10. Eugene Henry Lowman died April 7, 1895.

11. Mary Bostick and her daughters are listed in the Christ Church Parish roster, vol. 1 (William Jackson Wilson, *Christ Church South Pittsburg, Tennessee: The First 100 Years 1876–1976* [South Pittsburg, 1976]: 8, 23).

12. The Reverend Joseph H. Blacklock emigrated to America to settle on a farm near the Rugby, Tennessee, colony. Mr. Blacklock entered the priesthood under the personal influence of Bishop Charles Todd Quintard. He served as rector of Christ Church from 1887 until 1890.

13. The foundry manufactured sinks, sad iron, grate fronts, shoe lasts, and stands.

14. Kelly, *History of South Pittsburg*, 13.

15. The recession caused by the move of Tennessee Coal Iron & Railroad Company to Birmingham was offset somewhat by the establishment of the nearby Dixie Portland Cement Company in 1906 and the completion of Hales Bar Dam in 1910.

16. The *Lebanon Herald* of October 21, 1865, identified Thomas Bostick as one of seventeen lawyers practicing in Lebanon.

17. James Vaulx Drake, *Life of General Robert Hatton* (Nashville: Marshall and Bruce, 1867): 448, 450–52.

18. *The Daily American*, Nashville, August 21, 1880.

19. Wilson had lost an arm at Chickamauga while serving in the Confederate Army (Robert H. White, Ph.D., *Messages of the Governors of Tennessee, 1869–1883, Volume Six*, [Nashville: Tennessee Historical Commission, 1963]: 638).

20. Mary (Bostick) Wilson was survived by her husband, Samuel F. Wilson; her sister, Catharine (Bostick) Pennybaker; and four children, S. F. Wilson Jr., Litton W. Wilson, Miss Mary Wilson, and Mrs. W. O. Gloster (*Nashville Tennessean*, May 31, 1920).

21. *Lebanon Democrat*, January 2, 1890.

22. A fourth Halbert sibling, Margaret, died in infancy.

23. Catharine's grandchildren were Mrs. J. C. Dugon of Pasadena, California; Mrs. Charles R. White of Chicago; and Mrs. F. A. Butler, E. B. Lewis, Rush T. Lewis, and Pauline D. Lewis, all of Nashville.

24. Unidentified Nashville newspaper article.

25. Nothing is known of Mr. Davis' life during the Civil War. The absence of any reference to him in Bostick letters suggests that he married Mag after the war was over.

26. John A. Davis' remains were buried in Nashville's Mount Olivet Cemetery on September 11, 1899. When Mag died September 16, 1911, her remains were cremated in California. Her ashes were moved to Mt. Olivet in 1947 by a daughter, Mrs. S. C. McClung, of Long Beach, California.

27. Dr. William Topp's real estate was estimated to be worth $68,000 in 1860 and $30,000 in 1870. He had thirty-six slaves in 1860.

28. William Bostick and Susie Smith's marriage bond was signed December 5, 1889, in the presence of J. T. Armstrong, Circuit Court Clerk of Lowndes County, Mississippi.

29. Hardin Bostick had three children, all born in Marin County, California. His daughter, Ozella, was born in 1902, while his sons, Roy P. and Howard P., were born in 1904 and 1908 respectively.

30. Rosedale, which is located at 1523 9th Street South, was one of the antebellum homes featured on Columbus' Spring Pilgrimage, April 9–23, 1994.

31. Nashville City Directories, 1882–85.

32. *Christian Advocate*, November 8, 1894: 13.

33. *Nashville Sun*, June 14, 1897.

34. Margaret married Hubert Wyatt, a salesman for Nashville's Neely-Harwell Company on June 2, 1927. At the time of their marriage, Hubert's territory was Western Kentucky. For many years, Margaret and Hubert lived at their beautiful farm, Wyatt Hall Farm, on the Nashville Pike in Franklin, Tennessee. There, they bred, raised and raced trotting horses, many of which were very successful on the track.

35. John married Katherine Killebrew. His business career was with the Standard Oil Company.

36. Kay married Fred Russell in 1934. They still live in Nashville where Fred continues to write sports articles for the *Nashville Banner*, where he is vice president and sports editor emeritus. The dean of Southern sports writers, Russell is the author of three books and the recipient of many awards, including the 1981 Amos Alonzo Stagg Award from the American Football Coaches Association.

37. Lib married Robert A. McGaw in 1937. They still live on Brighton Road in Nashville across the street from where the Fred Russells lived for so long. Bob is secretary of Vanderbilt University emeritus.

38. John Early was elected president of the Montgomery Bell Academy Board of Trustees on June 23, 1923. He served until he resigned at the board meeting on August 19, 1930.

39. Unidentified Nashville newspaper, October 23, 1905.

BIBLIOGRAPHY

Alderson, William T., ed, "The Civil War Diary of Captain James Litton Cooper, Septmeber 30, 1861 to January, 1865." *Tennessee Historical Quarterly*, vol. XV, June, 1956, No. 2.

Allen, Jack and Herschel Gower, eds. *Pen and Sword, The Life and Journals of Randal W. McGavock, Colonel, C.S.A.* Nashville: Tennessee Historical Commission, 1959.

Bailey, Fred Arthur. *Class and Tennessee's Confederate Generation.* Chapel Hill: University of North Carolina Press, 1987.

Barrus, Ben M., Milton L. Baughn, and Thomas H. Campbell. *A People Called Cumberland Presbyterians.* Memphis: Frontier Press, 1972.

Bowman, Virginia McDaniel. *Historic Williamson County: Old Homes and Sites.* Blue and Gray Press, 1971.

Buck, Irving A. *Cleburne and His Command.* New York: Neale Publishing Company, 1908.

Burns, G. Frank. *150 Years Cumberland University, 1842–1992.* Lebanon: Cumberland University, 1992.

Butler, Carl. "Rosedale: Past and Present" Columbus: Mississippi School for Mathematics and Science, 1993–94.

Carter III, Samuel. *The Siege of Atlanta, 1864.* New York: Bonanza Books, 1973.

Catalogue of the Literary and Medical Departments of the University of Nashville 1858–9. Nashville: John T. S. Fall, Book and Job Printer, 1859.

Childs, James Rives. *Reliques of the Rives.* Lynchburg, Va.: J. P. Bell Co., Inc., 1929.

Christian Advocate, November 8, 1894.

Clayton, W. W. *History of Davidson County, Tennessee.* Philadelphia: J. W. Lewis & Co., 1880.

The Daily American, Nashville, August 21, 1880.

Daily Nashville Patriot, 1858, and 1861.

Drake, Dr. Edwin L. *Annals of the Army of Tennessee and Early Western History.* Nashville: A. D. Hayes, 1878.

Drake, James Vaulx. *Life of Robert Hatton.* Nashville: Marshall & Bruce, 1867.

Durham, Walter T. *Nashville The Occupied City.* Nashville: Tennessee Historical Society, 1985.

Fitch, John. *Annals of the Army of the Cumberland.* Philadelphia: J. B. Lippincott, 1864.

Freeman, Douglas Southall. *Robert E. Lee*, vol. 1. New York: Charles Scribner's Sons, 1934.

History of Tennessee from the Earliest Time to the Present; Together with an Historical and a Biographical Sketch of Maury, Williamson, Rutherford, Wison, Bedford and Marshall Counties. Nashville: Goodspeed Publishing Company, 1886.

Hood, John Bell. *Advance and Retreat: Personal Experiences in the United States and Confederate Armies.* New Orleans: G. T. Beauregard, 1879.

Horn, Stanley F. *The Army of Tennessee.* Norman: University of Oklahoma Press, 1941.

Johnson, Robert Underwood and Clarence Clough, eds. *Battles and Leaders of the Civil War*, vol. 1. Secaucus, N. J.: Book Sales, Inc.

Johnston, Joseph E. *Narrative of Military Operations, Directed During the Late War Between the States, by Joseph E. Johnston, General C.S.A.* New York: D. Appleton and Company, 1874.

Johnston, William Preston. *The Life of Gen. Albert Sidney Johnston.* New York: D. Appleton and Company, 1878.

Kelly, Martelia Cameron. *History of South Pittsburg, Tennessee.* South Pittsburg: Hustler Printing Co., 1973.

Lebanon Democrat, January 2, 1890.

Lindsley, John Berrien. *Military Annals of Tennessee Confederate.* Nashville: J. M. Lindsley and Co., 1886.

Lossing, LLD, Benson J. *A History of the Civil War.* New York: War Memorial Association, 1895.

MacDonald, John. *Great Battles of the Civil War.* New York: Macmillan Publishing House, 1988.

McDonough, James Lee and Thomas L. Connelly. *Five Tragic Hours: The Battle of Franklin.* Knoxville: University of Tennessee Press, 1983.

McGee, G. R. *A History of Tennessee from 1663 to 1900.* New York: American Book Company, 1899.

McMurray, M.D., W. J. *History of the Twentieth Tennessee Volunteer Infantry, C.S.A.* Nashville: Publication Committee, 1904.

Mims, Edwin. *History of Vanderbilt University.* Nashville: Vanderbilt University Press, 1946.

Nashville Sun, 1897.

Nashville Tennessean, May 31, 1820.

Nashville Tennessean Magazine, April 25, 1948.

Neff, Robert O. *Tennessee's Battered Brigade.* Nashville: Historic Travellers Rest, 1988.

Official History of the War of the Rebellion, Series I, vol. 20, Part 1, and vol. 30.

Parlow, Thomas E., comp., *Wilson County, Tennessee Marriages 1851–1865.* Lebanon: Tenn., 1980.

Passenger Arrivals at the Port of Philadelphia, 1800–1815. General Publishing Co., 1986.

Richardson, James D. *Tennessee Templars, A Register of Names with Biographical Sketches of the Knights Templar of Tennessee.* Nashville: Robert H. Howell & Co., 1883.

"Southern Historical Society Papers," IX.

Southwestern Christian Advocate. Nashville, July 3, 1846.

Tennesseans in the Civil War, A Military History of Confederate and Union Unites, Part 1. Nashville: Civil War Centennial Commission, 1964.

Tennessee Historical Quarterly, vol. 15, June 1956.

Thomas, Miss Jane. *Old Days in Nashville, Tenn.* Nashville: Publishing House Methodist Episcopal Church, South, 1897.

Tigert, John J. *Bishop Holland Nimmons McTyeire.* Nashville: Vanderbilt University Press, 1955.

Warner, Ezra J. *Generals in Blue.* Baton Rouge: Louisiana State University Press, 1964.

Warner, Ezra J. *Generals in Gray.* Baton Rouge: Louisiana State University Press, 1959.

White, Ph.D., Robert H. *Messages of the Governors of Tennessee, 1869–1883, Volume Six.* Nashville: Tennessee Historical Commission, 1963.

Wilson, William Jackson. *Christ Church South Pittsburg, Tennessee: The First 100 Years 1876–1976.* South Pittsburg, 1976.

Windrow, John E., ed. *Peabody and Alfred Leland Crabb.* Nashville: Williams Press, 1956.

Wyatt, Margaret Early. *Nothing Happens by Chance.* Franklin, Tn.: Privately published, 1992.

Wyeth, John Allen. *That Devil Forrest.* New York: Harper & Brothers, 1959.

INDEX

Bold numerals indicate references in endnotes.

A

Agatheridan Debate
Society, 9
Alexandria, Va., **159**
Aline (Bob Bugg's girl-
friend or wife), 39, 42
Allatoona, Ga., 135
Allen, Capt. John,
C.S.A., 58, 162
Alley, Erasmus, 148
Alley, Capt. Levan,
C.S.A., 170
Anderson, Elizabeth
"Anne," 10, 152
Anderson, Hardin
Bostick "Hardie," 10,
84, 91, 100, 153
Anderson, Mary Anne
"May" (Bostick) (Mrs.
William J.) (see also
Bostick, Mary Anne),
10, 59, 65, 69–70, 74,
81–82, 84, 90–94, 100,
106, 127, 129, 152–153,
164, **166**
Anderson, Gen. Samuel
R., C.S.A., 19, 30, 32,
39, 44, 48–49, 53–54,
56, **159–161**
Anderson, Col. William
J., C.S.A., 10, 81, 84,
91, 106, 153, **164**, **166**
Anderson, William J., Jr.
"Willie," 153
Archer, Gen. James J.,
C.S.A., 54, 57, **161**
Armies. See Confederate
and U.S. Armies
Armstrong, J. T., **170**
Armstrong, W. H.,
Chaplain, C.S.A., 43,
160
Arum City, Ca., 4
Athens, Al., 69
Atlanta, Ga., 26, 96,
108–110, 115, 130,
134–136, 151, **167**
Athenaeum Theater
(Atlanta), 110
Augusta, Ga., 144
Avenues. See Roads, etc.

B

Baines, Mort, C.S.A., 58
Baird, Lt. M. V., C.S.A.,
39, 56, **160**
Baldwin, Ms., 70
Baldwin, Rev. Samuel
D., 77

Baltimore, Md., 15
Bardstown, Ky., 87
Barrow, George
Washington, 76
Barrow, Anna Maria
(Shelby) (Mrs. George
W.), 77
Bate, William B., Gen.,
C.S.A., 98, 109
Bath, Va., 38, 52, **161**
Battle, Col. Joel A.,
C.S.A., 34, **159**
Battles: Atlanta, 108;
Bentonville, N. C., 144;
Cedar Creek, **162**, **166**;
Chicka-mauga, 100, 102,
109, **166**, **170**; Ezra
Church, 108; First
Manassas (Bull Run),
20, 31, 37, 45, **158–160**;
Fishing Creek (Mill
Springs), 53, 68, 70,
159–160, 162; Fort
Donelson, 53, 68, **161**;
Fort Henry, **161**;
Franklin, 141–145;
Gaines Mill, 80, **162**;
Gettysburg, 96, **161**;
Hoover's Gap, 89–90,
92, 94; Jonesboro, 108,
167; Kennesaw
Mountain, **167**, **169**;
Knoxville, 99; Liberty
Gap, 94, **165**;
Missionary Ridge, 107,
167; Nashville, 143–145,
161; New Hope Church,
108–109, **167**; Peachtree
Creek, 108; Perryville,
87; Pickett's Mill, **167**;
Port Gibson, 96; Second
Manassas, **159**, 162;
Seven Days', **162**; Seven
Pines, 54, 58, **161–162**;
Shiloh, 70, 74, 77, **168**;
Stones River, 88, 90, **160**,
165; Thompson's
Station, **167**; Vicksburg,
93, 96, **165**
Baucum, Col., George F.,
C.S.A., 121–122
Bayless (C.S.A. soldier
from Nashville), 30,
35, 40
Baxter, Judge Nathaniel,
71, **163**
Bean Station, Tn., 68
Bear Creek Station, Ga.,
134

Beauregard, Gen. Pierre
G. T., C.S.A., 19, 70,
107, 135–137
Becky (a Bostick slave),
149
Bell, Hon. John, **157**
Bell, Gen. Tyree H.,
C.S.A., 143
Belle Buckle, Tn., 89, 94
Benham, Major, C.S.A.,
118
Bentonville, N. C., 144
Bernard, Mr., 83, 84
Big Sewell, Va., 34
Big Spring, Va., 30, **159**
Birmingham, Al., 150–151
Blacklock Foundry, 149
Blacklock, Henry
"Harry," 149–150
Blacklock, Rev. Joseph
H., 149, **170**
Blacklock, Catharine
Warren "Kate" (Bostick)
(Mrs. Henry) (see also
Bostick, Catharine
Warren "Kate"), 149–150
Blount, Mr., 75
Blythe, Mr., 40
Bostick, Abe, xii, 3, 9, 12,
18–22, 24, 26–28, 30–31,
34, 36, 38–40, 43–44,
46–47, 49, 52, 54, 56,
58–65, 67, 70, 75, 80–83,
85, 145, **158–162**
Bostick, Absalom, xi
Bostick, Alta Ann, **170**
Bostick, Andrew
Jackson, **170**
Bostick, Bethenia
(Perkins), xi
Bostick, Cannon, 143
Bostick, Catharine (see also
Halbert, Catharine
Bostick), 11–12
Bostick, Catharine
"Kate" (see also
Pennybacker,
Catharine "Kate"), 7,
81, 92, 151
Bostick, Catharine
Warren, "Kate," (see
also Blacklock,
Catharine Warren
"Kate"), 147–148
Bostick, Catherine
"Belle," **170**
Bostick, Cora Annie
(Wish) (see also Wish,
Cora Annie), 148

Bostick, Ed, C.S.A., 81
Bostick, Eliza Jane (see
also Early, Eliza Jane
Bostick), 10–12
Bostick, Elizabeth C.
"Bettie" (Topp) (Mrs.
J. Litton) (see also
Topp, Bettie C.) 3, 6–7,
34, 68–69, 74, 84,
90–91, 99, 101,
105–106, 109–110, 112,
116, 124, 126, 128–131,
153, **159**
Bostick, Elva Lelan, **170**
Bostick, Hardin Perkins,
3, 7–8, 10, 12–13, 15–17,
156–158
Bostick, Hardin Perkins
II "Hardie," 3, 7, 84, 91,
99, 104, 106, 109, 114,
128, 153
Bostick, Howard P., **171**
Bostick, James Alfred,
xi, **156**, **157**
Bostick, John (son of
Absalom), xi, xii, 8, 15–
16, 80, 152, 155, **157**
Bostick, John (son of
Richard), 143
Bostick, John (Miss), xii
Bostick, John Franklin,
170
Bostick, John Litton xii,
3–7, 10, 17, 28, 34–35,
44, 52, 55–56, 65, 68–72,
74–75, 84, 87–88, 90–92,
94, 98–102, 104–106,
109–111, 114, 116, 124,
126–132, 138, 145, 153,
156, **163**
Bostick, John Litton Jr.,
68, 84, 91, 99, 105–106,
109, 114, 128, 153
Bostick, Johnathan,
M.D., **156**
Bostick, Joseph, M.D.
"Joe," xi–xii, 3, 7–9, 15,
30, 56, 58, 67–68, 70, 75,
84, 86, 88, 91, 92, 95,
99–102, 104–105, 109,
114–116, 125, 127, 129,
130, 137, 140, 142–152,
159, **161–162**, **164**, **166**,
170
Bostick, Joseph, Jr.
"Joe," 147–148, 151
Bostick, Joseph II "Joe,"
3, 7, 84, 91, 99, 106, 109,
114, 128, 153

173

Bostick, Joseph Litton, **170**
Bostick, Linnie (Mrs. Hardin P. Bostick II), 153
Bostick, Manoah James, **157**
Bostick, Margaret Rebecca "Mag" (*see also* Davis, Margaret Rebecca), 10–12, 27, 35, 42–43, 47, 55, 62, 65, 69, 70, 74, 84, 91–92, 100, 104, **157**, **159–160, 164**
Bostick, Margaret Litton "Maggie" (*see also* Wilson, Margaret Litton), 8–9, 20, 148–150
Bostick, Margaret Litton, **170**
Bostick, Margaret Rebecca (Litton) (Mrs. Hardin P.) (*see also* Litton, Margaret Rebecca) 3, 7, 10, 12–16, 30–31, 35, 38, 40–41, 45, 50, 55–56, 60, 62, 64–65, 68–74, 78–85, 89–92, 94, 100–101, 104, 106, 110, 114, 124, 126, 129, 130, 132, 144, 152, 154, **158–162, 166**
Bostick, Martha "Mat" (McClain) (Mrs. Thomas) (*see also* McClain, Martha "Mat"), 7, 21, 62, 64– 66, 75, 81–83, 92, 110, 151–152, **160, 162, 165**
Bostick, Martha Elizabeth (*see also* Ransom, Martha Elizabeth), xi
Bostick, Mary (Jarvis) (Mrs. John), 15, **157**
Bostick, Mary Ann, **170**
Bostick, Mary Anne "May." *See* Anderson, Mary Anne Bostick
Bostick, Mary Hunt (*see also* Lowman, Mary Hunt), 9, 148–149
Bostick, Mary Litton (*see also* Wilson, Mary Litton), 7, 81, 92, 151
Bostick, Mary Louisa "Bub" (Hunt) (Mrs. Joseph) (*see also* Hunt, Mary Louise "Bub"), 8–9, 75, 84, 104, 116, 124, 127, 129, 147–149, 151, **164**

Bostick, Nancy Woolsey (King) (Mrs. James Alfred) (*see also* King, Nancy Woolsey), **156**
Bostick, Ozella, **171**
Bostick, Rebecca Letitia (Mrs. Richard W. H.), 143
Bostick, Richard W. H., 143
Bostick, Roy P., **171**
Bostick, Susan "Sue," 10–12, 69, 78–79, 83, 91, 116, **157, 159**
Bostick, Susan "Susie" (Smith) (Mrs. William Thomas) (*see also* Smith, Susan "Susie"), 153, **171**
Bostick, Thomas H. "Tom," xii, 3, 5, 7, 18–23, 26, 28, 34, 36, 38–42, 48, 50, 52, 56–57, 61–63, 66–67, 75, 81–83, 87–88, 90–93, 99, 101–102, 104–105, 109–110, 114–116, 124–125, 128–132, 137, 142–145, 151–152, **156**, **164–166, 170**
Bostick, William Claud, **170**
Bostick, William Hunt "Willie," 9, 147
Bostick, William Thomas "Willie," 3, 6, 84, 91, 99, 105–106, 109, 114, 128, 153, **170**
Bostick, Wilson, **170**
Bostick Family Tree, 2
Bowron, James, 148
Bradley County, Tn., 21
Bradshaw, Lt. Col. Oliver A., C.S.A., 125, 145, **166**
Bragg, Gen. Braxton, C.S.A., 70, 86–87, 90, 93, 95–99, 102, 104, 107, 137, **160, 162, 164–166**
Branches. *See* Rivers, etc.
Bransford, Maj. John S., C.S.A., 138
Brasier, Colonel, C.S.A., 118
Breckenridge, Gen. John C., C.S.A., 70, 88
Brennan, Joseph, 76
Brennan, Thomas M., 76
Bridgeport, Al., 67, 98, 102, 136, 149, **159, 165**
Bristol, Tn.-Va., 20, 99, **158**
Brock's Cove (Tn.), 8
Brown, Gen. John C., C.S.A., 142

Brown, Gov. Neill S. 3
Brown's Ferry (Tn.), 98–100, **166**
Buchanan, Dr. A. H., 128, **168**
Buchanan, Mrs. A. H., 128, 130, **168**
Buell, Gen. Don Carlos, U.S.A., 86–87, **164**
Bugg, Robert S. "Bob", C.S.A., 39, 49
Bully (Abe's childhood friend), 31, 34, 36
Burnside, Gen. Ambrose E., U.S.A., 97, 99, **166**
Bush, C.S.A. (Abe's childhood friend), 28, 30, 34
Butler, Gen. Benjamin F., U.S.A., 26
Butler, Mrs. F. A., **170**

C
Callaway, Mrs. M. V., 128–130, **168**
Carrick's Ford (Va.), 26
Carter, Capt. Theodrick "Todd" C.S.A., 142
Cedar Creek, Va., 147
Cemeteries: City (Nashville), 152, **158**, City (South Pittsburg, Tn.), 149–150; Mount Olivet (Nashville), **170**.
Champneys, J. T., 153
Champneys, Ozella (Topp) (Mrs. J. T.), 153
Charleston, S. C., 44, **160, 168**
Charlottesville, Va., 20, 23, **158, 160**
Chattanooga, Tn., 19–20, 60, 62–63, 65, 70, 83, 86, 91, 93–94, 96–102, 135, 147, **162, 164, 168**
Cheatham, Gen. Benjamin F., C.S.A., 87, 92, 126, 127, 135, 137, 140,–142, 146, **160, 168**
Cheatham, Mayor Richard B., 76
Cheney, Hampton J., **170**
Cheney, Capt. Hampton J. Jr., C.S.A., 146, **170**
Cheney, Mary E. (Mrs. Hampton J.), **170**
Cherokee, Al. (or Cherokee Station, Al.), 136–138
Chicago, Il., **170**
Chickamauga, Ga. (or Chickamauga Station, Ga.), 90, 92–93, 100, 102, 105

Churches: Cherry Street Baptist Church (Nashville) 77, Christ Episcopal Church (St. Pittsburg), 149–151, **170**; First Baptist Church (Nashville), 77; First Presbyterian (Nashville), **159**; King's Chapel Methodist Church (Arrington, Tn.), 15; McKendree Methodist Church (Nashville), 9, 13, 152, 154; Methodist Church (Lebanon, Tn.), 151; Methodist Church (Staunton, Va.), 43, **160**; St. Andrews Episcopal Church (Birming-ham), 150
Churchill, Gen. Thomas J., C.S.A., 86
Churchwell, Col. William M., C.S.A., 67
Cincinnati, Oh., 78, 86, 136
Claiborne, Mr., 63
Clair, Maj. C.S.A., 95
Clarksville, Tn., 28, **158**
Cleburne, Gen. Patrick R. "Pat," C.S.A., 86, 88, 112–113, 116–118, 121, 126–127, 141, **168**
Cockrill, Mrs., 30
Cobb, Gen. Howell, C.S.A., 134, **168**
Columbia, Tn., 8, 139–140
Columbus, Ms. 3, 6, 55, 65, 68–70, 72, 83–84, 91, 99, 106, 109–110, 131, 147, 153, **156, 171**
Confederate Armies: Army of Mississippi, 69, 73; Army of Northern Virginia, 53–54, 107; Army of Tennessee, 14, 96–97, 99, 107–109, 134–135, 139, 142–145, **169**
Confederate Army Camps: Sneed (Tn.), 67; Moore (La.), 73, **164**, and Trousdale (Tn.), 18–19, 34, **159, 162**
Confederate Army Corps: Cheatham's 137, 141; Hardee's, 88, 96, **165, 167–168**; Lee's, **166**; Longstreet's, 97; Polk's, 88, 92, 96; Stewart's, 137; Wheeler's, **167**

Confederate Army Divisions: Breckenridge's, 70, 88, **164**; Cheatham's, 87, 92, **160**, **168**; Churchill's, 86, Cleburne's, 86, 88, 116, 126, **167**–**168**; Hill's, **161**; W. H. Jackson's, 135, 143; Polk's, 87

Confederate Army Infantry Brigades: Anderson's, 19, 22, 44, 56, **160**; Archer's, **161**; Bell's 143; Donelson's, 44, **160**; First Tennessee, 19, 57; Gordon's, 137, 142; Govan's, 111, 114, 119, 121, 124–126; Granbury's, 112–113, 119–123, 125; Hatton's, **161**; Liddell's, 111; Lowery's, 121–123, 125, **167**; Maney's, 92, 99; Palmer's, 143–144, 146; Polk's, 117–119; Preston's, **165**; Quarles' 121, 125; Second, 88; Smith's, 137; Tennessee, 53–54, **160**; Texas, 123; Tyler's, 14, 137–138; Zollicoffer's, **159**

Confederate Army Infantry Companies: Blues, 19; Davis Guards, 67, **159**, **163**; Gate City Guards, 26; New Orleans Tigers, 31; Rock City Guards, **158**; Williamson Grays, **168**

Confederate Army Infantry Regiments: 3rd Alabama, 58; 6th Alabama, **162**; 33rd Alabama, 121; 1st Arkansas, **168**, 121; 2nd Arkansas, 118, **167**; 3rd Arkansas, 27; 6th Arkansas, 119–121, 123; 7th Arkansas, 119–121, 123; 8th Arkansas, 87, 113–114, 121–123, **167**; 19th Arkansas, 121–123; 1st Tennesee (Maney's), 19, 28, 32–33, 42, 44, 51, 53, 57, 61–62, 99, **158**, **160**–**161**, **167**–**168**; 1st Tennesee (Turney's), 53; 1st Consolidated Tennessee, 144; 4th Tennessee, 67, 92, 95,

125, 7th Tennessee, 19–20, 22, 28, 38, 44, 53–54, 57, 59, **158**–**162**; 14th Tennessee, 19, 28, 32–33, 42, 44, 51, 53, 57, **159**–**161**; 20th Tennessee, 12–14, 18–19, 67, 70, 88–89, 92, 138, 142, **158**–**159**, **161**; 34th Tennessee, 67, 144, **161**, **165**; 5th Texas, 54, 57

Cooper, Ann (Litton) (Mrs. Washington B.), 12, 78–79, 81, 85, 89, 111, **157**, **164**–**165**

Cooper, James Litton "Jim," 12, 67–68, 70, 88–89, 91–92, 97, 99, 109–111, 137, 139, 142–143, 145–146, **165**–**167**, **169**

Cooper, Samuel, Gen., C.S.A., 109, 111

Cooper, Washington Bogart, xii, 10, 12–13, 72, 79, 89, **157**, **163**

Corinth, Ms., 70, 73, 136

Cotton Hill, Va., 37

Court of Chancery Appeals, 152

Crawfordsville, Ga., 82, 164

Creeks. *See* Rivers, etc.

Crittenden, Gen. Thomas L., U.S.A., 97

Cruces, New Granada, 4

Cumberland Ford, Ky., 67–68, **159**

Cumberland Gap, Ky.-Tn.-Va., 19, 22, 68, 87, **161**

Cumberland Plateau, 16

Curd, Capt.William E., C.S.A., 61–62, 162

D

Dalton, Ga., 99–100, 107–108, 111, 114, **166**–**167**

Davidson County, Tn., 7, 14, 16, **156**, **158**, **169**

Davis, Capt., C.S.A., 74

Davis, President Jefferson, C.S.A., 21, 26, 40, 87, 96, 99, 107–108, 134–135, 137, **160**, **166**

Davis, John A., 152– 153, **170**

Davis, John A. and Company, 152

Davis, Mrs. Kittie, 153

Davis, Kittie Litton, 152

Davis, Margaret Rebecca "Mag" (Mrs. John A.) (*see also* Bostick, Margaret Rebecca "Mag"), 152–153, **170**

Davis, Margaret "Margie," 152

Davis, Mary, 152

Decatur, Al., 70, 136

Dekalb County, Tn., 19

Demoss, Col. William E. "Bill" C.S.A., 144, **169**

Dickens, Maggie (Bostick family servant), 148

Dixie Portland Cement Company, **170**

Donelson, Andrew Jackson, C.S.A., **160**

Donelson, Gen. Daniel Smith, C.S.A., 44, **160**

Douglas, Capt. Dewitt Clinton, C.S.A., 46, 75, **160**

Dowell, Capt. Jonathan S., C.S.A., 58, **162**

Dranesville, Va., **160**

Drury's Bluff, Va., 57, 59

Dublin, Ireland, 13

Dugan, Mrs. J. C., **170**

Dumfries, Va., 53

Dunham, Miss., 30, 49

Durham Station, N. C., 144

E

Early, Eliza Jane (Bostick) (Mrs. John F.) (*see also* Bostick, Eliza Jane), 10, 23, 28, 34, 36, 40, 42, 52, 62, 65, 69, 70, 75, 81, 83, 91, 105, 109, 116, 124, 130, 144, 153–154, **157**–**160**, **163**–**164**, **166**

Early, Elizabeth, 110

Early, Elizabeth Drennon "Lib" (*see also* McGaw, Elizabeth Drennon "Lib,"), 155

Early, Frances "Fannie," 22, 74, **158**

Early, Hardin Bostick (son of John Fletcher), 69, 74, 154, **164**

Early, Hattie (Mrs. Hardin Bostick), 154

Early, Bishop John, **157**, **164**

Early, John (son of John Fletcher), 154–155, **164**, **171**

Early, John, Jr., 155, **171**

Early, John Fletcher, 10–11, 43, 69, 73–74, 82, 109, 114, 134, 137, 143–144, 153–154, **157**–160, **163**–**164**, **166**, **168**

Early, Joseph Horton Fall, 154

Early, Katherine (Killebrew) (Mrs. John) (*see also* Killebrew, Katherine), **171**

Early, Katherine Wyche "Kay," (*see also* Russell, Katherine "Kay," 155

Early, Lila, 154

Early, Margaret (*see also* Jackson, Margaret Early), 155

Early, Maj. Orville Rives, M.D., 74, 82, **164**

Early, Orville Rives, Jr., 74

Early, Rev. Thomas, 43, 74, **160**

Early, Willie (Fall) (Mrs. John) (*see also* Fall, Willie), 154

Early-Mack Company, 155

Eastman, Carrie C., 49

East Nashville Family YMCA, 157

East Tennessee Mining and Manufacturing Company, 8

Eatonville, Ga., 130, 137

Eatonton, Ga., 137, **169**

Ed (a slave), 49, **161**

Edgefield, Tn., 69

Edwards, R. O., **165**

Edward's Depot, Ms., 83, **164**–**165**

Elliott, Rev. Collins D., 77

Ellis, Mrs., 128, 130

Ellsworth, Col. E. Elmer, U.S.A., 31, **158**

Empire Coal Company, 153

Ewin, Capt. William G., C.S.A., 138, **169**

Ewing, Andrew, 58, 84, **162**

F

Fairfax County, Va., **160**

Fairfield, Tn., 89

Fall, J. Horton, 153

Fall, Willie (*see also* Early, Willie (Fall), 153

Farms. *See* Homes)

Farragut, Admiral
David G., U.S.N., 69,
164
Fayette County, Va., 34
Fayette Court House,
Va., 37
Fayetteville, Tn., 69, 72
Fenner, Lt. Charles E.,
C.S.A., 69, 134, **159**,
163, **166**
Fife, Tisle, Porter &
Company (Nashville),
169
Fishing Creek, Ky. (*see
also* Battles: Fishing
Creek), **159–160**
Fisher, John, 84
Flora City, Fl., 151
Florence, Al., 136–138
Floyd, Gen. John B.,
C.S.A., 27, 37
Fogg, Francis, 6
Forbes, Col. W. A., C.S.A.,
32, 42, 44, 51, **159–160**
Ford, Rev. Reuben, 77
Forrest, Gen. Nathan B.,
C.S.A., 78, 97, 135–136,
139, 141
Forts: Buckner (Ky.),
159; Delaware, 90, 144;
Jackson (La.), **164**; St.
Philip (La.), **164**; and
Sanders (Tn.), 99
Fort Worth, Tx., xii
Frankfort, Ky., 87
Franklin, Tn., 3, 5, 15,
140–144, **171**
Fredericksburg, Va., 53,
55–56
French, Gen. Samuel G.,
C.S.A., 134
Frye, Capt. John D.,
C.S.A., 61, 63, **162**

G

Gallatin, Tn., 151
Gaines Mill, Va., 54, **162**
Garnett, Gen. Robert S.,
C.S.A., 25–26
Gauley Bridge (Va.), 37
Gentry, Meredith, 16,
158
Giles County, Tn., **157**
Gilgath Church, Ga.,
114, 116
Glasgow, Ky., 86
Gloster, Mrs. W. O., **170**
Goodner, Col. John F.,
C.S.A., 56–57, 161
Gordon, Gen. George
Washington, C.S.A.,
137, 142
Gorgas, Col. Josiah,
C.S.A., 90, 95, **166**

Govan, Gen. Daniel C.,
C.S.A., 109–114,
117–126, **167**
Grafton, Va., 25
Grainger, Gen. Robert
S., U.S.A., 78
Grainger County, Tn., 68
Granada, Ms., 81
Granbury, Gen. Hiram
B., C.S.A., 112–113,
119–123, 125
Grant, Gen. Ulysses S.,
U.S.A., 98–99, 107,
135–136
Grassland (Tn.), **169**
Green, Elizabeth "Bettie"
(McClain) (Mrs.
Nathaniel, Jr.), **168**
Green, Nathaniel, Jr.,
C.S.A., 110, 133, **168**
Greeneville, Tn., 144–146
Green Hills, Tn., **160**
Greensboro, N. C.,
144–145
Griffin, Ga., 110,
128–131, 134, **169**
Guntersville, Al., 136
Guthrie, Maj. John,
C.S.A., **169**

H

Halbert, Arthur, **157**
Halbert, Catharine
(Bostick) (Mrs. John
Bently), xi, 10–11, 28–29,
31, 34, 39, 42, 47, 50, 55,
64, 69, 71–72, 78–81,
83–85, 89–92, 101,
103–105, 116, 124, 126,
130, 137, 143, 151–152,
159–163, **164–166**, **168**
Halbert, Hardin
"Hardie," 10, 12, 40,
43, 49, 71, 78, 84,
151–152, **160–161**, **163**
Halbert, John, **163**
Halbert, John Bently 6,
10, 69, **157**, **163–164**
Halbert, John Bently Jr.,
10, 12, 40, 78, 82, 84,
152–153, **160**, **164**
Halbert, Margaret
Harper (Mrs. John),
163
Halbert, Margaret Webb
(*see also* Moore,
Margaret Webb), 78, 84
Halbert, Mary (*see also*
Lewis, Mary Halbert),
10, 12, 40, 78, 84, 152,
160
Halbert, Parmelia
Arnold (Mrs. Arthur),
157

Halbert, Percival P., 69,
82, 84, **163–164**
Hales Bar Dam (Tn.),
170
Halifax County, Va., **157**
Halleck, Gen. Henry
Wagner, U.S.A., 77
Hamilton, James M., 76
Hancock, Md., 38
Hardee, Gen. William J.,
C.S.A., 87–88, 96, 99,
107, 113, 122, 135, **168**
Hardeman Cross Roads,
Tn. (*see also* Triune,
Tn.), xii, 3, 7, 9, 15
Harding, Elizabeth
(McGavock) (Mrs.
William G.), 77
Harding, Gen. William
G., 76, 80
Harper's Ferry, Va., 26
Harris, Dr. J. H., 4
Harris, Gov. Isham G.,
58, 76, 134, 140
Harrison, Ainsworth,
160
Harrison, Mrs.
Ainsworth, **160**
Harrison, Clack, C.S.A.,
47, **160**
Harrison Landing (Tn.),
97
Harrison, President
William Henry, 16
Harrodsburg, Ky., 87, 154
Hatton, Gen. Robert,
C.S.A., 18–19, 22, 28,
38–39, 41, 54, 56–57, 60,
151, **158**, **161–163**, **169**
Hawes, Gov. Richard, 87
Hawkins, Gov. Alvin,
151
Haynesville, Tn.
(Johnson City, Tn.), 22,
158
Heeley, Mr., 79
Herriford, John, 72, **163**
Hill, Gen. Ambrose P.,
C.S.A., 54, **161–162**
Hill, George, C.S.A., 138
Hinds County, Ms., 69,
163–164
Hogansville, Ga., 106,
116, 124, 126–127, 146,
166
Homes: Blue Springs
Farm, 13, 89, 137, **157**,
163, **168**; Carter
House, 142;
Everbright, 143;
Forkland Plantation,
69, 73, **163**; Litton
Place, 14; Meeting of
the Waters, xi–xii;

Polk Place, 78;
Pontotoc, 154;
Rosedale, 153, **156**,
171; Two Rivers
Plantation, 77; Wyatt
Hall, **171**
Hood, Gen. John Bell,
C.S.A., 14, 97, 108,
117–118, 134–137,
139–143
Hooker, Gen. Joseph,
U.S.A., 98, **167**
Hoover's Gap (Tn.), 89,
166
Horseshoe Ridge (Ga.),
97
Hospitals: Central
Hospital for the
Insane (Davidson
County, Tn.), 144; St.
Louis City Hospital,
7; 3rd Alabama
(Richmond)
Hotels: Catharine Inn
(Birmingham), 149;
City (Nashville), 41;
Commercial
(Nashville), 52, **161**;
Edwards House
(Jackson, Ms.), **164**;
Lowman Inn (South
Pittsburg), 149–150
House, Col. John L.,
C.S.A., 132, **168**
Howard, George A.,
Adjutant, C.S.A., 58,
161
Howard, Col. John K.,
C.S.A., 59, 61–63, **162**
Howard, Gen. Oliver
O., U.S.A., 122, **167**
Howell, Rev. R. B. C., 77
Humphreys, Judge West
H., 84, **165**
Hunt, Henry W., 8
Hunt, Mary Darwin
(Mrs. Henry W.), 8
Hunt, Mary Louisa
"Bub." *See also*
Bostick, Mary Louisa
Hunt, William Barry
"Will," 9, 58, 67, 100,
146, **162–163**, **166**
Hunter, Gen. David,
U.S.A., 77
Huntersville, Va., 27–28,
30–31, 39, **159**
Huntsville, Al., 8–9, 72

I

International
Agricultural
Corporation, 155
Iuka, Ms., 70

J

Jackson, Alexander, M.D., 135
Jackson, President Andrew, 160
Jackson, Charles S., 155
Jackson, Granbery, 155
Jackson, Granbery, Jr., 155
Jackson, Henriette (Weaver) (Mrs. Granbery, Jr.) (*see also* Weaver, Henriette), xii, 155
Jackson, Irene (*see also* Wills, Irene), xi, 155
Jackson, James T., **159**
Jackson, John Early, 154
Jackson, Margaret (Early) (Mrs. Granbery) (*see also* Early, Margaret), 155, **164**
Jackson, Miss., 69, 82, 93, 163, **165**
Jackson, Gen. Thomas J. "Stonewall" C.S.A., 38, 46, 48, 54, **159–162**
Jackson, Gen. William H., C.S.A., 135, 143
Jackson County, Al., 67
Jackson Phosphate Company, 154
Jasper, Tn., 8–9
Jennings, Ann E. (Mrs. Henry A.) (*see also* Wise, Ann E.), **159**
Jennings, Rev. Obediah, **159**
Jerry (Gen. Hatton's body servant), 150
Johnson, Gov. Andrew, 76–78, 87
Johnson, Gen. Edward, C.S.A., 140
Johnson City, Tn. *See* Haynesville, Tn.
Johnson's Island, Ohio, 160
Johnston, Gen. Albert Sidney, C.S.A., 27, 53, 69, 70, 73
Johnston, Gen. Joseph F., C.S.A., 19, 53, 93, 107–108, 113, 122, 126–127, 135, 143–144, **162**, **165**
Jonesboro, Ga., **169**
Jones' Station, Tn., 68
Judie (a girlfriend of Abe's from Nashville), 28

K

Kanawha Valley (Va.), 27

Kelly, Gen. John H., C.S.A., 117–118, 121, **167**
Kennett, Col., U.S.A., 78
Kennett, Mrs., 78
Key, Capt. Thomas, C.S.A., 119–121, 125, **167**
Kidwell, B. D. "Bill," xii
Killebrew, Katherine (*see also* Early, Katherine Killebrew), **171**
King, Nancy Woolsey (*see also* Bostick, Nancy Woolsey), **156**
Ku Klux Klan, 144
Knoxville, Tn., 19–20, 22, 67–68, 75, 97, 99, 104, **161**, **166**

L

Lafayette, Ga., 97
LaGrange, Ga., 131
Langley, Louisa, **163**
Lebanon, Tn., 7, 18, 34, 62, 65, 78, 150–151, **158**, **161–162**, **165**, **170**
Lee, Gen. Steven D., C.S.A., 135, 137
Lee, Gen. Robert E., C.S.A., 25–27, 35, 54, 96, 98, 107, 136, **159**, **163**
Lee and Gordon Mill (Ga.), 97
Leiper & Menifee, (commission merchants), 72, **163**
Lewis, Mr. (husband of Lewis, Mary Halbert), 152
Lewis, E. B., **170**
Lewis, Mary (Halbert) (*see also* Halbert, Mary), 152
Lewis, Pauline D., **170**
Lewis, Lt. Col. Robert N., C.S.A., **166**
Lewis, Rush T., **170**
Lewisburg, Va., 36
Lexington, Ky., 86–87
Liberty Gap, (Tn.), 94
Liddell, Gen. St. John Richardson, C.S.A., 70, 87–89, 93, 98, 100–101, 109, 111, **166**
Lincoln, President Abraham, 28, 41–42, 87, 97–98, 145
Lincoln, Robert "Bob," 41
Litton, Abram, M.D., 7, 14
Litton, Benjamin, 14
Litton, Catharine S. (Warren) (Mrs. Joseph), 13, **157**

Litton, George S., 14, 91, 100, 109, 137, 143, 144, **165**, **169**
Litton, Isaac "Ike," 14, 58, 72, 78, 106, 110, 124, 129, 130, 131, **157**, **161**, **163**, **165–167**, **169**
Litton, Jacob, 15
Litton, Joseph L., 9, 13, **157**
Litton, Joseph L., Jr., 15
Litton, Margaret Rebecca (*see also* Bostick, Margaret Rebecca), 14–15, **157**
Litton, Mary, 81, **164**
Long Beach, Ca., **170**
Longstreet, Gen. James "Pete" C.S.A., 54, 97–99, 104–105, 107, **162**, **166**
Loring, Gen. William W., C.S.A., 26–28, 32–33, 38, 44–45, **159–160**
Louisville, Ky., 86–87
Love, Dave, 72
Lovell, Gen. Mansfield, C.S.A., **164**
Lowman, Ann Litton "Annie," 149, 151
Lowman, Catharine "Kate," 149, 151
Lowman, Eugene Henry, 149, **170**
Lowman, Mary Hunt (Bostick) (Mrs. Eugene Henry) (*see also* Bostick, Mary Hunt), 149–151
Lowman, Mary Louise, 150–151
Lowman Stove Works, 149
Lowndes County, Ms., 153, **170**
Lowrey, Gen. Mark P., C.S.A., 121–123, 125, **167**
Lowry, D. Henry, **156**
Lucas, Maj. Henry Clay, C.S.A., **138**, **169**
Lucinda (Abe's Aunt), 35
Lynchburg, Va., 10, 20, 22, 61, 63, **158**, **164**

M

McClain, Alfred P., C.S.A., 59, **162**
McClain, Josiah S., 7, **156**
McClain, Martha (Mrs. Josiah), 7

McClain, Martha D. "Mat" (*see also* Bostick, Martha "Mat"), 7, **156**
McClain, Panthea "Panth" C.S.A., 47, **160**
McClain, Rufus P. "Rufe," 18, 61–62, **158**, **162**
McClellan, Gen. George B., U.S.A., 24–27, 37, 53, 57, 62, 65, **158**, **161–163**
McClung, Mrs. S. C., **170**
McCook, Gen. Alexander McDowell, U.S.A., 97
McCook, Gen. Daniel, Jr., U.S.A., 89
McDowell, Gen. Irvin, U.S.A., 26
McGavock, David H., 77
McGavock, Randal William, 6–7, 10, 17, 70, **157**
McGavock's Ford, (Tn.), 143
McGaw, Elizabeth Drennon "Lib" (Mrs. Robert A.) (*see also* Early, Elizabeth Drennon "Lib"), 155, **171**
McGaw, Robert A., **171**
McKenzie, Ephraim L. F., C.S.A., 60, 82, **162**
Mackinac Island, Mich., 77
McMurray, Lt. Col. James A., C.S.A., 75, 92, **164**, **166**
McPherson, Gen. John B., U.S.A., **167–168**
Macon, Ga., **168**
Macon, Ms., 110, 132
Maddin, Thomas L., M.D., 89
Manassas Junction, Va., 19, 26, 41, 44, 53
Manchester, Tn., 88
Maney, Col. George E., C.S.A., 22, 28–29, 32, 42, 44, 51, 53, 92, 99, **158**, **160**
Maney, Maj. Lewis Meredith, 72, **163**
Marietta, Ga., 58, 63–64, 66, 78, 83, 100, 109, 124, 126, **161**, **167**
Marion County, Tn., xi, 8, 67–68, **164**, **166**
Marin County, Ca., **171**
Marshall, Capt., U.S.A., 79

Martin, Andrew, C.S.A., 58
Martin, Thomas, **156**
Martin, Col. W. H., C.S.A., **168**
Mason, Maj. A. P., C.S.A., 118, 140
Masonic Lodges: Cumberland Lodge #1 (Nashville), 16; Magnolia Lodge #30 (Lebanon), 151
Maury County, Tn., **158**
Mechanicsville, Va., 54
Memphis, Tn., 154, **164**
Meridian, Ms., 106, **163**, **166**
Military and Financial Board of Tennessee, 76
Millboro, Va., 41, 47
Miller, Mr., 4,
Miller, Mrs., 65,
Mingo Flats, Va., 31
Mitchell, Mr. Lewis, **168**
Mitchell, Mrs. Lewis, 128–130, **168**
Mobile, Al., 10, 93, 106, **166**
Monteagle, Tn., xi, 151
Monteagle Sunday School Assembly, xi
Monterey, Va., 26, **158**
Montgomery, Al., 106, **166**
Montgomery Convention, **168**
Montvale Springs, Tn., **160**
Moore, Margaret Webb (Mrs. John Bently Halbert, Jr.), 152
Morristown, Tn., 65, 68, 70, 75
Morton, Ms. **165**
Mountains: Allegheny, 25; Appalachian Mountains, 98, 145; Big Sewell (Va.), 34; Blue Ridge, 20; Brush (Ga.), 108; Buffalo (Va.), 38; Cheat (Va.), 27, 39, **159**; Cumberland (Tn.), 9, 20; Kennesaw Mountain (Ga.), 108, **168**; Laurel Hill (Va.), 26; Lookout (Tn.), 97–98, 105; Lost (Ga.), 108; Missionary Ridge (Tn.), 98–99, 101–104; Pine (Ga.), 108, **167**; Rich (Va.), 26; Sierra Nevada (Ca.), 3; Stone (Ga.), **168**; Talley (Va.),

31; Walden's Ridge (Tn.), 68; Winstead Hill (Tn.), 141
Mount Pleasant, Tn., 154
Muir, Ky., 155
Murfreesboro, Tn., 71–72, 78, 87–89, 94, **163**, **165**

N
Nashville, Tn. 3–10, 12–14, 16, 18, 22, 26, 34, 41–42, 53–56, 65, 67–70, 72, 76–78, 80–81, 83, 86–92, 107–109, 111, 120, 135–136, 138–141, 143–144, 147, 150–154, **157–163**, **165–166**, **167–171**
Nashville School Board, 155
Neely-Harwell Co., **171**
New Grenada (*see also* Panama), 4
New Hope Church, Ga., 112
New Orleans, La., 10, 31, 69, 72–73, **156**, **159**, **164**
Newsom, Col. James E., C.S.A., 144
Newsom, Sallie N., 144
Newsom Station, Tn., 144
Newspapers: *Daily Nashville Patriot*, 68; *Memphis Appeal*, 125; *Memphis Public Ledger*, 152; *Nashville American*, **165**; *Nashville Banner*, **171**; *Nashville Patriot*, 17; *Nashville Sun*, 149
New York City, N. Y., 4, 154
Nolen, William, Jr., 17
Nolensville, Tn., 45
Norfork, Va., 54
Norris, Capt. Archibald D., C.S.A., 56, **161**

O
Oktibbeha Co., Ms., 69, **157**, **163**
Old English Company, 148
Orchard Knob (Tn.), 98
Ozark, Ark., 148

P
Palmer, Gen. Joseph B., C.S.A., 143–146

Palmetto, Ga., 134
Panama (*see also* New Grenada), 4
Parham, Mr., 75
Parham, Mrs., 75
Pasadena, Ca., **170**
Pate, John F., 4
Pearl (Abe's friend from Nashville), 30
Pearre, Joshua, **157**
Pennybacker, Catharine "Kate" (Mrs. Edward R.) (*see also* Bostick, Catharine "Kate"), 152, **170**
Pennybaker, Edward R., 152
Pennybaker, Edwin, 152
Pennybaker, Frank, 152
Perkins, Thomas Hardin, xi
Perryville, Ky., 87
Petersburg, Va., **160**
Peyton, Bailie, Jr., 62, **162**
Peyton, John S., 57, **161**
Philadelphia, Pa., 13, 16, **157**
Phillipi, Va., 25
Pickensville, Al., 91, 106, 114–115, 127, 137
Pikes. *See* Roads, etc.
Pikeville, Tn., 86
Pittsburg Landing, Tn., 70
Pittsylvania County, Va., **157**
Plantations. *See* Homes
Pocahontas County, Va., 28
Polecat Hollow (Va.), 29
Polk, Sarah (Childress) (Mrs. James K.), 77
Polk, Gen. Leonidas, C.S.A., 87–88, 92, 96, 107, 113, 117–119, 122, 124, **167**
Polk, Capt. Marshall T., C.S.A., 77–78
Porter, Mr., 71–72
Porter, William, 5
Port Gibson, Ms., 96
Powell, Lt. B. D., C.S.A., 34, 39, 41–42, **159–160**
Preston, Gen. William, **164**
Prisons: Andersonville (Ga.), 134; Chase (Ohio), 68, **163**; Johnson's Island (Ohio), **161**; Tennessee State, 76–77, 80, 85
Pulaski, Tn., 139
Putnam County, Ga., **169**

Q
Quarles, Gen. William A., C.S.A., 121, 125, **167**
Quintard, Bishop Charles Todd, **170**

R
Ragansville, Ga., 131
Railroads: Atlanta & West Point, 134; Baltimore & Ohio, 25; Chattanooga & Atlanta, 93; East Tennessee & Virginia, 20, 26, 145; Louisville & Nash-ville, 18; Memphis & Charleston, 69, 136, 146, **169**; Mobile & Ohio, 93; Nashville & Chattanooga, 19, 26, 69, 105; Nashville & Decatur, 154; Nashville & North-western, 12; New Orleans, Jackson & Great Northern, **164**; Southern & Mississippi, **165**; South Florida, 154; Virginia Central, 26; Western & Atlantic, 135
Ramage, Priv. Henry L. C., C.S.A., 124, **167**
Ransom, Mr., 71
Ransom, Martha Elizabeth (Mrs. George W.) (*see also* Bostick, Martha Elizabeth), xi
Ransom, George Washington, xi
Ransom, John B., xi
Rappahannock, Va., **160**
Ray, Anderson, C.S.A., 138
Raymond, Ms., 65
Read, Alex, C.S.A., 35
Readyville, Tn., 88
Resaca, Ga., 108, **167**
Rice, Capt. James L., C.S.A., 72, 128, 130, **162**, **168**
Richmond, Va., 26–27, 30, 48, 53–54, 56–61, 64, 72, 83, 90, 95, 111, 137, **161**, **164**
Ridley, Pvt. John, (musician), 8th Arkansas Infantry, 114, **167**
Ridley, Pvt. M. V., (musician), 8th Arkansas Infantry, 114, **167**

Rivers/Streams/
Creeks/Branches:
Alabama River, **166**;
American River, 3;
Arrington Creek, **157**;
Battle Creek, 9, 147;
Brown's Creek, 78;
Chattahoochee River,
108, 127; Cheat River,
26; Chickamauga
Creek, 97–98;
Cumberland River, 69,
87; Duck River, 88, 139;
Elk River, 88;
Greenbrier River, 39;
Harpeth River, 13,
140–141; James River,
53; Kanaba River, 37;
Knapp Creek, **158**;
Lick Branch, 16; Mill
Creek, 78; Mississippi
River, 93, 96, 98, 111;
New River, 37; Ohio
River, 7, 16, 25;
Peachtree Creek;
Potomac River, 26, 38,
43, 50, 53, **161**;
Rattlesnake Creek, 4;
Round Lick Creek;
Sam's Creek 4; Shivers
Fork, 26; Stones River,
157; Tennessee River, 9,
86–87, 96, 101, 136,
148–149, York River, 53
Rives, Henry, 74
Rives, John Fletcher, 74,
83, **164**
Rives, Orville C., 69, 74,
163
Roads/Pikes/Streets/
Avenues: Asylum
Street, 153; Bostick
Street, 12, 78; Brighton
Road, **171**; Carter's
Creek Pike, 143;
Charlotte Pike, 10,
12–13, 16–17, 68, 78,
160–161; Church Street,
152; Gallatin Pike, 14,
157; Murfreesboro Pike,
78; Nashville-Lebanon
Turnpike, 78; Moran
Road, **157**; Nashville
Pike, **169**, **171**; Natchez
Road, 13; Ninth Street
South, **171**;
Nolensville-College
Grove Road, **157**;
North Cherry Street,
6, 17; North Market
Street, 155; North
Summer Street, 6;
North Vine Street, 155;
Pearl Street, **157**;

Robertson Street, 12;
South Cherry Street,
168; South Market
Street, 153; South
Spruce Street, 76;
Spring Street, 76, 78;
Sumner Street, 165;
Twentieth Avenue
North, **157**; West End
Avenue, 152, 154;
Williams Avenue, 154
Robertson Association
6–7
Robinson, James C.,
13–14, 55, 58, 71, 83,
157, **161**, **163–164**
Robinson, James C., Jr.
"Jim," 14, 145
Robinson, Kitty Litton,
14, 137–138, 145, **169**
Robinson, Susan
(Litton) (Mrs. James
C.), 13–14, 81, **164**
Robinson, William
Joseph "Bill," 14, 18,
68, 70, 88–89
Romney, Va., 38, 47–48,
50–51, 144, **159**, **161**
Rosecrans, Gen. William
S., U.S.A., 26–27, 34–35,
37, 87, 96–98, **165**
Rugby, Tn., **170**
Russell, Fred, **171**
Russell, Katherine
"Kay" (Mrs. Fred). *See*
Early, Katherine
Wyche "Kay," **171**
Rust, Col. Albert B.,
C.S.A., 27
Rutherford County, Tn.,
4, **158**

S
St. Louis, Mo., 153
Sanford, Fl., 154
San Francisco, Ca., 4
San Rafael, Ca., 153
Savannah, Ga., 135, 144
Sawrie, Mr., C.S.A., 91
Sawrie, Rev. W. D. F., 77,
91, **165**
Schofield, Gen. John M.,
136, 139, 141, 143, **167**,
168
Schools: Athenaeum, 8;
Dr. Blackie's School
for Girls and Young
Ladies, 148; Bostick
Female Academy, xii,
156; College of New
Jersey, 9; Columbus
Female Institute, **156**;
Cumberland
University, **159**, **168**;

Cumberland
University Law
School, 7, **168–169**;
Harpeth Union Male
Academy, 15; Harvard
Law School, 3, 6; Mrs.
Holcombe's School,
91; Isaac Litton High
School, 14, **157**;
Montgomery Bell
Academy, **155**, **171**;
Nashville Female
Academy, 11, 77;
Nashville University,
3, 9, 14, **157**, **160**, **168**;
Mrs. Ripley's School,
3, 5; St. Louis
University, 7, 14;
Vanderbilt University,
14; Western Military
Institute, 9
Scott, Gen. Winfield,
U.S.A., 37
Seddon, James A.,
C.S.A., 107
Sehon, Bishop E. W., 19,
77, 80, 85, **165**
Selma, Al., 106, **166**
Sequatchie Valley (Tn.),
86, 150
Setts, Dr., (Marietta, Ga.,
physician), 100
Sewanee, Tn., xi
Sewanee Mining
Company, 16
Shannon, Lt., C.S.A.,
119, 120–121, 125
Sharp, Thomas, 76
Shelbyville, Tn., 69,
71–72, 88, 90–92, 95
Shenandoah Valley, 25,
38, **160**
Sherman, Gen. William
T., U.S.A., 98, 108, 127,
134–137, 144–145, **165**,
167–168
Ships: *Sally*, **157**;
Tennessee, 4
Shy, Col. William M.,
C.S.A., 138, 145, **169**
Smith County, Tn., 19
Smith, Gen. Edmund
Kirby, C.S.A., 58,
86–87, **161**
Smith, Col. Sam, C.S.A.,
120
Smith, Susan "Susie" (*see
also* Bostick, Susan
"Susie"), 153, **170**
Smith, Gen. Thomas
Benton, C.S.A., 70, 89,
137, 145, **169**
Smith, Gen. William F.,
U.S.A., **166**

Smyrna Station, Ga., 108
Sneed, Tom, C.S.A., 139
Southern Methodist
Publishing House, 10
South Pittsburg, Tn.,
148–151
South Pittsburg City
Company, 149–150
Sparta, Tn., 86
Springfield, Va., 51
Spring Hill, Tn., 140
Standard Oil Company,
171
State Bank
(Chattanooga), 70
Staunton, Va., 19, 23,
25–26, 38, 40–45, **158**,
160
Stevens, Vice-President
Alexander H., C.S.A.,
160
Stevenson, Gen. Carter
L., C.S.A., 102, **166**
Stevenson, Al., 136, 147
Stewart, Gen. Alexander
P., C.S.A., 110, 135,
137, 142, **167–168**
Stockton, Ca., 4
Stocton on Tees,
England, 150
Stokes County, N. C., 15
Stone Mountain, Ga.,
168
Stones, Joe, 30
Strasburg, Va., 44–46,
160
Streams. *See* Rivers, etc.
Streets. *See* Roads, etc.
Stuart, Gen. James E. B.
"Jeb" C.S.A., 54
Stubblefield, Terry, 153
Stubblefield, Mrs. Terry,
153
Summers, Thomas
"Tommy," 48
Sumner County, Tn., 19
Surry County, N. C., 15
Swett, Capt., C.S.A., 119,
125

T
Taliaferro County, Ga.,
164
Tarver, Lt. B. J., C.S.A.,
41, **160**
Taylor, Jane (Litton), 14
Taylor, Gen. Richard,
C.S.A., 135
Tennessee Botanical
Gardens and Fine Arts
Center, **157**
Tennessee Coal, Iron
and Railroad
Company, 150, **170**

Tennessee Historical
Society, 13
Thomas, Ann "Anna,"
49, 56, 62, 64, 66,
161–163
Thomas, Catharine
"Kate," 62, 64, 66,
162–163
Thomas, Elizabeth
(Litton) (Mrs. Jesse),
12–13, 78, 85, **162–163**,
165
Thomas, Gen. George
H., U.S.A., 86, 97–98,
108, 135–136, 140, **168**
Thomas, Jacob "Jake,"
13, 30, 31, 34–35, 40,
137, 143–144, **159–160**,
169
Thomas, James W.
"Jim," 13, 18, 64,
67–68, 70, 74, 88–92,
94, 137, 144, **162**, **164**
Thomas, Miss Jane,
78–79
Thomas, Jesse, 13, 58,
62–63, 66, 78, 91,
162–163, **169**
Thompson, Mr., 6
Thompson, John, 128,
130
Thompson, Mary
(Hamilton) (Mrs.
John), 79
Thompson, Zack,
C.S.A., 51
Tillson, Gen. Davis, 145
Toliver, Lt. Newnan,
C.S.A., 23, 30, 41, 49,
51–52, **158**, **160**
Topp, Bettie C. (*see also*
Bostick, Bettie C.) 3,
5–6
Topp, Dickson, 102, **166**
Topp, Eugene, C.S.A., 102
Topp, Hugh, C.S.A., 102,
114, **166**
Topp, Mary (Mrs.
Dickson), **166**
Topp, Mary (Mrs.
William W.), 6
Topp, Dr. William W., 6,
131, 153, **156**, **168**, **170**
Topp, Kezia G. (Mrs.
William W.), 153

Torbett, Col. G. C., 84, **165**
Trimble, James, 9
Triune, Tn. (*see also*
Hardeman Cross
Roads, Tn.), xii, 28,
88, **156**, **158**
Tule Ranch (Ca.) 4–5, 7
Tullahoma, Tn., 88–89,
94, **165**
Tunnel Hill, Ga., 110
Tupelo, Ms., 70, **160**
Turney, Peter, Col.,
C.S.A., 53
Tuscumbia, Al., 136
Tyler, Gen. Robert
Charles, 14, 138, **169**
Tyne, Mrs., 35

U
Union Bank of
Tennessee, 15
United Confederate
Veterans, **161**
United Daughters of
the Confederacy, 150
U.S. Armies: Army of
the Cumberland,
96–98, 108; Army of
the Ohio, 108; Army
of the Potomac, 37,
44, 53, 97; Army of
the Tennessee, 108
U.S. Army Brigades:
Wilder's, 89
U.S Army Corps:
Crittenden's, 97; Fourth
(Howard's), 122, **167**
U.S. Army Division:
Wood's, 97
U.S. Army Infantry
Regiments: 11th New
York (First Fire
Zouaves or
Ellsworth's Zouaves),
159; First
Pennsylvania, **160**;
Sixth Pennsylvania,
160; Ninth
Pennsylvania, **160**;
Tenth Pennsylvania,
160; Twelfth
Pennsylvania, **160**
U.S. Military Academy,
139, **160**
U.S. Steel Company, 150

V
Vanderbilt University
155, **171**
Vaughn, Hiram, **169**
Vaughn, Martha
(Johnson) (Mrs.
Hiram), **169**
Vaughn, Sara, **169**
Vick, Alexander W.
"Rex", Quartermaster,
C.S.A., 34, **159**
Vicksburg, Ms., 64, 70,
74, 93, **162**, **165–166**

W
Walsh, Capt. Marcus L.,
C.S.A., 61–62, **162**
Warm Springs, Va., 29,
38, 41
Wartrace, Tn., 88–90
Washington City, 16, 23,
28, 37–38, 41–42, 46,
53, 87, 98, **157**
Washington County,
Tn., 22
Weaver, Henriette (*see
also* Jackson, Henriette
Weaver), 155
Webster, Hon. Daniel, **157**
West Point, Ga., **169**
West Point, Ms., 68, 137
Wheeler, Gen. Joseph,
C.S.A., 87, 99, 135–137
White, Mrs. Charles R.,
170
Whitsett, Elisha, C.S.A.,
77
Whitsett, Johnny, C.S.A.,
77
Wilder, Col. John T.,
U.S.A., 89
Williams, Adj. Gen. G.
A., C.S.A., 88
Williamson, Capt.
William H., C.S.A., 32,
59, 61–62, **159**, **162**
Williamson County, Tn.,
xi, 3–4, 13, 137–138,
156–158, 163, **169**
Wills, Elizabeth Meade,
xi
Wills, Irene (Jackson),
155
Wills, William Ridley II,
155

Wills, William Ridley,
IV, xi
Wilson, John, 150
Wilson, Litton W., **170**
Wilson, Margaret
Litton "Maggie" (*see
also* Bostick, Margaret
Litton "Maggie"), 150
Wilson, Mary, **170**
Wilson, Mary Litton (*see
also* Bostick, Mary
Litton), 151–152
Wilson, Samuel F., 152,
170
Wilson, Samuel F., Jr., **170**
Wilson, Woodrow, 148
Wilson County, Tn., 7,
18–19, 150, **156**, **160**
Winchester, Va., 38, 44,
48–53
Wise, Ann E. (Jennings)
(Mrs. Henry A.) (*see
also* Jennings, Ann E.),
159
Wise, Gen. Henry A.,
C.S.A., 27, 35, **159**
Wish, Cora Annie (*see
also* Bostick, Cora
Annie), 148
Witherspoon, Anne
Lacy (Topp), 153
Wood, Capt. C. H.,
U.S.A., 77
Wood, Mrs. C. H., 77
Wood, Gen. Thomas J.,
U.S.A., 97
Woodson's Station, Tn.,
68
Woodstock, Va., 45, **160**
Wool, Gen. John E.,
U.S.A., 26
Wright, George
Washington 3, 4, **156**
Wright, John V., 152
Wyatt, Margaret (Early)
(Mrs. Hubert), **164**,
171
Wyatt, Hubert, **171**

Y
Yorktown, Va., 53, **161**

Z
Zollicoffer, Gen. Felix,
C.S.A., 19, **159**